MARGUERITE VALENTINE began w
women's group which established
refuges in the U.K. Subsequently,
at the University of Warwick, bef
in Social Services with a special 1...._
By this time she'd become fascinated by what makes peopic
tick, hence her decision to train as a psychotherapist. Often
moved by the accounts of those she worked with, it is their
experiences which inspire her. The characters she writes of,
though imagined, share a struggle to survive and to overcome
what life throws at them.

Between the Shadow and the Soul is Marguerite's debut
novel and is the imagined story of Flori, whose traumatic
childhood history drives her to snatch a baby as an attempt to
overcome her tragic past.

For more information about Marguerite and her work,
vist her website at www.margueritev.org

To David a Anna
with love from Marguerite
Sept. 24th 2014

BETWEEN THE
SHADOW
SOUL AND THE

MARGUERITE VALENTINE

SilverWood

Published in 2014 by SilverWood Books

SilverWood Books Ltd
30 Queen Charlotte Street, Bristol, BS1 4HJ
www.silverwoodbooks.co.uk

ISBN 978-1-78132-225-3 (paperback)
ISBN 978-1-78132-226-0 (ebook)

British Library Cataloguing in Publication Data
A CIP catalogue record for this book is available from
the British Library

Set in Sabon by SilverWood Books
Printed on responsibly sourced paper

For Marcus and Justin

Acknowledgements

Without the continuing interest and support from friends and colleagues, especially Diana Turner and Brigid Holdsworth, this story wouldn't have left my computer. My heartfelt thanks also to Robin Gordon Brown and Richard Carvalho, both of whom showed an early interest in my writing. Finally my thanks to jay Dixon, whose editing of the final version was truly impressive.

1

It was the early hours. The heat of the day had dropped and there was a chill in the air. Flori was awake. She was sober. She was alone. She sat up, looked around. The party was over. The garden silent, in darkness, there was no one else around. Even Phil had gone. She sighed. Somewhere, sometime, somebody leaves; one of life's inevitabilities and unavoidable, it must happen all the time. She'd been asleep, but for how long, she didn't know. She looked across the lawns. Facing her was the black outline of the mansion flats, looming into a night sky stained sulphur yellow by the street lamps and, breaking the still of the night, the sound of a diesel engine of a black cab passing in the street.

She looked at her watch, pressed the back light. Three twenty-three a.m. Her bag lay on the bench, a small business card jammed in the clasp. She picked it out, read the name. Philip Georgiou B.Sc. Melbourne Electronics. Turned it over. Written in small handwriting was a message, but it was too dark to see. She put it in her bag intending to read it later.

Last night, during the party, she'd gone into the garden and had sex with someone, then she'd fallen asleep. Was his name Phil? She'd hardly known him but they'd fancied each other so whatever. She paused. She'd called him Matt. Several times. She remembered that. But he hadn't been Matt, he'd said his name was Phil. Maybe she'd mixed them up because

9

she missed Matt and still thought about him, or maybe it was the drink. It could have been that. She'd drunk too much and she should have stopped after she and Rose left the Greek restaurant, *The Muse*. Anyway, Phil, Matt, or who ever, they'd gone and they'd left her. Both of them.

She began checking the contents of her bag, for speed tipping everything out. Yesterday had been hot, but the coolness of the night air left a delicate film of dew on the grass. Money, oyster card, notebook with attached pen, visa card, spare tampax, small folding hair brush, keys, the Estée Lauder navy mascara she'd bought for herself, the handbag-sized Miss Dior perfume. All was there, nothing had been taken. She ran an experimental finger across the grass and traced out a question mark. It quickly faded.

She looked up and across the lawns to the ground floor flat where the party had been held. It was over. Nothing but silence. No laughter, no conversation, no music. The French windows with the interior white-painted, burglar-proof grille were closed, the curtains tightly shut. She was locked out. She sat thinking. She wouldn't knock on a window and ask to be let in. It would look weird, and besides she'd have to bang hard. Everybody would be asleep.

She was gripped with fear but with that came excitement. She had a sense of her potential power. She was alone and no one knew she was there. She felt capable of anything, just like burglars must feel. She stood facing the block of mansion flats.

Then the reality: she was trapped. She shivered, pulled her wrap tightly around her shoulders and began walking idly round the gardens, thinking, wondering what she should do.

Large grounds, extensive, well-trimmed lawns, shrubs, some in flower, but all beautifully maintained, probably by a professional gardener. One plant glowed white in the darkness, its scent hanging heavy in the night air. It was exotic looking, its fragrance reminding her of a visit she'd once made to Seville. Was it orange blossom? Rose would have known if she'd been here, but she'd left, too. At least she'd told her she was going, unlike Phil who'd abandoned her while she slept. That's how it felt, a painful abandonment and it hurt.

She continued her walk. It was peaceful on her own. She had time to enjoy the garden's solitude. There was no bird song. It was too early. She noticed how carefully the weathered oak benches had been placed under the mature trees. She paused under an oak tree, before sitting down. She imagined she lived there and that this was her favourite place in the garden. It was a poetry type of garden, reflective, peaceful and tranquil. It would be here she could read her poems. I'd read, she thought, something by Sarah Teasdale or the Chinese poet, Li Po. Both were dead.

She became aware of the background hum of the city at sleep. She sighed, pursed her lips; she had to get out, she couldn't stay forever. She had to find a way. Her gaze continued round the garden and stopped at the gates the end of the building. They were not the usual type, wooden, set into a walled gothic arch, but high, made from ornamental iron, designed to protect the garden and the flats from intruders. She looked carefully at the height and estimated it as about four metres high. The gate was padlocked. Perhaps she could climb over it, but as she got closer, she saw it would be difficult. The design consisted of a number of vertical bars set into an arch and these were topped with vicious-looking finials. Difficult, certainly, but maybe, maybe she could still do it and there was a way. She'd been a good climber as a young girl and she didn't intend giving up that easily.

She got closer, there were only two horizontals and she could see straight away they were too far apart. There was nowhere to place her feet and hoist up her weight. The gate had been constructed so that it was impossible to climb. Up and over. She couldn't do it. She wasn't tall enough.

She was trapped. Well and truly trapped. She felt the beginnings of a panic attack. She felt claustrophobic. It was the realisation she was hemmed in. She was becoming breathless. She returned to the bench, sat down, wrapped her arms round her knees to keep warm, twisting and untwisting her hair round her fingers. She heard a distant church bell strike four. She looked again at the building. It occurred to her she could be seen from the flats and the police might be called. She moved to a bench in the far corner where she couldn't easily be seen.

She thought through her options. She could ring Rose to ask for help, but on reflection she discarded that. Last night Rose had left with Dave and she'd taken him to her London flat because neither of her parents were at home. It might be inconvenient this time of the morning. They'd clearly fancied the pants off each other and she wasn't going to interrupt them. It wasn't that bad. Perhaps she'd ring her for support, tell her what had happened, but when she looked for her mobile, she'd left it at home. She hadn't thought she'd be on her own and would need it. Another avenue closed. If the worst comes to the worst, she thought, she'd have to sleep here, wait until people get up, then knock on a window and explain why she was there. She'd look stupid, but at least she'd get out.

She noticed the night sky lightening. People would be waking in an hour or two, except it was a Saturday and for many their day off and they'd sleep in. Theoretically, she realised she could be here for a long time. She had to take more decisive action. She moved away from her bench closer to the flats and looked along the width of the building. She noticed then something she hadn't seen before.

At the opposite end of the building from where she'd been sitting was an iron fire escape. It ran up the side of the building, passing outside all the flats, including one with an open window on the second floor. The occupants, presumably because of the heat, had left this open. It was accessible. It would lead to the street. Perfect. Without thinking too much about it, she left her bench, stood for a moment at the bottom of the staircase, looked around once more, then silently made her way up the stair case.

She reached the flat, paused, looked around again, checking she hadn't been seen. There was no one. She was standing outside the open window. Long, white, voile curtains moving very slightly in the gentle breeze concealed the interior. She hesitated, then decisively pulled the window open a little further, pushed her way past the white curtains and climbed in. She was inside someone's bedroom. She stood, listening, wondering if there was a dog but then thought dogs are usually banned in flats.

A couple lay asleep in bed. She glanced at them. She could hear them breathing. Long, slow, steady, breaths, the sound of a deep, dreamless sleep. So quiet. She took off her shoes and holding them in one hand crept across the room. She walked with infinite care across the floor, her eyes travelling across the interior of the room. She had to be careful. No noise.

She'd almost reached the bedroom door when she stopped. It was partially open and the orange glow of the hall lamp lit up the bedroom's interior. What she saw distracted her. She stood. Stared. She felt as if she wasn't quite awake, that she'd woken in a dream and had been transported back in time and place to a country house. It was beautiful, the type of place she'd never been inside but she'd seen photographed in *Country Life*, the magazine for the affluent which sometimes she flicked through at work. She was surprised that such homes existed near the centre of London. She glanced quickly at the occupants, who were still asleep. She continued to gaze at her surroundings.

She observed the wide oak floorboards, burnished dark honey, polished by hand, by someone's hard work, probably not those of the owners. It must have taken years to get them to that sheen. They glowed as the light caught them and they creaked as she walked over them as old floor boards do. They were works of art, like the glowing deep red Persian carpets that lay on them.

An enormous ornate gilt mirror hung over the massive white marble fireplace, and on one side of this was placed a chaise longue, and on the other an opulent arm chair covered in a William Morris linen fabric. Both were strewn with clothes. Everything in that room exuded taste, high-class gentility, and breeding. The furniture hadn't been bought but probably had been passed down through the generations.

She felt in awe of their obvious wealth. Were they 'traders' she wondered, did they work in the city, buying and selling currency back and forth across the globe? Would this have paid for the white-painted antique French 'shabby chic' style bedroom furniture, the wide, sage green, striped wallpaper, the faded water colours of the English countryside hanging from the picture rail, and the old sepia prints of people in silver frames? They stood in groups, the children at the front, embarrassed, smiling. They seemed to look straight at her. She gave them a wink, and a 'thumbs up', for old time's sake. She moved into the hall.

She was making her way to the front door when she heard the cry of a baby. Its sudden wail broke the silence. The baby was inside the flat and its cry brought her back to reality. She was an intruder and she had to get out before the baby's parents woke to attend to their baby. Carrying her shoes, she moved quickly towards the front door. She bent down, pulled them on, the door facing her. She tried opening it. It was locked. She pulled at it. It didn't give way, it was definitely locked. The keys, the keys, the keys, where were they? She couldn't see any.

Fuck, fuck, fuck, now what, she thought. They'll catch me. There was no place to hide in the hall. She moved swiftly to another room. The lounge. Large, floor-length windows with huge, lined silk curtains, framed the street outside, plenty of room to hide behind them. Her breathing was fast, shallow, noisy. She might be heard. She slowed her breathing down. She'd leave as soon as the baby stopped crying. The cover was temporary.

The street lights were still on and they were shining directly onto her. They'd switch off when dawn broke so not long to wait. No one would see her. No one would be out on the street at this time, not even the dog walkers, not unless they were insomniacs. As soon as the baby was settled, she'd find the keys, open the door, creep out. No one would be the wiser. She had a few minutes reprieve. She made another effort to calm herself, slowing her breathing down.

She could hear the baby clearly. He was agitated. His crying grew louder. No one was coming to him.

He'd stopped. Why didn't anyone come to him, what was going on? She had to stay where she was for the moment. She'd give it fifteen minutes then she'd make a move. He didn't seem far away. She could hear him sucking frantically on his dummy. He was so close, he must be in the next room. The doors had been left open. She wondered how old he was, guessed by his cry he was very young. His cry sounded like the wail of a new born, persistent, frightened, 'waa-waa-waa' over and over again. But still no one came.

As she stood there, hiding, it crossed her mind that her behaviour was mad, that she shouldn't be here, that she should have attracted someone's attention at the start to get out of those gardens, but it was too late now. She had to finish what she'd started.

Her eye was caught by a large moth moving up the inside of the curtain. So close to her, she could see its eyes and its antennae. It was crawling as if towards her and as if it knew she didn't like moths and it was going to get deliberately close to persecute her. She watched fascinated as it slowly came near. Its antennae were moving and it was so near, she could squash it. But she couldn't do that. She didn't like killing things, even insects and especially if they were harmless. All the same it was annoying her with its relentless crawling passage. She was thinking, please God, don't crawl on me, but she knew she'd have to tolerate it. She could do nothing. It wouldn't bite. It wasn't a vampire. Look on the bright side, she thought, it could have been a wasp.

She watched the moth for what seemed forever, until it lost interest in the curtain and in her, and after flapping about aimlessly for a second or two, it flew off into the hall, attracted by the light.

Just as she thought the baby had fallen asleep because he hadn't hollered for a while, he started again. His cries were louder, more persistent, to the point it was painful to hear. At first he'd cried with sad, long, wails, but when no one came, his cries became piercing, and he gasped for breath as if in extreme distress or in pain with hunger and was desperate for someone to come and pick him up.

Flori wanted to go to him, pick him up, hold him in her arms, comfort him. He was frightened, lonely while she was becoming increasingly angry. How could his parents continue lying in bed and do nothing? It was unbearable having to listen to his distress. She felt as if she was an accomplice to his murder; the murder of indifference. She thought she could stand it only for another couple of minutes, when she was jolted out of her dilemma.

A woman screamed out. Her voice so loud, so ugly, so penetrating it felt like an assault to her.

'How long are you going to lie there? You lazy bastard. You deaf or something? Can't you hear him? Get the fuck up.'

There was silence, broken only by the baby's continuing cry. No one responded.

'Did you hear me! Get the fuck up. Go on. Get the fuck up. Your son is crying. Your. Son. Is. Crying.'

'Where's the nanny?'

'Are you stupid?' The woman was contemptuous, her voice dipped in sarcasm. 'You prick, she doesn't work Saturdays, don't you know that by now? That means you get him. Get it. You go. Because. He's. Your. Son.'

She left gaps between the words as if talking to an imbecile, or as if he didn't speak English and didn't understand her words.

A man's voice. 'What about you? You go. Are you a cripple or something? He's your son as well.'

This comment inflamed the woman further, she became

hysterical, her accusations wilder, more vicious.

'My son? My son? You say he's my son!' She paused, as if thinking what to say next and then another volley of hate, resentment and spite was let loose. 'Let's get this right, shall we? Shall we? I had him because of you. You. You wanted him for your precious family. That's right, isn't it? Why? Because you wanted an heir and it had to be a boy. So that's what you got. A boy. So. Look after him.' There was a sneer in her voice.

The husband's response seemed weak in comparison. It showed his upset. 'But you wanted a baby. That's what you said. It wasn't just me.'

'Hah! Hah! Hah! Right. But that, I remember, was before we got married, before I knew you, before I knew the truth. That you're a bastard.'

He spat out, 'Me, a bastard? You can talk. Bitch.'

Hearing their destructive rage was almost unbearable. Flori covered her ears with her hands but it couldn't block out their verbal violence. All resemblance to a civilised discussion had been lost; there were no limits to the expression of their hatred. She trembled with fear. The woman was so murderous she was the type to hang, draw and quarter her if she was discovered.

The man was shouting again. 'How do you think I feel? Married to you? Treated like a fucking stallion. A sperm donor to be discarded. You think that makes me feel good? Do you?'

'Well, thank you, thank you very much. What about when one of your oh-so-nice city friends, referred to me as a bitch on heat. That made me feel really good.'

'Drunk. He was drunk. You know that. We've been through this many times.'

'Oh, that makes it alright, does it? That he was pissed?'

'Fuck off. Piss off and take your son with you. Give me a break. It's my flat anyway, so you can get out.' He paused, before adding, 'And when you go – don't come back.'

There was silence for five minutes. Their hatred and

poisonous venom for each other seemed to have worked its way through, even if only temporarily. The baby had gone quiet. Maybe he was listening, terrified, not knowing what the shouting was about. But then he started crying all over again. His cries were becoming evermore frantic. She had to do something, she couldn't leave him any longer. She was at the point of going to pick him up, facing the consequences, when the woman shouted, 'I'll make his bottle. Since you refuse.'

There was no answer but she must have got up and gone into the kitchen because Flori could hear her crashing around. She stayed where she was, hoping she wouldn't be long. She had to get out as soon as she could. She felt a deep sense of foreboding. She could hear the mother shaking the bottle. She sounded like a lunatic. She must have put the bottle in the microwave because she heard the microwave turntable rotating.

At last she heard the woman go to the baby. She heard her say coldly, 'Here's what you want, pest. It's your fault, so you can shut up now.'

That was all. There was no warmth or affection in her voice. The baby made no further noise. Flori imagined her standing over him, glaring down, not touching and not holding him, leaving him where he lay in his cot, while she irritably held the bottle as he hungrily sucked on it. Her baby was of no significance and of no importance. Both she and her husband saw him as a nuisance. They assumed he couldn't see or hear the violence of their rows, let alone be affected by their rows. It was as if he was an irritating animal, and, like feeding an unwanted cat, was fed only to shut him up.

The woman began crying. She cried with loud sobs that racked her body. It was awful to listen to, as if she was in the depths of despair. But the husband slept through his wife's distress, snoring so loudly nothing could be heard, let alone the sobs of his partner. Eventually she stopped and she must have gone to bed in another room, because Flori heard a door across the hall close softly. For ten minutes she heard nothing. The silence was sinister.

Standing listening for every sound but hearing nothing, it crossed Flori's mind that the baby was dead, that she'd murdered him, put a pillow over his head, but then she guessed what might have happened. His mother had no patience, she didn't want to care for him, didn't want to feed him, didn't want to hold the bottle while he sucked, so she'd left it propped up on a cushion and left him to it. She expected him to feed himself, on his own, tiny, desolate and uncomprehending. Flori felt again a familiar flame of angry distress burn through her. She had to get out of this flat, leave and as soon as possible.

She moved into the hall. All the doors were shut so any noise she might make wouldn't be heard. She paused. Before she left, she had to see the baby. She wanted to see what he looked like, wanted to reassure herself he was still alive.

She'd been in the flat long enough to know where he was.

She went straight to his room. She pushed the door open quietly. Little by little. She peered round the door. She entered the room. The room smelt of new carpet and fresh paint. It was almost in darkness. The pale light of dawn could be seen round the edges of the curtains. She could see well enough.

The baby was at the far end, underneath a window with the curtains drawn. He was lying in one of those swinging cribs. She crept across the room and stood looking down at him. He was sleeping, dressed in an all-in-one, and lay on his back. It was just after six now and getting lighter. A police siren passed at high speed down the street. The baby was startled, jumped, opened his eyes, looked straight at her and for a second she thought he'd cry, but he sighed, rubbed his eyes with his fist, turned his head to one side and fell back to sleep. He was exhausted and satiated with milk. He hadn't registered there was a stranger in his room. She stood smiling at him, listening to his breathing, staring at him, noticing every tiny detail about him.

He had fine, dark, straight hair. It occurred to her how like Tids he was. Her brother, Tids. Baby Tids. Did he smile the way Tids used to? She wondered what he looked like when he was awake, what colour his eyes were. She'd always liked it when Tids smiled. She couldn't resist it. She delicately and lightly pushed the crib with one finger. Watched it swing. Just a little. She wanted to see what he looked like if he did wake up, but he didn't wake, even when the crib swung gently back and forth. He was too exhausted. She watched him until the crib stopped swinging.

She turned. Looked round the room. A wet nappy hanging over a bin. An empty bottle left on a mahogany chest of drawers. A clock ticking. The noise irritated her. Each hour painted with a different bird. She took it off the wall, removed the battery, placed it on a chair, covered it with a cushion. A baby monitor. She walked across to see if it was on. The room was quiet. Any noise would be heard. She felt nervous. His parents might hear her, maybe see her. They might be watching her. But it was switched off. Their first priority was to themselves, so why would it be on? There was a colour photograph in a silver frame on the chest of drawers. It was of a woman, presumably his mother, the one she'd just heard screaming. It must have been taken after she'd given birth. She was holding a tiny baby swaddled in a white cot blanket. She was smiling, looking down at the baby. Her husband had his arm round her. She studied it. Happy families, she thought. She put the photo face down on the chest of drawers, then on second thoughts, picked it up, opened a drawer, pushed it inside. Better. Out of sight, out of mind. She wouldn't have to look at it.

She went back to the crib. Back to the baby and noticed he had a toy giraffe. It lay next to him and was one of those soft baby toys that people give to newborns. Not like a real giraffe, because they're all legs and necks. This one was short legged, chubby, with big brown eyes, and a smiley, happy face. She picked it up, looked at it closely. It was like a baby because it was round with short limbs and big eyes. It was

20

sweet. She put the giraffe back in his crib next to him and watched his hand curl round it. It must be his favourite. Tears pricked her eyes. She knew him, all about him, and he knew who she was. He needed her like Tids had needed her.

She stared at him, standing absolutely still, looked intensely at him. After all this time, he was back. That made her happy. She loved him. He must know that. She wanted to tell him she'd come back and that he'd be safe now. She'd look after him. She wouldn't leave him. She'd protect him. She'd make him happy.

But his name. What was it? She didn't know his name. He wasn't called anything. He was nameless. He wasn't their baby. He could be anybody's baby. He could be her baby. He was her baby. He was Tids. He was her brother.

She moved closer. She knelt down and looked into the crib. She could see him properly. She was so close she could feel his soft breath and the rhythm of his breathing. His breath was her breath. That's how close she was. As if they were joined and were one. He was adorable. Innocent, helpless, vulnerable, totally dependent, he had thick, dark hair, and he'd fallen asleep on his back. He was surrounded with soft bright toys, and the giraffe that was his favourite. But he really wanted her. She knew that.

She knelt by him and looked at him for a long time. She didn't know how long she was there. Crouching by him. Listening. The room was quiet, almost peaceful, but not in her head. Thoughts, sounds, images from her past came. Crowding through her mind. The sound of traffic in the distance. Fading until a long way off. Her heart beating. Filling the room. Shouting. She could hear shouting. Crying. Her mother sobbing. A man pushing her against the wall. Her mother falling. She was falling. Putting her hands over her head to protect herself, screaming for help, calling for her, 'Flori, Flori, Flori.' A terrible, long scream.

No. She covered her ears. She wouldn't listen to them. She must get out. She stood up. Her breath came in short gasps.

21

She had to act. Save him. Rescue him. Protect him. She must. Before it was too late. She pulled away the blanket covering him. Slowly, gently, quietly, she picked the baby up. He was tiny. So tiny. She brought him close to her. She was crying. Silent tears flowed down her face. She bent down, picked up his little fat giraffe, put it next to him, then she wrapped them both, the baby and the giraffe, tightly in his blanket. She put his bottle and his dummy in her bag. He didn't wake up.

She held him close to her until she felt the warmth of his body. She was going to keep him. He was real and she was going to look after him forever. He belonged to her and no one else. She was the only one who could keep him safe. No one could harm him now. They didn't deserve to have him. She hated them. She hated them for not loving him. They wouldn't get him. Not this time. She walked silently into the hall, holding him in her arms, still crying. It was right to take him. She'd love him, protect him.

She stood by the front door looking for the keys. She could see them on the floor under the hall table. She picked the keys up, turned them in the lock and let herself and the baby out of the flat. She was as silent as possible. She noticed the brass plate on the door was polished but there were fingerprints on it. This alerted her. Using the corner of her wrap, she wiped the keys and the brass plate clear of finger prints and left the door slightly open.

She moved across to the lift shaft. It was directly in front of her. She pressed the button to call the lift. It came straightaway. It was old-fashioned, lined with mahogany, with more polished brass and with metal trellised doors.

She got in holding the baby, pulled the doors across and pressed the button. It glided silently down, jerked to a stop at the bottom. She pulled the door open. It was stiff and she had to balance the baby on one arm while she did that. She wiped all traces of her fingerprints from the lift. She left the inner and outer lift doors open so the lift couldn't be used. The baby remained sleeping in her arms.

She opened the front door, stood for a moment in the doorway, looking out and along the street. There was no one. She would go now. Holding the baby in her arms she walked down the steps. It was that easy. They were free. A wave of happiness passed through her. They knew nothing about her. She'd left no trace, no fingerprints. She was anonymous. They were about to disappear. They'd never be found. The early morning air was cool as she walked away holding the baby in her arms.

From the moment she'd seen him and held him against her, she'd thought of him as her own. Though she hadn't carried him inside her body and so didn't know how it felt to be pregnant, it made no difference; she felt she was his mother. The woman who'd actually given birth to him, she had little thought for. She was irrelevant because she, Flori, deserved him, and from now on she was going to look after him and keep him safe.

Driven by something she didn't understand, she was in the same state of mind that had led her to snatch him. She'd protect and care for him but her over-riding aim was to avoid getting caught and she was prepared to do anything necessary to achieve that. Her mind began focusing on the practicalities. Although she was short of sleep, she was also high on adrenaline, which meant she felt disconnected from what she was doing. It wasn't really her. It was as if she was floating above the general melee and as if she wasn't part of the real world.

What should she do first? She reasoned the baby would need feeding, but she had no baby milk. She hadn't thought she'd be looking after a baby. She didn't know how old he was but she assumed he must be not long born because he didn't weigh much. She stood inside a shop doorway and pulled the wrap away from his face to look at him. He was tiny, a little thing, sleeping peacefully, his eyes tight shut, his dark hair curling over his forehead, his hands curled. He could cry any moment. When new babies got hungry and cried, they had to be attended to quickly, otherwise they got into a state. They made a noise. They roared. They woke the neighbourhood from their sleep. She stared hard at him. It was difficult to know for sure his age but she guessed he was less than two months. His precise age wouldn't matter too much because as long as she got baby milk for the newborn to three months that would be suitable. But she'd have to get it quickly.

As she walked towards the tube, she remembered there was an all-night chemist close by. It was big and it would have everything she needed for him. It was still early, before seven, but already there was traffic and pedestrians, so she wouldn't be too conspicuous shopping with a baby at this time. She reached the chemist's shop, looked around for the CCTV. She didn't want to be filmed and appear on *Crime Watch* at some later date so, keeping her head well down, she walked along the aisle looking for baby formula. She knew enough to be aware of the cameras, the police, and not to get into conversation which might draw attention to her and make her memorable. She had to avoid raising suspicions.

The baby stuff was easy to find. There were racks of it and she was in luck. A special offer; a collection for newborns which included a feeding bottle, formula, steriliser, dummy, cotton wool, and baby cream; everything was there. She looked for nappies, hesitated, deciding to buy them nearer to her flat in Paddington. That way, she wouldn't have so much to carry. She stood and waited to pay at the counter. The chemist was arguing with a drug addict who'd brought in his script, but had got into a row with another customer. The police had been called and in the general uproar, he hardly looked at Flori. She paid cash and hurried out. Keeping her head well down, she drew the baby closer to her. She could feel his body heat, and felt a wave of love for him but she remained anxious and nervous. She imagined people looking at her, wondering why she was up so early and why she carried a baby in her arms without a buggy.

She was still too close to where she'd taken him and with every passing minute was aware that once his parents were awake, they'd go to the baby's room and find him gone. The police would be called and they'd swarm all over Earls Court looking for women with a tiny baby, especially one with no buggy. She had to get home quickly. She quickened her pace, avoiding looking anyone in the eye.

She had to get back to Paddington, disappear into the background and leave no trace of her presence. It was too far to walk, but still too early to ring Rose and ask her for a lift. There was also the potential problem of how Rose would react to her baby. She'd have to explain to her why she'd taken the baby and how it had happened.

She began thinking through how to get back to her flat. The tube was quick and wouldn't be too crowded at this time of the morning, but there were too many cameras around and people sitting opposite her in the carriage might notice her agitation and remember her so she decided against that. It was too risky.

Black cabs were a possibility. But black cab drivers were smart and they were often curious about their passengers and had a habit of starting conversations with their fares, especially after a night shift. Tiredness seemed to make them more talkative, and she didn't want a stream of comments or questions directed at her over their shoulder. They might ask where she'd been, the name of her baby and why she was up with a baby so early.

As she thought this, she noticed the revolving red neon sign of a minicab office. She'd give them a try. Minicab drivers didn't ask questions, half didn't speak much English and the other half were students, trying to increase their income. Whoever they were, and wherever they were from, most didn't give a damn who was in their car as long as they got paid. Their minds were always elsewhere. She walked into the office.

The controller must have been working all night. He

was watching early morning television, and looked bored and irritable. He asked Flori where she was going. When she said Paddington, he called a car straight away. Flori gave the driver an address two streets away from where she lived, just in case he was ever questioned. But as she'd predicted he didn't look at her, even when she paid him and gave a small tip so as not to draw attention to herself.

Once she was dropped off and began the walk back she became panicky that she'd be caught before she reached her flat. But if she rang Rose for help, her call could be intercepted by the police. For all she knew she could already have been spotted and was being followed. Making a call on her mobile would mean she could be traced and although it was unlikely they already had her mobile number, she had to cover her tracks. She'd watched enough American crime films to know how to be anonymous. She had to change her phone.

Near her flat she'd noticed a kiosk advertising the sale of mobiles, 'unlocking' mobiles and new Sim cards. She walked in and, avoiding the man's eyes, bought a new phone and Sim card. She planned to discard her own phone when she got home. She'd conceal it and put it in a public bin as far away as possible from where she lived or, alternatively, she'd ask Rose to dispose of it when she returned to Uni in Oxford. But now she had this new mobile, any calls couldn't be traced back. It would take the police time to find out her number by which time it would be too late. She'd be gone.

Twenty-five minutes later carrying the baby she walked up the steps to where she lived, entered the hall and opened the front door to her flat. She looked around; everything looked the same. She lay the baby down in a chair and packed cushions round him to keep him from falling. He was asleep. She stood watching him. He was so still that for a moment she feared he'd died, but no, he was still breathing.

It was two hours since he'd been fed and it must be getting close to when he'd wake up for another feed.

She smiled to herself. He was so perfect, so beautiful.

She placed his little fat giraffe next to him and looked at her watch. Surely his parents would have woken by now and seen he was missing? But she felt triumphant, and whispered, as if his parents were in the room and she was addressing them directly, 'He's mine. I'm going to look after him. It's too late, you've had your chance.'

He began wriggling. He was waking, becoming restless, his hands came up to his eyes, he rubbed them, then whimpered, and with his fingers curled round his giraffe, pulled it to his mouth and started sucking one of the horns. He must be hungry. Flori was immediately panicky and wondered what she should do. It was so long since she'd looked after Tids, but then she realised, all she had to do was care for him as she had her brother all those years ago. She picked him up, and holding him cradled in her left arm, carried him into the kitchen. As soon as she held him, he stopped crying. That pleased her and, speaking to him softly, she told him what a lovely boy he was.

That his mother hadn't breast fed him made it easier for her. She'd read babies knew the smell of their mother, so with time, he'd get used to her. She prepared the milk, sat down in an armchair and, cradling him closely, began feeding him. He sucked strongly on the teat of the bottle. He seemed ravenous, even though it wasn't so long since he'd been fed, and as he fed he looked deeply into her eyes.

Just looking at him fascinated her. He made her smile and she began baby talking to him, telling him how beautiful and how clever he was. She was sure that he was listening to her, because when he'd almost emptied the bottle his hands came up uncertainly to her face. She caught one of them, waved it with her own, and laughed. Once he'd finished his bottle, his eyes drooped but he was struggling to keep them open. He looked briefly at her, then closed them and immediately dropped off asleep. She put him over her shoulder to wind him and obligingly he gave a loud burp.

Flori was pleased. This had been his first feed, but she'd

managed to settle him and he seemed to have accepted her. She couldn't take her eyes off him. He reminded her so much of Tids the way he lay asleep. Satiated with milk, he'd become transported to nirvana and like a baby Buddha he now lay asleep in his own milky, happy world. No one need ever shout at him again or leave him to cry and that made her feel good. She would love him.

She became aware that the front of her dress was wet from where she'd held him. She put him on his back, unbuttoned his baby grow and as she expected, his nappy was saturated. In her haste to get back she'd forgotten to buy nappies and neither had she rung Rose.

Needs must, she thought. She pulled his wet nappy from his inert little body, found a clean, dry towel, cut long narrow strips from it, wrapped a piece round his bottom, and then secured it with a pair of her own pants. These were small and kept the towelling in place. It would do, she thought, until she got the nappies. While she did this, he hadn't woken or cried. She put him back on the sofa and again surrounded him with the cushions. He remained asleep. Flori laughed and said, 'You're my tiny king and you hold the key to my heart, I love you so much and you're beautiful and you're clever.'

But she must ring Rose and ask her to bring some nappies. She needed her help, but she'd been so focused on looking after the baby, she'd hadn't thought how she'd react. That might be difficult, but she thought she could persuade her to see it her way. It was how she told her. She'd have to break the news gently and wondered what was the best way to do this. She'd have to give an initial reason, one that was believable.

An explanation came to her. It was simple and believable. She'd tell her she was unexpectedly looking after a neighbour's baby, but his mother had forgotten to leave her any nappies. She'd say she couldn't take the baby out because he'd just fallen asleep. She'd ask Rose to get them and afterwards ask her to come and have a coffee with her. Then she could tell her the whole story.

She picked up her new mobile and rang her. She stood watching the baby's perfect smallness while she waited for her to pick up. Rose didn't answer straightaway, which made her anxious. She began pacing up and down. She became impatient, and said, 'Come on Rose, pick up, pick up, it's urgent.' She became more agitated. Maybe she wasn't there or was deeply asleep or because she wouldn't recognise the number, she wouldn't pick up. It rang for what seemed a long time, before Rose finally answered, 'Hello, who is this?'

'Rose, sorry to wake you up early but I lost my mobile last night. This is my new one but listen, there's an emergency, I'm unexpectedly looking after my neighbour's baby and she's forgotten to give me his nappies. Would you get hold of some?'

There was a silence before Rose answered, 'What? Now? I've only just woken up, and Dave's only just gone.'

'Please, Rose, it's urgent, the baby needs them, I haven't got a buggy to take him out, I've just fed him and he's saturated already. Look, you could pick up croissants from the cafe down the road and I'll make you coffee.'

Rose sounded reluctant but she said, 'Okay, if I must.'

'That's great, but make sure to get the right size, the one that comes after newborn, you know, the three to six months and he's tiny, a little boy, so get the right shape, but thank you so much, Rose. I really appreciate it.'

Rose didn't ask any more questions. She said she'd be there soon and began telling her about Dave, how he'd stayed the night, how much she'd liked him but she was fed up because he was flying out to Athens soon. Flori wasn't listening. Her mind drifted off and she was back to admiring her baby. She couldn't take her eyes off him. It was as if he was a wonderful present, but one that miraculously behaved like a real baby.

She was barely aware of what Rose was saying until she heard her say, 'Flori, you're not listening. I can tell.'

'Sorry. I am, well, most of the time, I am, but you will get them, won't you? You won't forget.'

She switched off her mobile. Rose was right, she wasn't really interested in what she'd been up to. How could she be when she had her new baby to look after? She sat down to wait. She wasn't sure what to do. There was so much to think about, so much to organise and it would all take time. One step at a time, she thought, luckily today's one of my days off, but I can't return to work, not now I've got a baby but I'll sort this out later with Rose.

She glanced again at the baby lying asleep. She didn't know his name. She couldn't introduce him to Rose when she didn't know his name. The woman in the flat hadn't called him anything but Rose would be sure to ask what he was called. Maybe she could call him Tids? The name she'd given her brother, but, if she called him that she could get muddled up. She decided against it. She continued to worry about his name and what she should call him until eventually she came up with an idea.

A Naming Ceremony, one that would be secret, just for the two of them.

It had to be memorable, one the baby wouldn't forget. She wanted a bond between them. A bond that would last forever. It would be her ritual and although right now she didn't know his name, she'd choose one at his Naming Ceremony. It would come to her. All she had to do would be with him and the right name would come into her mind. But she had to do this quickly. Rose would arrive soon, and she didn't want anyone else here for the Ceremony, not even Rose.

She stood up but was beginning to feel strange, as if she'd given birth to him. She remembered Matt and how he used to smile at her. It was so long ago since they'd last seen one another. She wondered what he was doing and wished he was with her and that this baby was his. She sighed and picked him up, but as she held him close to her, he woke. He pulled away from her and was staring at her, but he didn't cry. What

30

was he thinking? She had no idea. She wished he'd talk. She carried him into the kitchen and looked at the clothes she'd taken off.

They were wet, they'd have to be washed. His 'baby grow' was pale lemon, a colour she didn't like. It wouldn't have been her choice and every time she saw it she was reminded of his past and what they'd come through, but there was no time to buy new clothes now.

Holding him in the crook of her arm she walked into her bedroom and lay him in the middle of her bed where she could see him while she chose something from the store of baby clothes. She pulled the cane screen away from the corner of the wall. Tids wouldn't mind if she used his clothes, after all, they were like brothers. She began sorting through the various combinations of baby clothes until she found one she thought would be right. Striped navy leggings, with a matching navy top, it was embroidered in red with the logo, 'Don't mess with me.' A fierce-looking baby glowered on the front. She laughed. 'Now you'll look like a real boy.'

She began dressing him in this outfit, but noticed when she laughed, he didn't, and this made her despondent. Why didn't he? Maybe, she thought, it was because he was too young to respond. Or maybe he didn't like her. But once he knew her and she'd looked after him longer, he would, she felt sure of that.

'What chubby legs you have, I could eat you up,' she said, as she pulled the striped tights onto him. He was holding onto his giraffe so tightly she had to wrench it out of his hand to get his top on. 'You're so attached to your fat giraffe,' she said and laughed and waved it at him. His eyes followed the movement, but not for long. He switched his gaze back to her again. She wondered again what he was thinking, and whether he was puzzled who she was, but she came to the conclusion that babies probably don't think. Not when they're so little. After all, they don't have words, so they can't speak. But still she was curious. She wondered whether he had images of the woman she'd heard screaming and he sensed she was different to her.

Her mind went back to the flat, replaying what she'd overheard. She imagined how he must have felt hearing the rows, the shouting, the hatred and aggression. He wouldn't have been able to make sense of it and would have been frightened. She knew herself how it felt to be frightened and her eyes filled with tears. She tightly swaddled him in the small, white cot blanket with the fleece she'd found behind the screen, putting his giraffe close to him and where he could see it and said, 'Now you're ready, you're safe with me and you don't have to cry anymore, baby.'

She began to look for candles for the Ceremony. She knew she had some but she wasn't sure where, and she began looking for them in a cupboard. It was untidy but after pulling out all the old papers and magazines, she found them. There were two of them, both decorative and they'd been pushed right at the back.

She also came across the old scrapbook and a wave of anxiety swept through her. She stood up, holding it in her hands as if it would contaminate her, asking herself why she kept it.

It was from the past and that woman had made her, but she'd never asked her if she wanted it. Seeing it now and unexpectedly made her feel light headed and breathless. It was an old feeling but she also felt fear. Not ordinary fear but worse, terror, as if she was going to die. That was familiar, too. That horrible, horrible feeling from the past. She hated that scrapbook. She hated it as if it would infect her. It reminded her of the bad times. She pushed it to the back of the cupboard so it was hard to find. One day she'd burn it.

She picked up the candles and looked closely at them. She'd been saving them for a special occasion. They were deep green, with an abstract red, gold and green pattern embossed on them. She placed them on a glass plate, put them on her table and carefully lit them. Within minutes they gave off the fragrance of a forest in the summer, of warm pine trees and bracken, crushed underfoot. Immediately she felt a sense of peace. She picked up the baby and held him to her but as she did, he woke up. He began watching her, his eyes wide.

She laid him on a large cushion on the table by the two candles, and surrounded him with more cushions. She turned towards her music centre. She knew the music she wanted as the background for the Ceremony. It was the music of the sitar, a classical Indian Raga called *Shahana*, and was one of her favourites. She played it only occasionally, when she was searching for an inner peace. It was so beautiful, and as she heard it play, Flori began to dance.

Slowly, slowly, she moved round the room and round the baby. She felt she was going into a trance. She lifted up her arms and spun round in time to the music. For Flori, it was the music of love, of tranquillity, of nature, of the deep forest, of the sound of water tumbling over boulders, and of distant birdsong. It was dreamlike and for that moment she was transported away. The sound of the London traffic disappeared, leaving only the beautiful melody of the sitar. She turned up the volume, ever so slightly and noticed the baby's head turn towards her. He was watching her.

She bent her head close to her baby, whispered to him, 'The mists rise and carry the gods and goddesses of the mountains. The spirits of the forests and of the seas carry you. You hear the music of the sun, the shadows of the leaves, and the blue of the sky crossing the heavens. You have been chosen to interpret nature's wildness. You are free, a magic baby, poetry is in your soul and may it always be with you.'

As she said this, an image came to her of a bearded warrior in a coat of arms. He was sitting on a beautifully coloured chestnut horse standing high on a mountain and against a clear brilliant blue sky. Flori paused. The warrior's name. Owain. It was his name she'd call the baby. The name of the warrior. She hesitated briefly, then she said, 'I name you, Owain.'

She lightly kissed him once on each cheek, then crossed

over to her vase of red carnations. She selected five perfect flowers, arranging them in a circle round his head on the cushion. He looked up at her. She smiled at him and then read these lines from Pablo Neruda's *Love Sonnets.*

'I do not love you as if you were salt-rose, or topaz
Or the arrow of carnations the fire shoots off
I love you as certain dark things are to be loved
In secret, between the shadow and the soul.'

She gazed at him, thinking how beautiful he was. She whispered, 'You're mine,' and to capture the moment, she picked up her camera, was about to press the shutter when she heard the flat's buzzer. It was loud, buzzing incessantly. The noise brought her back to reality. A flash of fear. But she had to answer it. She walked over and looked through the flat's intercom. Rose. She pressed the button to let her in.

2

Flori was alone on the island with Owain. She felt desolate. She hadn't wanted Matt to go. He was her anchor. He listened to her. He understood her and without him, she felt like an automaton, going through the daily routine of feeding, bathing and dressing Owain but all the time preoccupied with thoughts and feelings for him. Powerful feelings of loss would sweep over her, catching her when she least expected them. She feared she'd never see him again and wished fervently she hadn't promised not to contact him.

But gradually, as time passed, the responsibilities of caring for Owain distracted her and her dark mood began to lift. Today though, Rose was coming and she was looking forward to her visit.

She'd taken to standing outside the croft's front door and looking at the wild fuchsia bushes. They seemed to grow everywhere; their brightly coloured purple and pink flowers cheering the low light of dusk. Sometimes there was no wind, no bird call, and without the sounds of traffic or the police sirens, she could hear the hum of electricity through the wires, and the silence. It surrounded the croft. Eerie and dreamlike it reminded her of Wales. Although it was over two years since she'd lived in the caravan by the sea at Newgale, and it had been quiet there, she'd forgotten how silent the countryside was at night.

She didn't miss London. She recognised without the shops, buses, cars and taxis, she now had the time and the space to think. She loved the island's solitude , but sometimes, being on her own, she felt moody, and then she'd remember things, events, people from her past. She'd tried to avoid thinking about it, but it was unsuccessful.

Her mind continually went over the past six weeks and she'd wonder if she could survive living on this remote Scottish island without the constant support and friendship of Rose. There was the loss of her flat, too. It had been her home and she loved it. She'd decorated it and furnished it with care and style and it had provided her with security. Every now and again she'd think she must have been crazy to have given it up to live on a remote Scottish island with a baby, even if only temporarily.

And at night she'd begun to dream. They were bad dreams. She'd tried reassuring herself that the dreaming was because of her fear of loneliness and of the unknown, but the reassurance didn't work. The reality of the recent past would hit her and she had a sudden insight into how others might see her and she didn't like it. It was disorientating and confusing and she'd ask herself, why were Rose and Matt helping her? Were they mad too? And the nights were the worst, that's when she hated being on her own. The loneliness, solitude, and bleakness of the island wound round her like the damp sea mist, until she felt saturated with its atmosphere.

The dreams were becoming repetitive and they frightened her. They were always the same, but that didn't make them any easier. Memories and images from when she'd been a child, none of them seemed real; visual fragments from the past, the sea ferry approaching the island, the high mountains in the middle, a single track road with grass and weeds growing in the middle, a desolate house, being told a famous writer had lived there long ago, and always, the wild vivid red and purple fuchsias growing in the hedgerows.

After these dreams and she'd woken up, the panic attacks

would start. She'd be gripped by fears of abandonment that Rose wouldn't come and she was left waiting. Waiting for people that might not arrive, might let her down, anxieties that put her on edge and seared into her. They reminded her of when she was waiting for Matt to drive her and Owain here and she'd retrace in her mind the night she'd left London with him. Not that that made her feel any better. It was a compulsion, an obsession. The thoughts were just the same. Matt was going to let her down.

The night they were to leave London she'd placed everything she'd packed just inside her flat door. She'd checked and re-checked that she hadn't forgotten anything. Owain had been asleep in his buggy and he hadn't woken when she moved him. She'd been looking out of the window as Matt had driven up and she'd watched him reverse into the space she'd marked out with two large dustbins on the road. She'd run down the steps to greet him.

'Alright, Flori?' he'd said and as she nodded, he'd put his arm round her shoulder and given her a brief hug, but she could see he was tense and preoccupied. 'We must be quick,' he'd said. They'd packed the car within the hour and he'd placed Owain in his buggy, which he detached from the frame onto the floor of the Land Rover, just behind the front seats. Owain had woken up and he'd stared at the roof of the Land Rover, but when she'd climbed in and spoken to him, his little face had lit up with a smile of recognition. His trust in her had made her feel tearful and she'd touched his cheek and spoken softly to him but there had been tears in her eyes.

'I'll check round the flat, make sure nothing's forgotten before we go,' she'd said, and she'd climbed slowly up the steps back to her flat. Entering each room for the last time she'd felt again a rising panic, but it was too late then for regrets; there was no turning back. As she'd walked away from the tall, white building, her legs felt like lead and she'd glanced back at what had been her home for over two years, forcing herself to walk towards the Land Rover. She was only half-aware that Matt was sitting in the driver's seat and that he was observing her closely. She'd smiled at him as she shakily climbed into the front seat of the Land Rover. It had taken three days to get here but they'd made it.

Now she was waiting again. This time for Rose. She went back inside the croft and looked around the room. She was here now and whatever happened, she'd have to make the best of it. The whole croft needed brightening up. It was so dark and dismal. She'd asked Rose to bring coloured emulsion and paints with her. She planned then to paint the walls, put her belongings, books and pictures around, make it look more like her own place.

The wait made her feel impatient and she went upstairs to check on Owain. He was asleep. She returned downstairs and went outside to sit on her favourite bench. It was still warm enough. She loved sitting outside at dusk. She'd watch the occasional deer walk slowly through the bracken, and she'd keep so still it wouldn't see her.

She'd been outside ten minutes when she heard it. Loud music. Salsa, the music incongruous against the backdrop of the heather and bracken hills of Jura. The silence of the countryside ripped apart. It could only be Rose. It was her type of music. She must have her car window wide open and be very near. She'd reached Lagg and was almost here, driving off the road and making her way down the track towards the croft. It sounded that way. Flori smiled. Knowing that, cheered her, made her smile. Within seconds a car came into view, halted, and Rose jumped out.

Flori stood up and laughing with delight, she said, 'Hey, look who it is, turn it up, turn the music up, it's not loud enough, I want the neighbours to hear, they can join in the party.' She clicked her fingers and gyrated around in time to the music.

'Neighbours? What neighbours?' Rose looked around blankly, then realised Flori was joking, 'Very funny. How you doing? Long time, no see.'

Flori put her hands on her hips, looked her friend up

and down, said. 'I see you've dressed for the part.'

'What's wrong with how I'm dressed? I like this outfit.' Rose looked down at what she was wearing.

'Absolutely nothing. You look as if you're about to do some hunting, shooting, fishing. Not.'

'I can change. It's just what I travelled in.'

'Yeah, well, it's just that people round here don't usually dress in vivid blue dresses with pearls, and paint their nails scarlet. It looks odd on the hills.' She smiled at her friend. 'I'm kidding you. And you look great. Anyway, welcome. You can't imagine how pleased I am to see you. Really pleased.'

She gave Rose a hug and, glancing towards the back seat of the car, saw it was piled with the things she'd asked her to bring. Tins of different colours of emulsion paint, books, pictures, CDs, and one of her favourite rugs.

'Rose, that's great, you've brought it, all that stuff, thank you. After I'd asked I thought it might be difficult to get into my flat, in case the police were watching it?'

'Thought the same. I checked it out first. Hung around but no sign of them, so they can't know. I let myself in, rooted round and found what you wanted behind the cane screen. Uh, those baby clothes you asked for, wasn't sure what you wanted, you didn't say, but I thought that's funny, they're all baby boy clothes.'

'Funny? What's so funny? And why are you giving me the evil eye, staring like that?'

'I'm not. Don't take on. No need to get uptight. Here's my present.' Rose passed her a beautifully packed flat parcel.

Flori unpacked it. It was a linen tablecloth in pale, duck-egg blue. She held it up, stroking it with her hands, 'Beautiful, Rose. So classy. Just like you.'

'Well, it's for you.'

'Thank you. I really, really appreciate it.' She leaned forward and gave Rose a quick kiss on the cheek. 'Now come inside and I'll show you Owain and I want to hear all about your journey.'

'It's great to see you, Flori. Really, really good, but I'm exhausted, it's a hell of a journey, takes forever, and getting round Glasgow was a nightmare, but I'm here. And Owain? How's he doing, your pride and joy.'

'He's thriving, put weight on since you last saw him. Follow me. He's upstairs asleep.'

They stood looking at him.

Rose whispered, 'He's gorgeous, gorgeous, gorgeous, good enough to eat. Flori. Congratulations.'

Flori beamed. 'I love him to bits and he knows that. He'll wake up soon, then you can see him properly. Let's go down.'

'Well, how's it going then?'

'Fine...well most of the time. I'm so happy you're here, Rose and when you're ready I'll show you the metropolis of Lagg and look,' she said pointing to a flask on the side of the dresser, 'I'm even making my own yoghurt. I'm turning into a country person and I'm thinking of joining the Women's Institute soon.'

Rose laughed, 'Give me a break, that'll be the day. Not your style.'

They went back outside and unpacked the car. Rose had brought more presents for Flori; a book about the Hebrides, a box of wine, and a quirky-looking clock for the wall and by the time they'd finished, Owain had woken up.

Flori ran upstairs to get him, picked him gently out of his crib and brought him down. She held up the sleepy baby for Rose's approval. Seeing someone he didn't know, Owain clung to Flori, staring at Rose over his shoulder with his wide eyes, while holding onto his giraffe. Flori smiled, 'He likes to keep his giraffe close to him and he's started sucking his thumb.'

'You know, Flori, he's made a really strong attachment to you and, funnily enough, he looks like you, almost as if he's your baby, and you've given birth to him. How weird.'

'What are you talking about? Of course, he looks like me, we've got the same mother, after all.'

There was a silence before Rose said, 'The same mother. What do you mean?'

Flori didn't answer, Rose's comment didn't appear to register with her. She said, 'Do you think he's grown since you last saw him?'

Rose looked puzzled. She said, 'I'd say. Doubled his body weight, by the look of him. How much does he weigh now?'

'How would I know? I'm not sure. Maybe I should get some scales, but it has crossed my mind, that if he falls ill, I can't take him to a baby clinic. Can I?'

'Oh, I wouldn't worry about that. You'd probably be alright here, you could say you were a visitor, or you could lie, they wouldn't know.'

'But they'd want records, they'd want to know where he was born and who was the GP, and what could I say? Nothing.'

'Well, let's hope it doesn't happen.'

Flori looked apprehensive. 'What are they saying now? In the press, Is there much in the papers about him?'

'Apparently his name is Bertie, but it's all gone quiet, and that's ominous. It makes me wonder what's going on. Why do you ask?'

Flori stared at her. 'What do you think?'

'Well, what I was thinking was, on the way here, that maybe, maybe, Flori, we should watch *Crime Watch*. I read in *The Independent* that this next episode was about the 'baby snatching', and that makes it even more important to watch. It makes sense. We should know, see what the police are up to, and how much they've find out. What do you think?'

Flori saw Rose was watching her. What she'd just said made her feel suspicious, uneasy. She didn't want to face the reality of how Owain came into her life. She was silent, looked closely at her friend, tried to read what might be going through her mind.

She said, 'It'll spoil your visit if we watch *Crime Watch* and I don't want to, I don't want to watch it. Besides, it's probably not on here.'

'It is, I checked it. It's tomorrow, I think. We have to, Flori. We have to know how much they know. Isn't it wise, not to bury our heads in the sand?'

Flori sighed, looked reluctant and then said, 'If we must.'

'You know we must. I have to look after you and Owain. I don't want them to find you, so we have to be one step ahead. Now, let's eat, then you can show me around outside and we can walk down to the water and look across to the mainland.'

3

It was calm; a day with little wind and the late summer sun cast a soft light over the hills. Flori and Rose were taking Owain for a walk. Heading towards the north end of the island, they pushed him in his all-terrain buggy along the deserted road. Flori glanced at Owain lying on his back in the warm depths of his buggy. He was facing them both and watching them with his large dark eyes, and with, they both agreed, an intelligent interest. They'd discussed how much he might understand, but decided as he was only a few weeks old, it wasn't much.

He'd become the centre of their attention so when Rose commented that Owain's buggy was fit for a king or like a Roman chariot and wasted on a mere baby, this started Flori off in fits of giggles. He enjoyed having their attention so much that when Flori began to prepare him for bed, he still wanted to be part of the fun and protested loudly and vigorously at being put down. Only his bottle pacified him and Flori had to stay with him in the quiet of her bedroom until he fell asleep.

Returning down stairs she found Rose sitting in the lounge in one of the dark green moquette armchairs. Flori looked round the room's décor. 'Rose,' she said, 'This room is drab, drab, drab so I for one, need a glass of wine.' She went to the case of wine Rose had brought with her and opened one of the bottles, while Rose looked for two wine glasses.

'There's plenty of small whisky glasses but no wine glasses. People here drink more whisky than wine,' Flori said, and passed over to Rose two rather ugly tumblers.

Rose filled one to the brim and handed it back to her. 'So how did Owain take to being put down? Was he alright about it?'

'No, he wasn't, he didn't want to go, he wanted to stay up and be with us, but when I gave him his bottle, he was okay.'

'That's good, because I want to show you something, Flori. A letter I found in my mother's bureau. I'll get it. I'd like you to read it and tell me what you think. It won't take long, then we can watch *Crime Watch*.'

Flori looked at her friend. She'd been hoping Rose would forget about the programme but clearly she hadn't. She said, 'You know what, I tried putting on the television earlier, but the reception was so bad, I couldn't see the picture. It's like that round here, a bit intermittent.'

'So what do you do?'

'Wait for the weather to improve. The television is old, but I'm used to it. Maybe we can try later. I'll show you.' She walked over and turned on the TV. The screen was filled with what looked like a snow fall, 'See what I mean.' She turned to face Rose. 'Show me the letter instead, that sounds much more interesting.'

'Okay,' Rose said and left the room. She returned five minutes later and handed it to Flori. 'I've wanted to show you this since I found it. Read it. It's a handwritten copy of a letter addressed to my father. She must have kept it as a reminder because the original was sent through the diplomatic bag. It's kind of self-evident.'

Flori sat down, took the letter from Rose and sipping her wine began reading.

26 Kensington Church St
London W8
April 25th

Nicholas,

Following our last conversation when your language was unbearably vulgar, I consulted my family solicitor to consider my options, one of which is divorce. He advised we should communicate in future by letter, hence for security reasons; I am sending this by diplomatic bag. The fewer who know of our marital problems, the better. After all, you still have some years left in the service, and as ever, I would like to maintain some semblance of civilised behaviour. To the last, I have taken my responsibilities as a wife married to a diplomat seriously. I have always worked to uphold the best standards of the Foreign Office, even though, I am well aware this may sound archaic.

It grieves me greatly, that you have no conscience regarding the consequences of your philandering behaviour. To have received a letter from your ex-lover telling me of your affair, and further that you fathered and now maintain a child, was devastating. Have you no imagination? Of course, I would be upset. I am not made of stone.

I was made aware from when we first met at Oxford, that you had a weakness for attractive women. You did after all, cheat on me twice, and each time I forgave you, and put it down to your youth. You begged me not to give up on you, and I, against my better judgement, didn't. I see now how misguided that was.

It is particularly painful to me the timing of your affair. The birth of Rose was one of the happiest days of my life, and I presumed, perhaps naively, it was for you too. I remember very clearly that you and I had considerable discussions, that given you were about to be posted to Moscow, whether Rose and I should accompany you.

We decided against it on the grounds that the Moscow posting was likely to be challenging, and that you would need a clear head without the additional pressures of a wife with a new baby. It was fortunate for me that subsequently my mother offered to move into our London home on a temporary basis and help with the care of Rose. The first two or three years of Rose's life were very hard. As you know, she was difficult. From the start she refused to bond with me, and her subsequent elective mutism made it difficult for me to love her. However she seems now, having received considerable and costly psychological help, to have overcome all her difficulties, which leaves me to face our own.

The subsequent discovery, that you took my absence in Russia, as an opportunity to be unfaithful I find intolerable, particularly as I had just given birth to Rose.

You tell me that Natalya, is now seven and that you have no idea where she and her mother now live. I am not sure whether I find this believable, but ultimately it is of little consequence either to myself or to Rose. You also tell me you have every intention of continuing your maintenance of her. I must say I admire your principles, even though they seem lacking in relation to your London family.

I write to inform you that as far as I'm concerned, our marriage is over. I am prepared to act, for the sake of appearances, as if this is not the case, but I shall continue to be in frequent contact with my solicitor. I should also add that on your return to London, I shall expect you to move forthwith out of the marital bed.

Jane

Flori read it twice, slowly and carefully. She looked at her friend. 'Rose, heavy, this is heavy. I'm sorry, really sorry. How long have you known about this?'

'Only recently. I found it in the bureau, one she always kept locked. I wanted to know why and what was in it and then I found the key.'

'Did you know that he was having an affair?'

'I'd always suspected. He's the type, a ladies' man. He's my father, but we've never got on, really. I've never trusted him. Now I know why.'

'It's devastating. What a bastard, betraying your mother like that and so soon after she'd given birth to you.'

Rose avoided Flori's eyes. She looked across the room. 'I've been brought up against a background of them constantly bickering and having arguments. The holidays when they were together were hell. It was constant. I knew they didn't get on, but even so, it's horrible. Knowing your father is unfaithful.'

'Bickering is one thing, but fathering a child with your lover, that's something else. What are you going to do? Will you tell them you know?'

'What's the point? No, or at least not straightaway. But what she says gets to me, when she says "elective mutism" as if I suddenly made a decision not to speak to anyone, and as if I wanted to prove a point…but it wasn't like that and it hurts. I just couldn't, you know, speak. I don't know why. After I was sent for play therapy, it came back.' She looked at Flori. 'And there's the bit where she says it's been difficult to love me. I'd always thought that. I thought she hated me, that I was a failure, or that maybe she wanted a boy, and that's why. She never put her arms round me and told me she loved me.'

'But she must love you, Rose, all mothers love their children…well, most do. But if she didn't, it was her problem, not yours. You're not responsible for how she felt. Sometimes the mother can't bond with a child but it's not the baby's fault.'

'Flori, don't make excuses for her. Even if that was true, I wanted her to like me, but she never did. She never liked me. It's never been like, well, you know, a good mother-daughter relationship. Is there something wrong with me?'

She looked away from Flori, put her hands under her body and, sitting on them, rocked gently back and forth as she cried. Flori moved across to sit down besides her. She put her arm round her. 'Rose, don't cry. It's not true. There's nothing wrong with you.'

Rose looked at her. 'And what about my half-sister. Do you think Natalya knows of me?'

'Your half-sister? I wouldn't know, but do you want her to know?'

'Yes, I want to find her. I want her to know about me. I've always wanted a sister.'

There was a moment's pause, before Flori said, 'But Rose, this'll affect us. Won't it?'

'What do you mean?'

'I thought we were like sisters, we've always said that, that we're as good as sisters.'

Rose hesitated. 'Flori, what we have together, no one can take away. We'll always be the same. If I ever do find Natalya, you'll be part of that. There'll be the three of us. I love you, Flori. You know that….look, let's leave this for a while. I can see it's upsetting both of us. I want to talk about something else. Tell me about Matt. You've told me virtually nothing. All I know is that he brought you here.'

There was a long silence. Flori walked over to the wine, poured herself another glass, then turned to look at Rose. 'Okay, I'll tell you about him. But only if you tell me about Dave. After the party you left with him, then what happened?'

'We went back to my place. He told me he was travelling with Phil and they were about to fly to Athens. I liked him. He's the only Greek guy I've ever known, not that that's the reason. He's not about to move to London, he made that clear. He's going back to Australia. That's where his family emigrated from, an island called Halki.' She paused. 'At least he was straight with me. You know, when you sleep with a guy, he means more to you, and I really did fall for him. It

48

was his crazy sense of humour. It was good, but it didn't last long enough. End of story.'

'What was good? The sex or him?'

'Either or both. But, finis.' She smiled. 'What about Phil? What happened there? I left you sitting on the bench with him and it was obvious he fancied you. Did you make out with him?'

'Make out with him? What do you think? But I was pissed, so I can't remember much about it. It was embarrassing. I called him Matt.'

'Christ, how did he take that?'

'It didn't seem to register as far as I remember.'

'Matt. Isn't he the one you once told me about, the one who gave you flowers, some carnations? You've never said much about him, so tell me about him. I want to know.'

Flori twisted her wine glass round in her hands and took another sip before she spoke. She sighed. 'It's difficult, talking about him, but if I do will you promise me you'll keep it to yourself? I don't want him implicated. If it's a secret you think you can't keep, tell me now.'

'How scary you are, Flori. I promise. None of it will go outside this room.'

Flori paused before she began speaking. 'It's hard, because I still love him. I met him in Wales. I was spending the summer on my own in Newgale and one day I'd been to Haverfordwest but I missed the bus back so I was hitch hiking back to my caravan along the St David's Road and he picked me up. He was driving a Land Rover. I was young then, eighteen and impressionable, or that's how it seems now.'

Rose interrupted her with a laugh. 'You still are young.'

'Yes, but I know more now, about life, about relationships.'

There was a long silence, before she continued, 'We spent the whole of that summer together. He's a few years older than me, a marine biologist and I began helping him. He was doing research on marine contamination from an oil spill in Dyfed, as it was then called. Summer ended, and that's when it fell apart.

'He was an activist for Greenpeace, and he told me he had to keep on the move. He wasn't an ordinary activist, fund raising, selling flags or something, or collecting data, oh no, nothing like that, but, more like an ecological warrior. That's how I saw him. He travelled all over the world, Russia, Norway, Canada, illegally boarding ships and boats, trying to block the hunting of seals, dolphins, whales. He was involved in planning the campaign which opposed the exploitation of coral reefs. You name it, he was there. The rows had already started big time and I wanted him to give it up. But he wouldn't. I said his priority was to the environment and not to me. I felt used. I told him that. One night he walked out on me. I couldn't believe he'd do that and it broke my heart. I'd thought of him as my first, my only true love, and it would never end. Maybe that was childish, but that's how it felt.'

'Why didn't you tell me this before?'

'It was before I met you, and it's still painful. Even to speak of it now tears me apart. He'd always said what he did was secret, and nothing was more important than the campaigns he was involved in. He told me there were police infiltrators and that he couldn't trust anybody. It's big business, killing marine creatures, they get sold on, and there's a lot of money involved. It's nasty and it's bloody.'

'But what about now? How did he come to bring you here, to Jura? Did you ring him?'

'It was strange, a coincidence. He'd rung me out of the blue, said he wanted to see me again, and that he'd missed me. I agreed, after all I was in a mess. We met in my flat and I asked for his help. That's when he told me. That he was in another relationship and he wasn't happy. But that's what they all say, isn't it?'

She bit her lower lip, her eyes filling with tears.

'He was unhappy because of his other relationship?'

'Yes, that's what he said, that he had a partner and he'd met her soon after we'd finished. She's a marine biologist, the same as him, and they have a baby.'

'How old?'

'About fifteen months, I think he did say, but I can't remember. I don't want to know really.'

'That could only have been on the rebound. But I'm sorry, Flori.'

'Whatever.' She smiled a brittle smile. 'It's all too late, but there's more. I should tell you. It's hard because it's a consequence of meeting up with Matt again, but I need to tell you.' She looked away, avoiding Rose's eyes.

'Consequence? What kind of consequence?'

Flori stared hard at Rose, their eyes meeting for an intense moment. 'I'm overdue, and Matt has to be the father. I've worked it out. It can only be him.'

Rose said 'How do you know it's Matt's? It could be Phil.'

'I'd had a period after Phil and before I met Matt.'

'So when did you sleep with Matt, if you don't mind my asking and it's not too personal?' There was a slight tinge of sarcasm in Rose's voice.

'The first night. We'd just arrived and it was after I'd asked him for help. One thing led to another and we slept together.' She added, 'Then again when we got to Jura. Before he went away. By then I knew it wouldn't matter. I was already late.'

Rose stared at Flori. She looked furious. Her eyes bored into her. 'Are you stupid? No. I won't say what I'm thinking. You must like playing Russian roulette? Does it add excitement? Is that why you didn't use a condom?'

'Condoms? I don't know why we didn't, but so what? I hadn't seen him for a long while, remember, and I'm still in love with him.'

'For fuck's sake, Flori!' Rose sprang up out of her chair and, raising her voice, shouted, 'How old are you? Aren't we in enough trouble, without this?'

'Don't shout. Don't shout. Don't shout, I can't bear it.'

'Look, I'm sorry, but do I have to spell it out?'

'Spell what out?'

'The consequences. The consequences. Think. Think. Think, Flori.'

Flori turned her back on her friend and looked out of the window. Rose remained standing and glaring down at her wine. She said, 'Let's imagine, just for a moment, you are pregnant. What do you plan to do?'

Flori returned to face her. 'What do you think? What would you do?'

'I have no idea. If it were me, I wouldn't have got pregnant in the first place.'

'Well good for you. Mrs Saintly, Mrs Mother Superior.'

Rose just sighed. 'Okay, no insults, what are you going to do?'

'Keep the baby.'

'Oh, are you? And what about Owain? What'll happen to him?'

'He'll have a little bother or a sister.'

'Flori, do you live all the time in la-la land? How lovely. Living in fairy land, but reality isn't quite like that. Here we are, exiled on a remote Hebridean island, your future on hold, while you play at being mummy, and fuck the consequences.' There was silence. They stared at each other. Flori was looking shocked at this outburst. Rose continued, 'Sometimes I wonder if you're nuts.'

'Well, I'm not. It's just, oh well, never mind. It doesn't matter.'

'What were you going to say?'

'It doesn't matter.'

'Go on. Say it.'

'No.'

'Go on. Say it. I want to hear it.'

'Well, that first night, after our long separation, I wanted to get pregnant. I was thinking I'd always have him even if he left me, because I'd have his baby and I could look after both of them, Owain and, I'd like a girl. I'd call her Cerys. It's a Welsh name, like Owain.'

'Are you taking the piss, Flori, because I don't find it funny. Shall I tell you something? I hope you're not pregnant. I really hope you're not. I don't want to be nasty but you can't have a baby and look after a stolen baby at the same time. For one thing, we don't live in the Amazonian jungle, so there aren't any native midwives who'll deliver the baby, and let's assume you had a wonderful, problem-free birth where there was no need for a doctor or a midwife, and you just followed an instruction manual for home birth, how wonderful that would be, but highly unlikely. I wouldn't take bets on it. So you have this baby, your love-child, and then you have to register it, so you can get medical assistance and all the wonderful goodies this country's welfare state can offer. And that's just for starters.'

Flori said nothing. She didn't dare. She could see how angry her friend was. 'I'm not aborting it, if that's what you think I should do.'

'Who mentioned abortion? I didn't. You have other choices.'

'Like what?'

'You could give Owain back.'

'No. I don't want to, don't say that. He's mine.'

'Look, I'm not arguing with you. It's crazy, the whole situation, from start to finish, and who knows how it's going to end. I've said what I think. You're not stupid, not usually. It's time you wised up, and stopped being so fucking impulsive and self-centred.'

Rose had never spoken to her like that before and it shocked Flori into silence. She walked into the kitchen, leaving Rose angrily sitting in her chair. Neither spoke. Rose could hear Flori banging about in the kitchen and when she returned Rose was holding up her wine to the light as if to study its clarity.

Flori silently replaced the chenille-bobbled table cloth with Rose's present but she made no reference to their conflict.

Speaking normally, she said, 'Thanks for the cloth, Rose,

it's beautiful, and thanks for the paint, too. I'll paint the walls with the terracotta, it's one of my favourite colours. It'll make a huge difference.'

'That's why I got that colour. I know you like it. Do you want any help?'

'There's no room in the kitchen, so no, but thanks.'

The atmosphere was strained. Five minutes later, they were sitting opposite each other eating. Flori looked at Rose and said, 'That's the first time, the one and only time you've ever sworn at me.'

'Well, now you know. I can.'

'You're right, by the way.'

'About what?'

'I am impulsive, or as you said, fucking impulsive.' Flori grinned at her friend, who returned the grin. 'Sorry.'

'No one's perfect, I guess, and let's hope you're wrong, that you're not pregnant.'

'Do you fancy a walk tomorrow into the hills?'

'That sounds good. But I need to go to bed soon. I'm exhausted.'

'Of course, the bed's made up and I just put a hot water bottle in it, in case it's cold. I'll listen to the weather forecast for tomorrow.'

'Flori, one more thing. Have you ever been late before? Your period, I mean.'

'Yes, when I'm stressed.'

'Good, let's hope this is one of those occasions. You can have your baby with Matt another time.' She walked out of the room before Flori could reply.

With Compliments

With best wishes, Mayasiri

Marguerite Valentine

www.margueritev.org

marguerite@margueritev.org

0794 104 2916

Write your Story

4

Saturday, 14th August

Flori stood in the doorway of the croft. It had rained, steadily, slowly, persistently through the night and the smell of yellow flowering gorse mixed with the wet dankness of the earth reminded her of the fragrance of coconuts. She watched the early morning sun catch the flashes of water droplets hanging off the vivid purple red fuchsia flowers. She looked at her watch. She was impatient to be off. They'd planned a walk to the Paps of Jura, the mountains which soared up in the middle of the island. Their inaccessibility made them appear magical and, as she stood waiting, she imagined, like the child she'd once been, that strange fairy-like creatures lived in the caves high up the mountain.

She'd have liked to climb them but with Owain on her back, she knew it was unrealistic. Still, she thought, they could get close. She planned to walk using the Bushbaby carrier, the one Matt had recommended for the hills. It was the same make he'd used for his baby, Nami, and she'd felt momentary jealous when he told her. She hadn't wanted a reminder he was in a relationship and he was a father.

She looked up at the bedroom window. The curtains were still drawn. Rose and Owain must still be asleep. Owain had woken at five and after she'd fed him, he'd taken a while to get back to sleep.

While she waited, she thought to wander down the track

towards the water's edge. It was where she'd stood watching Matt's boat disappear into the mists of the Sound when he'd returned to Tayvallich on the mainland. She still thought about him and longed for him, despite what Rose had said last night. She wanted to be pregnant and she'd didn't care if this made her life more difficult. Rose's anger had surprised her, but ultimately she thought, it was of no consequence; Rose always helped her and she'd come round to her way of thinking.

She stood daydreaming until the sound of an approaching vehicle interrupted her. A large four-wheel drive vehicle was travelling slowly along the narrow road towards her. It came to a stop on the steep bank that ran just above her and a man with a rifle slung over his shoulder stepped out. He struggled down the grass to where she was standing. He had the red face of a whisky drinker, a bulbous nose and faded, watery blue eyes, but he looked friendly enough. He reached the track and smiling walked towards her, holding out his hand. She shook his hand, noticing they were hard and dry like a workman's hands.

He had a loud voice which boomed as he greeted her, 'Morning, are you the lassie with the bairn renting Jamie and Morag MacLean's old croft?'

'Yes.' Flori immediately felt edgy. She remembered what Matt had told her, that she should be careful about who she spoke to, be conscious about what she said, how she responded, and above all, to hold off from appearing too friendly. She smiled briefly, shifting her eyes away from him towards the sea, thus subtly removing him from her line of sight.

'Well, you're most welcome to our island. I'm Andrew McPherson. If you want anything, if there's anything at all ye need, I can pass on a message to Jamie. I'll be visiting him later today in Craighouse. Jamie told me they left some fish and a rabbit for you. Did you find it? He shot the rabbit himself.'

'That was really nice of him and I'm grateful but I don't eat meat. I'm a vegetarian.'

'A vegetarian! Good god. I've heard about them, but I never met one before. We're all venison eaters on this island. Big carnivores. Plenty of deer, you see.' He laughed. 'Are ye from down south?'

'Yes.'

'That explains it. Well, enjoy yourself, it takes all sorts,' and with that he laughed again as if he'd just cracked a really funny joke, struggled back up the bank to his four-wheel drive and with a final toot and friendly wave, he drove off.

Flori found his comments about her vegetarianism irritating and as he disappeared down the road, she stuck her two fingers up in a V sign. 'Prat,' she said. She bent down to dip her fingers into the water to test the temperature, noted how cold it was and eventually meandered back to the croft.

Rose was up now and standing in the doorway drinking her morning coffee.

'Morning, Flori, what a stunning morning,' Rose said. 'I'm almost ready for our walk. I slept like a baby.'

'Great, glad to hear it. Talking of which, did you hear Owain stirring?'

'I did. He was cooing to himself, but I didn't go in, just in case he cried. After all, he doesn't know me.'

Flori ran up the stairs to her bedroom and drew back the heavy dark curtains. The room was immediately bathed in the clear light of the Hebridean morning and as Owain caught sight of her, he chuckled with delight, kicking off his covers and waving his arms and legs vigorously in the air. His happiness made her laugh.

'Hello, my little man,' she said. 'Ready for your big walk today?'

She picked him up, nuzzled up to him, kissed his plump neck and, cradling him in her arms, took him downstairs to change and feed. She heated up his baby food and put this in a thermos for their walk later. She'd noticed how quickly he got hungry so she'd already introduced him to solids. He loved his food, especially the sweet custard with apples she gave him, which he ate smacking his lips with pleasure.

She retrieved the Bushbaby carrier and as soon as Rose had eaten breakfast, they were ready to go. Flori stood by the old car, waiting for Rose to unlock the boot. They piled the walking gear in and placed Owain carefully in a baby seat. Rose handed her the key.

'You drive,' Rose said. 'That way you'll get used to the car for when I leave it with you.'

Flori looked at it apprehensively. 'It looks old and battered, sure it won't break down?'

'It may look as if it's past it, but it's been used by one careful lady driver and has a full service history.'

Flori took a look at her friend and began laughing. The comment had amused her and soon they were joking about what being a 'lady' meant, and whether they were 'ladies with a full service history'. By the time they set off they were in good spirits.

They were driving towards Craighouse, but after a couple of miles they came face to face with a car travelling in the opposite direction. Flori pulled over onto the verge so the driver could pass. He drew parallel with Flori and leant over to speak to her through the open side window.

'Halloo there, I'm Jamie and this is my wife, Morag. We're the owners of the croft you're staying in. Is everything alright?'

'Absolutely. Thanks, just what I wanted, peace and quiet to write. We love the view across to the mainland by the way.'

'Which one has the bairn?

'That's me. My baby's called Owain and this is Rose, my best friend.'

'Well, you couldn't find a quieter spot than Lagg. Used to be different years ago, busy, the post office was there, you know. Did you see, we left some rabbit and fish, hoped ye enjoyed it, couldn't be fresher, shot the rabbit myself the day you came. You don't get food that fresh in London.'

'Lovely thought but I'm a vegetarian, so I wouldn't eat it. Sorry.'

'Don't you eat any meat or fish?' He sounded incredulous.

'No, sorry. I don't.'

'Must be difficult, ah well, never mind.' He laughed. 'Are you off to Craighouse?'

'No, we thought we'd take a walk in the hills.'

He looked alarmed. 'Now? Be careful. Didn't you know the deer hunting season is in full swing? It'd be better not to. If you hear the guns firing, get out the way, fast. Make sure the ghillies see you and they know you're there.'

'What should we look out for?'

'The Argocats. Can't miss them. They're like army tanks. If you see flattened bracken and muddy tracks all over the hills, they're around. They carry the deer hunters, the guns, and like I say, keep out of their way. It's dangerous.'

Flori noticed his hunting rifle. It was propped between him and Morag.

'Thanks, will do. Maybe see you again.' And with a smile and a wave she drove off.

'Christ,' Flori said, 'that's the second gun I've seen in the space of two hours. Talk about the shooters in London, they should come here.'

'Yes, but a better class of people use them,' said Rose.

Flori glanced at her. 'You think so? You're being ironic, I hope.'

Once they reached the bend in the road where the map showed the beginning of the track into the mountains. Flori came to a halt. She parked the car off the road on a verge. This was the start of their walk. They were aiming to walk towards a bothy they'd located on the map. Set high in the mountains it was partly reached via a rough path running parallel to a mountain stream.

They loaded up their walking gear and with Rose leading the way, Flori walked behind carrying Owain on her back in the Bushbaby. The track was narrow, steep, and covered with uneven rocks and stones and it needed all their concentration to keep to a steady pace and not trip. After ten minutes of steady walking they passed through a small forest, and having cleared this they noticed the temperature dropping very slightly. Their progress was slow and after an hour the drizzle started.

'Let's stop soon,' said Rose, 'have a coffee and shelter under that tree.' She pointed to an old hawthorn tree with low branches which would give some protection from the fine rain and mist rising from the valley. She opened a pack of biscuits and poured hot coffee from the thermos for them and they sat quietly side by side watching the steam from the drink spiral into the cool air of the mountain. Flori turned to look at Owain. She'd propped him close to her under the tree in his Bushbaby. He was wide awake and looking around him with interest.

'My beautiful boy, Owain. You're as good as gold. I'm so lucky, don't you think, Rose?'

Rose hesitated. 'Well, I hope so, I mean I hope you're lucky.' She took a bite out of her biscuit and held it in the air pointing in the general direction of Owain. 'Do you think he'd like some?'

'Rose, he's not got teeth yet, so how could he eat a biscuit? Please. But how much further before we reach the bothy?'

'Sorry, I don't know about babies.' She looked at the map. 'It's about half a mile, but tough going. Here, take a look at the map.' She pointed to the route. 'See these, they're contour lines and they show it's a steep ascent up scree and rocks, then we have to find a way across a stream to get back to the track, and there's no bridge, according to this map. The crossing doesn't look too bad, it's narrow, but it depends how much rain there's been. If the stream's full, we could have problems getting over without trekking poles. I don't fancy balancing on a wet boulder, especially with you carrying Owain on your back.'

As she said this, there was a series of loud cracks. They

shattered the peace and silence of the mountainside. They looked at each other in alarm. Rose stood up.

'That must be the hunters Jamie MacLean was talking about. I'm going to climb that ridge ahead and see if I can see where they are. I won't be long.'

Without waiting for Flori to respond, she picked her way through the rough grass until she reached a path at the bottom of the ridge, then scrambled up, holding onto the protruding stone and tussocks of grass until she reached the top. She stood looking around her and then turned to beckon to Flori who, after checking Owain had fallen asleep and making sure she could still see him, joined her friend.

From the top, the land fell steeply down to a wooded valley and beyond that was open moorland. In the distance and to one side of the valley they could see an Argocat, the all-terrain, six-wheel drive vehicle which Jamie had told them about. It was travelling rapidly across the heather, carrying a shooting party over the rough ground.

They looked at each other.

Rose said, 'It's a different world here to what we're used to. They kill the deer and they justify it by calling it land management. I don't believe it and I don't like it.'

'Culling, that's another word for killing. An expensive sport more like it and it's a euphemism. What kind of people kill animals for fun? '

'They say we think like this because we live in a city, and we know nothing about their life and what these animals need. But you know what, they should keep to paint-balling.'

'Let's go. I don't like it. Men with guns, Jamie was right, it's dangerous. What if they take pot shots at us? They could, you know.'

'Don't be daft, they won't do that. But if we go now, we'll miss the bothy and I did want to see it, it's only another half mile. Shouldn't take too long.'

'Okay, let's walk until we see the bothy, then turn round.'

They continued toiling up the track. It was hard work,

especially for Flori who was carrying Owain on her back. He seemed to get heavier by the minute. Forty-five minutes later the bothy came into sight. It was a low, white building with two tiny windows equally spaced each side of the door and alongside the outside wall was a wide bench. There was no sign of any occupants.

Flori gazed at it, then she turned to Rose and said, 'It's so remote here, it's scary. But who'd be here, miles from anywhere? Does anyone live there?'

Rose said, 'No, not permanently. Don't you know? They're refuges for mountain walkers. When the mist comes down and the temperature drops and it's getting dark, it's a shelter for them. They're left unlocked and save lives, especially in the bad weather.'

Flori laughed. 'You sound so knowledgeable, but then you're an experienced hiker. But why be on your own, out here in the mountains? Doesn't make sense to me. Let's go, Rose. The place gives me the creeps. Makes me think someone might be there, hiding. A fugitive on the run, and the hunters are not really looking for deer but out to find him. He's watching us now, with his gun trained on us waiting for us to get near. Let's go.'

'Flori, don't think like that, it's horrible. Okay. Let's go. I'm ready.'

They turned and made their way down the mountain. It was easier retracing their steps and they didn't stop until they reached their car.

Rose wasn't to be dissuaded. She insisted that if the reception was good enough, they watch *Crime Watch* and all Flori's arguments, prevarications, pleadings that they should enjoy themselves, and ignore what might be being said about them, had no effect upon her. Rose was determined they'd watch the programme and she repeated the argument that they must see where the police were in their inquiry. It made Flori go cold but she knew she'd have to go through with it. Rose was refusing to back down so she reasoned with herself the programme only lasted an hour and she could put up with it for that long.

She went upstairs to put Owain down for the night. He fell asleep as soon as his head touched the pillow and it had just reached nine when she returned downstairs and sat down.

Rose poured two glasses of wine and passed one over to Flori. She took it but avoided looking at her and turning her face towards the television, she began biting her nails. She fidgeted in her chair, twisted locks of hair round her fingers and secretly hoped the reception would be bad so they couldn't watch.

But tonight it didn't fail. The picture was good and they sat in silence waiting for the start of the programme. The familiar signature tune to the programme played and as the music ended, the presenter Kelsi Walls walked across the studio towards the camera as if towards them, the viewers. She looked serious, and speaking directly to the camera, began her introduction.

'Tonight's edition is particularly important', she said. 'The case of the missing baby from Earls Court has touched the heart of the nation and what we are about to tell you will upset all parents,' she said.

She spoke slowly and urgently, saying all parents would identify with the fear their child could be snatched. She paused and Flori, in response, felt her anxiety rise.

She continued. 'The programme tonight concerns the abduction of baby Bertie. It was the early hours of June 26th. His parents lay asleep in the next room to him. While they were sleeping someone entered their flat and snatched him from his crib. Despite the best efforts of our police, he remains missing. It is of the utmost importance that this baby is found.'

She turned round to face police officers working in the background, some writing, others taking calls, then said, 'But first, we must tell you about our successes following the programme last month. I'll hand you over to Ian who'll bring you details of his gallery of villains.'

Ian stood smiling at the camera. It was a friendly smile, but one, Flori thought, similar to the smile on the face of a tiger. Powerful and potentially menacing, he pointed to a row of faces. These were, he said, 'mug shots'. They were mostly of men but also a couple of women were shown. He referred to each of them as a 'villain'. He described their crimes: the fraud, the violence, the assaults, the burgling, robbing, or their failure to turn up for a court hearing. Some already had been arrested but he stressed the importance of those remaining on the loose being found. He finished with the words. 'Take another look at these mug shots. See them, name them, cop them.' His work completed, he beamed to the camera as if exceptionally pleased with himself and said, 'And now I'll hand you back to Kelsi.'

For one horrific moment, Flori thought a photo of herself was about to be shown to the nation and that she, too, would be publicly branded as a villain. She felt physically sick, wanted to run out of the room but she knew Rose would stop her, so she stayed silent and sat motionless in her chair. It was like torture. She didn't see herself as a criminal but she knew what was coming up and why she didn't want to see the programme. She was about to be held up for scrutiny and in the public's mind, she was about to be classified as a villain.

The presenter turned to the various crimes of arson and rape. They were reconstructed using actors to engage the viewers' fears, concerns and sympathy, with the aim of encouraging them to ring in with information.

She waited for the inevitable, a description of the baby snatching, but listening to what preceded this seemed to last forever and Flori increasingly found herself unable to concentrate. She was aware of only a series of moving images randomly coming and going across the screen and it took all her self-control to remain in the room. But the worst was to come. It was the moment when Kelsi Walls began talking about the abduction of the baby. Flori was compelled to listen with a horrified fascination as the events of that night were described and pieced together for the nation. As she talked the presenter became particularly intense.

Looking straight into the camera, she said, 'Do you remember where you were and what you were doing the night of June 26th? It had been a hot day and London was sweltering. Children and teenagers played in the newly restored Trafalgar Square fountains. Cast your mind back to that night. Were you anywhere near the vicinity of Earls Court that night, or in the early hours of the following day? It was the night little Bertie was snatched from his parents. He hasn't been seen since. Where is he? Who is he with? It is imperative he's found as soon as possible. His parents are distraught. They're pleading you to help with his safe return.'

She walked over to a sofa where a well-dressed man and woman sat. They looked to be in their early thirties and as if dressed for the office, the kind of work associated with London's 'square mile'. Neat, cold, efficient, business-like, the man was dressed in a striped suit with his dark hair sleeked straight back from his forehead; the woman in a suit with black, high-heeled shoes. She was tall, slim and blonde with fine, straight hair that hung and swung like a curtain round her thin pale face.

It was then Flori spoke, unable to stop herself. 'So that's how they look, cool, controlled, ordinary. But the truth? They're full of hatred for each other. And to think, baby Owain had them as parents.'

Rose put her fingers to her lips, 'Sssh, Flori, I can't hear.'

Flori glared at her. She turned her attention back to the programme. The presenter had now sat opposite the parents and, leaning towards them, she said, 'Annabelle and Rupert, thank you so much for coming. I know how difficult it is for you. Will you tell the viewers what happened.'

Rupert spoke first. He had a deep, slow voice, his accent tinged with estuary English. He was used to getting attention and had a natural authority but what he said sounded like a script and one he'd rehearsed well.

'We'd been out for supper with friends, leaving Bertie in the care of a trusted baby sitter. On our return, which was about 11 pm, I drove the baby sitter home and returned half an hour later. My wife was already in bed. I switched on the television. I wanted to catch up with the cricket. I watched for about half an hour, then I went to bed. Sometime later, in the early hours, Bertie began crying for a feed. My wife got up, made him a bottle and returned to sleep ten minutes later. We woke at 8 am and my wife, as usual, went to fetch Bertie. He'd gone. Vanished. His crib empty. Since then, nothing. We've heard nothing.'

Annabelle began sobbing, dabbing at her face with a handkerchief, but her husband sat by, and made no attempt to comfort her. He seemed in a state of shock, and unmoved by her tears, his face was expressionless.

Kelsi bent towards Annabelle, her face full of compassion. 'As a mother myself, I know how awful this is for you, and you won't mind if I tell the viewers that you and your husband had tried for some time to conceive and that little Bertie was born as a result of your IVF treatment. It's tragic what both of you are going through. He was so wanted and you've had to wait for him so long.'

'Yes, he was. So loved and so wanted,' Annabelle said, and turning to look at her husband with her eyes full of tears, she added, 'By both of us. I can't believe it. We love him so dearly, he's so precious to us, we mourn every day he's not with us. Please,' she turned towards the camera, 'if you know where he is, go to the police. Tell them all you know. We must have him back. Our baby. We miss him so much.'

Flori jumped up, and exploded, 'Liars, liars, you didn't love him, I know why you had him, I heard, you had him for his family, an heir, that's what you said, he's like a trophy for you, you fucking liars, I told you, didn't I, Rose, didn't I say, they didn't love him.'

Rose stared at Flori, her response was mild in comparison to Flori's fury. 'Yes, you did tell me that. I remember. That's why you rescued him. You wouldn't have taken him, if they'd loved him.'

Flori began to pace up and down the room.

'Flori, sit down and stop shouting, otherwise we'll miss something.'

Flori glared at her. Rose had no idea. She didn't understand how she felt and what she'd gone through. She sat down but she was feeling more and more resentful. Rose didn't seem to care. She was too calm. She continued to stare angrily at the television screen. The woman was crying again and her husband continued looking impassive. He gave every impression of total indifference. It was as if he was a method actor and had been told to go through the motions of a father who'd just lost his child He seemed to have nothing empathic from within himself to draw on.

Kelsi stood up. She spoke briskly, almost as if she wanted to conceal the husband's indifference. Looking warmly at the mother she said, 'Well, let's hope the viewers can help. I have every confidence in them.'

She walked over to where a woman police officer stood. She was looking impassive as she waited for Kelsi to introduce her. 'This is DCI Ann Evans, she's heading up the enquiry. Ann, can you tell us what you know so far?'

'Yes, Kelsi. The baby was stolen from this block of flats near Earls Court tube.' She waited as a shot of the flats came onscreen. 'We estimate he was taken sometime between the hours of four and six. We have a number of leads, but we believe that somebody has essential information, somebody who isn't coming forward.'

'There was a party held in the flats that night, wasn't there?'

'Yes, an all-night party in the same block. The front door was left open for some time. This meant anyone could walk in and walk out and leave without trace.'

'Where was this flat in relation to Annabelle and Rupert's?'

'On the ground floor, further along the building. We think we've found most of the party goers, but there are still some people we haven't traced or haven't been interviewed. It was a birthday party and food had been laid out in the dining room. Someone got in there and helped themselves to food. Maybe someone homeless. We just don't know. There was at least one but it could have been two or even more but whoever it was vandalised the food. The birthday cake had been spoilt and food thrown round. Someone must have seen them enter that room.'

Flori and Rose looked at each other.

'We want to find them. We don't know who they are. There may be a link between them and a young woman seen by one of the flat's residents in the early hours. She was seen twice, once with a male at the end of the garden before the party was over, and then sitting by herself on a bench in the garden at about 4 am.'

'And you have forensic evidence, don't you?'

'Yes, we have considerable forensic evidence. Firstly, from the half-eaten food in the dining room. Secondly, from hairs we have found, we suspect there were at least two young women, one dark haired, one with red hair.'

'Thirdly, from the man in the garden. He left considerable evidence. We've run his DNA through a computer but we've found no match. It's likely he has no previous and he's of Mediterranean origin. We think the person who stole the baby came up the fire escape from the garden, climbed through the open window of Annabelle and Rupert's bedroom, and then hid behind the long curtains in the sitting room. She waited for Annabelle to feed the baby and go back to bed, then she snatched the baby. Forensic evidence indicates she's young with dark hair.'

'Might she be the same person seen sitting in the garden?'

'It's possible but we need to find her and eliminate her from our enquiries.'

Rose looked at Flori. She sounded accusing. 'You said you'd wiped all surfaces clean of fingerprints.'

'Don't look at me like that. I did, but I didn't vacuum behind the curtains. There wasn't time.'

Rose stared at her, and then she said, 'Very funny. So they have one of your hairs. Great.'

'And yours, too. Don't forget. You're implicated.'

Rose ignored Flori's comment. 'The "male" at the bottom of the garden, she referred to, was that Phil?'

'Must have been.'

'You didn't tell me.'

'I did, you forgot.'

'What were you doing?' Flori didn't answer. 'Well, I can guess, screwing with him.'

'You can talk.' Flori put out her hands in a resigned way, shrugged, and raised her eyes up. 'Whatever. What can I do? Nothing now.'

They looked back to the television. Kelsi was still talking, 'And do you have any other evidence?'

'Yes, we know from CCTV television around Earls Court tube, taken later, that an indistinct image of a young woman can be seen, and she's holding close to her what might be a baby. But then she disappears from camera view. We need to follow up all sightings. Somebody must know. Somebody is protecting her. We believe she has an accomplice, maybe her partner, male or female. We want to know who she is. We need to find the baby.'

Kelsi turned to the camera, and looking straight at the camera, she said, 'The footage from CCTV is on our website. You know what to do. If you think you recognise her, or if you have any information at all, ring, text, or email us at Crime Stoppers. The number is on the screen. You can also visit our web site. Your calls count. Help us find the baby and catch the abductor of baby Bertie. Your calls are valuable, and remember, there's a twenty-five thousand pound reward for information leading to the return of little Bertie.'

She paused and added, 'And if you are the young man or woman seen in the garden, or you know who she is, please get in touch. We need to eliminate you from our enquiries.'

Flori stared into space. Everything had become too real. She was terrified but she couldn't say this to Rose. It was all too awful. She'd been identified as a criminal, and grouped with arsonists, murderers, rapists, burglars, drug dealers. No longer could she see it as an adventure or as rescuing a child. She was trapped by a moment of madness, and aided and abetted by Rose, she would be seen by the public as a child abductor and the lowest of the low.

Rose stood up and switched off the television. She looked preoccupied and glancing quickly at Flori, said, 'It's only a matter of time before we're caught. There's forensic evidence. They know about us, and what we did with the party food. I said we shouldn't help ourselves, but you went straight ahead and ignored me. You were out of control. They know you were hiding behind the curtain, and probably that you had sex with Phil, and more they're not telling us about. They always hold back information.'

'What are you talking about, the party food?'

'The party food, for fuck's sake, when we found all that food and helped ourselves. Don't you remember?'

Flori was looking blank. 'No, I can't remember that.'

'Downstairs, in the basement. The room with all the food. We helped ourselves, we stuffed ourselves, we danced around the table, we threw it around. "Mutiny on the bounty", that's what you called it. At the time it was funny and I couldn't stop laughing. Surely you remember?'

'No, I don't remember.'

'You're not joking, are you? What's wrong with you, Flori?'

Flori shouted, 'I don't remember, so shut up.'

'Oh well, what's it matter, if you remember or not. The game's up anyway.'

She put her head in her hands, to avoid Flori's eyes, then

she looked up. She was staring at her, twisting her hands together, her face contorted with fear.

Flori felt a flash of anger sear through her.

'How can you say that? The game's up. How was I to know what was going to happen?'

'You have to remember. You were pissed. You had sex with Phil, you climbed into someone's bedroom, and you stole their baby on the way out. Then you rang me for help. Great. You said you'd left no clues, but that's crap. There's enough clues left to keep the dumbest police officer busy. Like a bleeding shower of confetti after a wedding.'

'I wasn't pissed, not then I wasn't. No, Rose, the game isn't up. I came here to escape. Nobody knows I'm here. There's no police on Jura. Don't let me down, not now, when I need you.'

'But what if someone here has watched Crime Watch? And what about Phil? They could track him down, or Dave. I slept with him, remember and maybe he didn't go to Greece after all.'

'Stop it. You're winding me up. They'll go back to Australia after they've visited Greece to see their family, and you told the owners of this place when you booked it, I was a writer and needed quiet.'

'Yes, but that's not enough, they're not stupid, they might put two and two together, and they might wonder about the father. You'd better have a story ready about Owain's father, who he is and where he is. They're nosy round here and they gossip. You've noticed it yourself, they're not used to visitors and a stranger sticks out.'

'Calm down. I'll say his father works abroad. As a diplomat.'

Rose laughed sardonically. 'A diplomat like my father? I don't think so. You're not the type to be a diplomat's wife, believe me. I know. Try again.'

'I'll ignore that slur. Long-distance lorry driver? Or maybe someone random. No idea of his name just overcome with passion in the garden. A fuck with a stranger. How about that?'

'Please, Flori, be sensible.'

'Freelance war reporter? Is that okay?'

'Leave out the sarcasm. It's better. That'll be hard to check out. We need to think where the weak link is, try and forestall it. The trouble is, if Phil and Dave are still in the UK and...'

She didn't finish her sentence.

'Well, they're not, they're on a tiny island in the Aegean, visiting family before they return to Aussie land and it's not likely they'll be watching *Crime Watch* even if they could. Why would they? You're getting paranoid.' Flori stared at her. 'I'm beginning not to trust you. Why so pessimistic? It's as if...of course. It's you. You. You're the potential. The potential leak. You're going to grass me up. Aren't you?'

She walked over to Rose and stood over her. Rose sat still, looked up at her, said, 'What do you mean?' She sounded nervous, uncertain, her voice shaky.

'That Kelsi woman. You heard. She said if you know who it is, get in touch. Well, you do know. There's a reward. Twenty-five thousand. You're going to betray me. For that money.'

There was a long silence.

'I don't need the money, Flori. I've told you, I'm with you all the way.'

Flori shouted, 'You don't need the money! That's not the point. The point is you wouldn't cop me, even if you did need the money. You say you're with me, but anyone can say anything and they don't mean it. It's what you do, isn't it? That's what matters. How do I know? How do I know I can trust you?'

Rose shouted back, 'Because I've said that I'm with you on this. What more can I say? I mean it, Flori.'

She stood up to put her arms round Flori but Flori pushed her away and flew to the other side of the room and shouted, 'How do I know? How do I know I can trust you? You don't know anything, do you? Not about me. You know nothing. Not about me and Tids.'

'Who the hell is Tids?'

'It doesn't matter, he's nothing to you. Forget I said it.

Anyway, if you cop me, you cop yourself and they wouldn't pay you. You're aiding and abetting a crime. We're in this together, all the way. So fuck you.'

She angrily stomped out the room and into the kitchen. Rose was silent and remained seated in the chair, waiting for her return. Half an hour later Flori reappeared with a plate of snacks.

She placed them on a side table and looked at Rose, 'I'm sorry, Rose, for shouting. It's just that watching *Crime Watch* made me feel edgy, particularly when Kelsi Walls said how Bertie must have been snatched. Then there was his mother's response. It's made me feel worse. I realise now it's going to be difficult to conceal the baby and I'm wondering what I can say as he grows up. He'll want to know how he came to be with me but I can't tell him the truth. Life is getting more and more difficult and complicated.'

Rose listened and nodded sympathetically. Flori continued, 'I want to go out tomorrow, even if the weather's foul. I'm feeling claustrophobic. I hate being seen as a criminal. I was rescuing him, Rose, and at the time I didn't think it through and if I can, I'd like to forget about it even if only for an hour or so.'

'Good idea. I'm up for that and yes, even if the weather's bad we'll go. We haven't been to the north of the island so let's go tomorrow.'

'What's there, other than the whirlpool?'

'There's that writer George Orwell. He'd dead now but he lived in a house at the end of the island. It's called Barnhill, I think. Have you heard of him?'

'George Orwell?'

'Yes. He wrote *Nineteen Eighty Four*. It's a great book, but scary. It's about a future totalitarianism. Did you ever read it?'

'No, but my mother did. She told me about it. She said Orwell didn't make it up. It was true.'

Rose made no comment other than saying she wanted an early night.

5

The following day they drove towards the end of the island. It was a little-used road which deteriorated into an uneven track full of pot holes, tussocks of grass and reeds, which scraped against the underside of the car forcing them to slow down. They stopped just outside Barnhill. It was as far as the car could go and the beginning of their walk.

Rose parked on a grass verge a short distance away and they walked in silence along a small and overgrown track towards the house. Flori had left Owain in the car. They wanted a quick look at the house before they began their walk and didn't intend to be long.

Barnhill was like a larger version of a croft, dark, long and dilapidated, built in stone with two outbuildings, one either side of the main house. Large overgrown bushes surrounded the windows. The windows at ground floor level were set symmetrically each side of the front door. It stood in extreme isolation, the nearest inhabited house being over two miles away. The back of the house looked out over the flat, slate-grey sea of the Sound of Jura.

Flori glanced over her shoulder to check there was no one following them. She was feeling uneasy, but there was no one around. She wished she'd brought Owain with her. She'd left him asleep in his car seat thinking they'd only be gone two or three minutes and she hadn't wanted to disturb him, but now she was so nervous she retraced her steps to double check he was still there. As she got nearer she was reassured that he was still asleep in the car. She ran back and caught up with Rose.

They walked tentatively round the building, their feet crunching on the gravel path shot through with weeds. Wild fuchsia and yellow broom had colonised what was left of the gardens and an atmosphere of neglect and despair enveloped the buildings. The atmosphere disturbed Flori. She felt as if the place had been taken over by a silent menace and as if the wild spiky bushes held a malevolent force. She looked into the sky, black crows were circling over their heads, occasionally scattering in raucous, angry, vicious dispute.

It was bleak. The expression 'god forsaken' came to her mind. She shivered. Anything could happen here and no one would know. The place had an unkempt, dark, desolate air. For some reason she began thinking about her mother. She was glad she hadn't read the book, *Nineteen Eighty Four*. She remembered how her mother had told her about Orwell's description of the 'proles' dwellings', but she said nothing of these thoughts to Rose.

Some things she had to keep to herself. She didn't want Rose to know what she was thinking, not after last night. After Rose had gone to bed, she found a slip of paper with the *Crime Stopper's* number on it. She'd left it where it was because she didn't want her to know she'd seen it but it had raised her suspicions even more. She'd thought more about Rose's reaction to *Crime Watch* and her paranoia. The programme had upset her because she feared being caught – at least that's what she hoped.

But despite trying to reassure herself with this explination, Rose's reaction was playing on her mind. Rose would be returning to London soon, maybe tomorrow, or the day after at the latest, and she dreaded being left on her own. She wondered when she was planning to go. She'd said nothing to her yet so she must be waiting for the right moment when to tell her. Her thoughts returned to the walk and she glanced again at Barnhill. It depressed her, but she didn't know why.

'I want to go, Rose. I don't like it and I wouldn't like to live here. No wonder it's empty. It's...' she struggled to find the right word, 'desolate, soulless.' She stared up at one of the upstairs windows, then turned to Rose, and said in amazement, 'Did you see that? There is someone, someone's inside.'

Rose looked at her. She had an expression of disbelief on her face. 'Where?'

Flori pointed at a window. 'There. Look. Someone passed quickly across the window.'

'No, there's nobody. There can't be. You're mistaken. It was a shadow.'

'I did see someone. It wasn't a shadow. Whoever it was, moved across the window quickly. They didn't want to be seen. We're being watched.'

'I don't think so. Flori, it's your imagination again. It's been empty for years. Look at the vegetation round the door. It's overgrown. No one's here.'

'Don't you understand? It's the thought police.'

'The thought police? What are you talking about?'

'Barnhill. It's their headquarters. My mum told me. It's all in the book. They lived here. She told me after I went back and I visited her.'

'What visit?'

'I was here with my uncle and auntie. They brought me here. I've told you that already.' Flori sounded irritated.

'I don't think you have. When was that?'

'When I was six. My mum stayed in London and I was on holiday with my aunt and uncle and when I came back, I saw my mum and she asked me if I'd seen the thought police. I told her I'd seen men with guns and she said that was them. She'd read about them in that book and she said they must still be there and Barnhill was their secret headquarters. They're employed by the government. Don't you remember, we've seen them before? On our walks. Three times. You've seen them, too. Spying on us. Listening to what we say. We have to be careful. We might be overheard. We'd better go. All of us, me, you and Tids.'

'Tids? Who's Tids? You haven't told me who he is.' Rose looked warily up at a window. 'Do you mean that window, is that where you think you saw someone?' She pointed up to one of the windows.

'For god's sake, Rose. Don't point. I've told you. Let's go. Quickly. It's Tids. I have to get back to him, make sure he's alright, in case he comes to harm.'

She turned and, half-running, half-walking, headed back towards the car. She gestured over her shoulder at Rose and shouted, 'Come on, faster, faster, we need to go. Quickly.'

She was running ahead and when she reached the car, she pulled the back door open and snatched the sleeping Owain from his car seat. The sudden, rough movement woke him. He looked at her uncomprehendingly, his eyes filling with tears. Then he began crying. He sensed there was something different about her and between his tears he was watching her apprehensively.

Flori spoke softly to him, 'Baby, baby, baby, I'm sorry. Flori won't hurt you, I promise, don't worry.' She smiled reassuringly, gently rocking him, until he quietened and began waving his tiny arms up and down.

Her mood seemed to pass as quickly as it came and she made no further comment but began preparing for the walk ahead, silently lacing up her boots and putting on her fleece and waterproofs. She took the Bushbaby from the boot, propped it on the ground and prepared Owain for his walk. Owain had his own walking gear, a tiny red and navy fleece balaclava with ears which Flori covered with a waterproof and then she stood back to admire him. He looked so cute peeking out from the warmth of his hat, he made them both laugh.

Rose leant forward to help Flori with putting the Bushbaby on her back. She pulled up Owain's hood, commenting that although the sun was out, the strong winds off the sea would keep the temperature down as the day wore on. Flori didn't reply.

A final check on the map and they set off. As Rose predicted, the path was rough, but the views spectacular. On one side of the path was an irregular, jagged range of rocks, bogs, and uneven tussocks following the contours of the hills and the moorland stretching across to the west side of the island. On the other side lay the sea. The path, a hundred feet up, closely followed the edge of the cliff. From there they could see across the Sound of Jura with its islands and skerries, tiny islets which punctured the surface of the green and blue depths of the sea, the intense colour reflecting that of the sky. Only the wind and the cry of the sea gulls broke the silence. Flori took the lead with Owain, who lay peacefully asleep on her back, his head falling against the edge of the Bushbaby, while Rose followed a little way behind.

Flori's gaze took in the restless movement of the sea, and a feeling of loneliness came over her. She knew Rose didn't believe her when she'd seen the figure at the windows and this unsettled her. Her thoughts turned to Matt, to the time when she and Matt had parted and he'd returned to the mainland. In her mind's eye she could see him on the boat as the early morning sea mist enveloped him and he disappeared from view. She put her hand in her Gore-Tex pocket, her fingers searching for the small white stone he'd found in Solva harbour, the one he'd given her as a keepsake when he left Jura. It was as precious to her as any gemstone, its beauty entirely natural, created by the ceaseless action of the sea.

She wondered if she'd ever see him again and what he'd meant when he'd said 'Until then'. He'd never finished his sentence and she hadn't wanted to ask because she'd been frightened by what he might say. The strength of her feelings for him had been overwhelming. She'd hoped these would lessen with time but they were resurfacing again, unbidden, and as powerful as ever. She needed him, she wanted him with her. Her need was even more urgent, knowing Rose would soon return to London, although she still hadn't said when that would be.

She turned round to check on Rose's progress. She'd fallen behind. She stopped and waved, waiting for her to catch up. Although Rose was smiling, she'd never seen her so angry as last night when she'd told her that her period was late. She'd reacted as if she'd been irresponsible to have unprotected sex and seemed to see it as a one-night stand.

A feeling of defiance came over her. It hadn't been like that. She didn't understand. It had been natural, spontaneous, and how it should be between two people who loved one another and who'd been separated by circumstances. When Rose swore at her, she'd been amazed. It wasn't her business if she was pregnant and in any case, the more she thought about it, the more she wanted it. As she'd said to her, if she was pregnant she'd always have a part of him and whether it was a boy or girl, wouldn't matter.

She looked up. Rose was behind and calling out to her. She stood waiting for her, deciding she'd respond as if everything was still normal between them.

'Wait, Flori. I need a break. A coffee. You're steaming ahead. I can't keep up with you.'

'Sorry. Okay, let's stop. We must be about halfway. I'll give Owain something to drink, too.' She swung the Bushbaby off her back and propped it with Owain inside against a large rock. Then she carefully pulled Owain out and held him to her.

Rose smiled. She said, 'He's enjoying his walk, Flori. He woke up just now and was looking around.'

Flori hugged him and kissed his cold cheek. 'What can you see baby boy, can you see the birds in the sky?' She pointed towards the seagulls but Owain kept his eyes fixed on her, his arms waving in pleasure at her attention. Flori laughed, waved her arms, too, and began baby talking with him.

They sat down on the grass. Rose looked at her

apprehensively, 'Flori, I was thinking. You know, I shall have to go back soon, probably tomorrow.'

Flori's response was measured. 'Well, I knew you would at some point, but I wish you weren't.'

'I know. I'm sorry, but I'll leave the car with you.'

'I'm not bothered by the car. If I had a choice, the car or you, I'd choose you.'

Rose looked down at the grass, pulling at it irritably. 'I can't help it, Flori. I have to, at least you'll be mobile with the car, you'll be able to get around and I'll come and see you again.'

'When?'

'I don't know. As soon as I can. The new term starts soon and I have to get up to speed with my reading. It's my finals next year and I want to do well.'

Flori was silent. Then she said, 'And what about Natalya?'

'What do you mean, "what about Natalya?"'

'You told me. You told me that you wanted to find her. Is that why you're going early, to leave time to try to find her?'

'Don't be jealous, Flori. It's a long shot that I find her, and besides I've told you, no one can replace you. I mean that. We've been through a lot together, you're special and always will be.'

'Promise? Do you promise, Rose, you won't disappear? And do you promise, if you find her, you'll tell me and we'll still be best friends?'

'Of course.' Rose leant over, hugged her, then stood up and looked around. 'Look, the sky's getting overcast and we haven't been walking very fast. I'm not trying to avoid anything, but we'd better get going pretty quickly or we'll be walking back in the dark and maybe the rain, and that's not a good idea on this path. We're so near the sea.'

Flori stood up and struggled with the Bushbaby, as she tried to put Owain on her back.

'Here let me help you. I'm sorry I have to go. I'll be back as soon as possible, but you'll be alright.' Rose tipped the dregs of her coffee away on the grass.

Flori said, 'I'll have to be, won't I?'

They continued the walk passing close to herds of red deer grazing the coarse grass. The animals didn't run but lifted their heads from feeding, watching with dumb interest as Flori and Rose slowly past them along the path. Flori stopped for a moment and glanced down over the cliff watching wild goats eating the kelp left fastened to the slippery rocks by the tide on the beaches below. As they neared the end of the island the wind picked up and the roar of the Corryvreckan whirlpool could be heard.

Flori came to a sudden halt. 'Rose, will you take Owain? I want to go ahead.'

Her voice was urgent. Rose stopped behind her just as Flori swung off the Bushbaby, rapidly transferring Owain to Rose, before she ran off. The speed of Flori's departure took Rose aback and she stared as she moved rapidly away over the bleak and rocky landscape. The path was uneven, potentially dangerous but without Owain she seemed able to skip with ease across the stones and splash through the streams coursing down the hill side. Sometimes she'd disappear, only to reappear moments later, scrambling up a gorse-covered slope, using the tussocks and rocks protruding from the hillside as handholds. By now she was moving so fast it was impossible for Rose to keep up with her.

With Owain now on her back Rose had to watch where she placed her feet and pick her steps with care. She looked up ten minutes later. Flori was way ahead and almost had reached the end of the island. She'd stopped and silhouetted against the skyline, sat balanced on a rock. She was hunched over, looking across the surging tide which raced between Jura and Scarba, the tiny deserted island which lay opposite.

Rose toiled towards her. The track was almost extinct, and as she came within shouting distance of Flori she called out, 'Hey. Hey. Flori. Can't you wait? What's the rush?'

Flori turned round. She had tears streaming down her face. 'Look,' she said, and pointed towards the whirlpool.

The tide was racing and at its maximum height, but it had a strange appearance. The water was turbulent with different levels and directions and this created collisions. Some of the waves stood stationary in the middle of the raging waters.

Rose stood staring, 'O, my god, how scary. It's hellish, no wonder it's called The Hag Goddess' Cauldron.'

Flori said, 'I don't mean the whirlpool, Rose, that's not what I'm looking at, it's the goats, look, can't you see them?'

She pointed towards two goats, a nanny with her kid, balanced on a skerry a short distance away from the coastline. It seemed as if they were trapped by the rising tide as they were looking bemused, watching the water part around them. But they remained standing on the rock and made no effort to swim away.

'Stupid animals.'

'Don't say that, Rose. They're going to die, while we watch, and we can do nothing. Nobody cares about them. The mother will drown and the baby will die with her.'

'Flori, that won't happen, goats can swim, they'll be alright. Why are you so upset? It's out of proportion.'

'Because they'll die. Don't you care? And how do you know anyway, that goats can swim?'

'I've seen them, not here, but in Greece. I'm not lying, you know.' Rose put her arm round her. 'Look if you come back here, maybe tomorrow, after I've gone, you'll see for yourself, they'll have survived.'

Flori looked at her doubtfully.

'Things are getting you down, Flori, you're over-reacting. I think you're upset because I'm leaving soon. Look, as soon as I can, I'll come back to see you.'

'Yes, but when will that be?'

'Not sure, it depends on how my work goes, but you can always ring me. Whenever you want. You know that.'

She smiled reassuringly. 'Let's go back now, Flori, time's running out.'

Flori gave her a look. 'Okay, but you go ahead. I want to stay a bit longer.'

'What for?'

'I don't know, I want to stay here, just for a while, maybe see the Hag Goddess.'

'It's not true.'

'I know that, I'm not stupid, just go, I won't be long.'

Rose decided to do what her friend asked and with Owain still on her back she slowly made her way back along the coast path. Ten minutes later Flori caught up. She made no comment why she'd wanted to stay longer and they continued the rest of the walk in silence. The light had faded fast and it was almost dark by the time they reached Barnhill, which added to its already sinister atmosphere.

They got into the car. Flori's mood was sombre. She sat unsmiling by her friend and in an attempt to lighten her mood, Rose said, 'I'll drive, Flori, but I have an idea. What about if we take turns to choose a piece of music that'll cheer us up.'

'I don't want to be cheered up.'

Rose persisted. 'Well, I do. For one thing I don't like the feeling of being dismal, it's horrible, so I'll choose first.' She paused, 'That is, if you don't mind?' There was no answer. She repeated, 'Do you mind?'

'Whatever.' Flori shrugged her shoulders and stared out the window.

'Good,' she said. 'You might like this, it's Madeleine Peyroux and you like her.'

Flori shrugged her shoulders. 'She's okay.'

She put on the CD. She knew despite Flori's surly answer, she loved Madeleine Peyroux, because she'd commented once that her voice was like Billie Holiday. She chose one of the songs which had a strong calypso beat and as the music began, Rose sang along with her hoping the words would cheer her. Flori was silent while it played, then she said, 'I don't want that, I want that song where she asks her lover to stay with her for the night.'

'Do you mean the one by Judie Tzuke when she sings "Stay with me until Dawn"?'

'Yes, have you heard it?'

'Of course I have. It's a classic and it's beautiful, Flori.'

'Have you got it?'

'I have.' Rose leant forward, to put on the track, but as the bittersweet words were heard by Flori, she began crying. Rose stopped the car, leant over and put her arm round Flori. 'Tell me what's upsetting you.'

'I can't, not now.'

'If you keep it to yourself, I can't help you.'

'Some other time.' She turned her head away, thus effectively shutting her friend out.

Rose persisted. 'Alright, I won't forget that you said, "some other time" and I'll ask you again. You seem troubled so I'm going to play something jolly whatever you say. This CD is by the Andrew Sisters. I like them because they're so retro.'

Flori looked at her. 'What's it called?'

'"Don't sit under the apple tree". It's really jolly.'

'Okay.' Flori sounded resigned but untouched by Rose's attempts to cheer her up she remained in a bad mood for the rest of the evening, although she did agree to drive Rose to the ferry the next day.

The following morning they arrived at Feolin, the point of departure for the ferry at the end of the island. Flori, holding Owain in her arms, accompanied Rose as she walked towards the ferry which was about to dock. Neither spoke but just as she got on the ferry, Rose, on an impulse looked directly at Flori, and said, 'Flori, I've been thinking about what you said about Tids. Who is he? I'm intrigued. You mentioned his name yesterday, but I don't know who he is. I'd like to know.'

There was a long pause before Flori answered, but when she did, the tone of her voice changed, almost as if she was a little girl. She said, 'Ask no questions, hear no lies,' and then she added coldly, 'You'll miss your ferry.'

She turned away from Rose and holding Owain tightly in her arms walked abruptly to the car without looking back at her friend. She put Owain in the car seat, got into the driver's seat and accelerated off. She drove away at speed without waving goodbye to her friend.

6

Twilight. The landscape was drained of colour. A depressing pall reached upwards as if there were no divisions between the sands, the sea, the sky. Flori felt she couldn't breathe. She put her hands to her throat. There was no air. She looked out at the brown, still waters of the bay. Two pregnant women were close by, standing motionless in a cave, their bathing costumes barely covering their swollen bellies. They were dwarfed by a castle of sand which soared above them many metres high and from its base snaking across the sands ran shallow channels of water. The water slowly drifted into tributaries, before being engulfed by the silent force of the sea. As she gazed at this surreal, silent landscape, the sandcastles, little by little, collapsed into nothingness.

She woke with a start. Startled, her eyes swept round the bedroom. First Matt and now Rose. Both. Gone. She was alone with a baby. The baby she'd stolen. She felt desperate for air. She had to breathe or she'd scream. She dragged herself out of bed. Went downstairs to the kitchen. Air. She had to have air. She felt as if she was about to be suffocated. She flung open the window. It was a clear night. She looked out over to the mainland. She could see lights across the water on the mainland. Scotland, fractured coast line, indented with lochs, marked with mountains. It was real and not a dream and here she was on Jura, an island, miles from anywhere with a baby that didn't belonged to her. She stood, trying to calm herself, breathing in the sharp, pure, clear air of the night.

That row with Rose about being pregnant. It had been on her mind before she'd fallen asleep, made her think about her pregnancy, about Matt, about how he'd respond if he knew, about how much she wanted his baby. She'd always dreamt she'd have her own baby, but the dream was weird and she didn't understand it. It was strange. A nightmare really. Those two pregnant women, the sandcastles that collapsed, the water running into the sea.

She felt a sensation, as if something was trickling down her legs. Something wasn't right with her body. Something was happening. Something warm, flowing down, trickling down her legs. Real. It wasn't her imagination. It was happening now. She could feel it. She could see it. Her white nightdress, it was red.

She pulled it up, inch by inch, slowly, slowly. She didn't want to look, she wanted to avoid what she might see. She had to force herself to look down. She stared at the stain of dark red blood was trickling down the inside of her legs. She couldn't believe it. This couldn't happen to her. Not a miscarriage. It couldn't be but it must be. Isn't that what bleeding meant, that if she was pregnant, she was losing her baby? But she had to be pregnant. That's what she wanted and her body couldn't let her down, not if she wanted it so much.

She stared at the blood. She hated it. She loathed it. She could smell it. It had the metallic smell of blood so it was real. It wasn't a nightmare, wasn't imagined. The iron in her soul seeping away. Her life's blood, her baby bleeding away as she watched.

She didn't respond at first. She was in shock. She pulled out a kitchen chair. Sat down. She began rocking, back and forth, in a daze, until the tears came. Bitter tears. She felt as if she was being punished, punished for what she'd done, for stealing a baby, for making love, for wanting a baby.

The words of Rose came back. She was shouting at her. 'Do you like playing Russian roulette?'

'You're crazy.'

'I really hope you're not pregnant.'

Cruel. She was so cruel. She was right not to trust her. But Matt. She could trust him and she needed him, he'd sustained her through everything. But he'd gone and there was no baby. There was no one for her. Not even Owain. Especially not Owain. He didn't belong to her. She shouldn't have done what she did that night, shouldn't have taken him.

Her sobs came, she leant over, holding her head in her hands until she felt empty and she could cry no longer and then that terrible feeling. Desolation, hopelessness, despair gripping her as if she was going to die. It was unbearable.

She got up from the chair. Unsteady on her feet, she leaned for a moment against the wall to get her balance, then she opened the front door. It was dark and there was a light, soft rain falling. The smell of the sea, the wet trees and the bracken filled her nostrils and a damp mist curled round the croft. Oblivious to the cold, the wet, the wind, she walked out into the rain still wearing her thin nightdress. She wore nothing on her feet. Her mind was blank. She ran down the track towards the sea. She'd submerge herself in the water where she'd last seen Matt when he'd left her. She'd be close to him then.

She reached the water, then she stopped. She stood watching the sea creeping in. Like a cat, she could see in the low light. The mist was rising like a grey pall from the dark waters. She looked across towards the mainland. She thought she could see him. He was in his boat, the boat that had brought them to Jura. She began to wade into the sea. She'd swim out to him. But the water was so cold, so deathly cold that it took her breath away. But she mustn't go back. She wouldn't, she had to let the sea water flow over her and wash away the salt of her tears.

The water was like ice. She was finding it hard to breathe and it was cold, cold, colder than she'd ever known.

Almost unconscious, she began slipping away into the

water when the voice of a crying child reached her. The child was so close, she could hear him clearly. She struggled to stand up.

'Flori, Flori, where are you? I want you. Please. Please, Flori.'

It was Tids calling for her. She must go to him. She looked up at the night sky as the waters closed round her. It was almost dawn, the sky lightening as the sun rose from the horizon but still the tide was rising inexorably. She knew then if she didn't leave now, she'd drown. Dragging herself up and through the water she struggled for the shallows of the shoreline. Her bare feet touched the wet sands and shivering, her wet nightdress clinging to her, she walked slowly back to Tids. She didn't want to die. He needed her and she had to stay with him. She wanted to care for him.

She looked down. Her feet were cut and bleeding; she hadn't noticed she wore no shoes when she ran down the track towards the water. The nightmares of the night were slowly going. Now she could hear the song of the early morning birds, notice the flowers of a late summer pink rose bush by one of the empty crofts and one in particular caught her attention. It reminded her of Rose. The petals were the colour of her hair, a golden, salmon pink. She bent over the stem to break it off. It was old-fashioned, neglected, un-pruned, but with few thorns it was perfect in its natural wildness. She stood holding it upright against the grey dawn sky. She saw the line of its stem and the clusters of flowers, imagined it as having come from an old masterpiece like the ones she'd seen in museums, where the artist had painted flowers cascading out of a vivid blue Chinese lacquered vase, and where the petals lay scattered around the base. But this flower was real, not a painting, its fragrance natural, unspoilt and beautiful.

She took the rose inside the croft, placed it where she could see it in a wine glass on the kitchen table. Its presence soothed her. She filled a hot water bottle and went upstairs to check on Tids. For a moment she was confused because it was Owain who lay there, not Tids and he was alive, safe, still asleep. She put the water bottle into bed, took off her nightdress, left it to soak in a wash basin, then took a warm bath, and stood drying herself with a soft white towel. She wanted Owain by her. He was her baby and she'd look after him. She went to his room, and carried him in the carrycot to her bedroom, and placed him next to her bed. She climbed into her warm bed and pulled the cream duvet over her and slept until the late morning.

She woke later, pulled the curtains back and looked into the big, blue sky. She felt the warmth of the sun. The world was different now; it was beautiful. She turned and looked at Owain. He was awake, staring at his fingers. She smiled. She lived only for him. The nightmares had disappeared.

She picked him up, carried him downstairs, changed and fed him. She talked to him all the time but he was dozy and after his feed he fell asleep so she placed him in his buggy, pulling it close to the edge of the table. She'd bought him a mobile before they'd left London and she wanted him to see it as he woke up. It was a replica of the solar system, and when wound up, the planets rotated round the sun, each planet giving out a different tinkling sound.

She glanced at him as she did her housework and as soon as he woke she wound up the mobile so he could see it in action. He was curious, his eyes following the movement. He reached out for the sun. It was the biggest and brightest and in the middle of the solar system. His hands hovered in mid-air as he tried to coordinate his hands with his eyes to reach the mobile. She stared at him. He fascinated her. He couldn't quite reach the mobile, but she wouldn't help him. She wanted him to do it himself. She wondered again how old he was. She didn't know. Not for sure. That reminded her. He wasn't her baby. He was stolen. He was falling asleep. She stood gazing at him, noticing the curve of his cheek, the eyelashes that closed his eyes, his tiny fist closed against his face.

She sat by him, whispered, 'Baby, my beautiful baby, you're mine. You'll never leave me, baby. You'll always be mine. I love you so much. You're such a little thing. I'll always be here for you. Don't worry, baby. No one will hurt you. I'm here and I'll keep you safe, safe from everyone.'

He woke up, looked around but when he saw her, something must have upset him and he began crying. She was surprised. He cried rarely, so why was he upset now? Did he think her strange? Perhaps he wanted another feed. She went into the kitchen and prepared his bottle but when she returned and put the teat into his mouth he spat it out. She was perplexed. 'Don't you want your milk, baby boy?' she said.

He continued staring at her. She picked him up and drew him close. He clung to her. She loved it when he did that, he reminded her of a little koala bear. She pressed her face close to his, and she began dancing around the room as she held him. As she danced, she sang one of her favourite songs. It was a song she'd sung once to Matt. She felt delirious with happiness, as if it was a hot day and she'd drunk too much champagne and the day would never end. Owain was hanging onto her and she pressed him close to her, holding him in her arms as she dipped and twirled round the room.

But when she reached the last line, she paused. She couldn't bring herself to sing *don't you know it can never be* because it was about an ending and it would make her low mood return. She'd had a premonition that shortly she might lose Owain so she began to talk to him. 'Baby Owain', she said, 'you mustn't worry. I'm going to take you to the end of the island and we'll see if Rose was right, whether the goats escaped off the rock or drowned.'

That cheered her up, that she had somewhere to go and that she could take Owain with her, so as she prepared for the walk, she hummed and sang baby tunes. She felt happy, she didn't rush, there was plenty of time, she couldn't get lost. All she had to do was park the car at Barnhill and follow the cliff path and retrace the steps she'd taken with Rose a few days ago.

It was late afternoon by the time they arrived. She'd driven carefully, avoiding the potholes and deep ridges. She had a horror of breaking down as this part of the island was very remote. She lifted Owain out of his car seat, then transferred him into the Bushbaby, leaving the buggy in the car.

She began the walk, but it was tiring walking by herself with Owain on her back and it took longer than she'd expected. Owain had been silent on the walk and the light had fallen by the time they reached the end of the island. She found a convenient place to stop, a hollow among the rocks, took him out of the Bushbaby and briefly played with him, making him laugh. Balancing him between her legs she sat with him on the grass as her eyes scanned the water towards Scarba. She was surprised to find she missed Rose, but Rose had been right. There was no sign of the goats. She was relieved. They must have swum ashore after all, as she'd said they would.

She looked in the other direction across the island's moor lands. In the far distance she noticed a bothy. They missed that when they first came. It was a good way off. It was tiny, looking rough, primitive and it stood alone in the bleak moor lands. There was no obvious path which led to it, but around its vicinity she could see flattened bracken and through the peat bogs, the signs of the massive wheel tracks of the Argocats. She was puzzled. Why would they be here, miles from anywhere?

She stood up, was just preparing to go, when she stopped. On the horizon, she saw an Argocat. It was moving rapidly across the bracken and heather in the direction of the bothy. A second followed and then another. It occurred to her they were like cockroaches; primeval scuttling black insects, moving relentlessly across the landscape, allowing nothing to stand in their way. They came to a halt outside the bothy and a moment later, men carrying guns slung over their shoulders got out and disappeared inside.

Instinctively Flori sat down and pulled Owain close to

her. What were they doing? The voice of her mother came to her. 'Flori, it's the thought police, it's their headquarters. You shouldn't be there. You're in danger. Get out fast. They'll think you're a spy.'

Her pulse raced as she stared across the bleak peat bogs and moorland. Could she be seen? She was a long way off, but they had binoculars and if they looked in her direction, they might shoot. 'You'll be shot. No one will know.' Her mother's voice again. Rose had said they were deer hunters, but she was wrong. She hadn't believed her. Her mother was right. These men were sinister, their hunting a cover for some secret government purpose. Inside the bothy they must be holding the prisoners, the people who'd committed a thought crime. She began trembling. She and Owain had to get away before they were seen.

Holding Owain in her arms, she bent down and dragging the Bushbaby in one hand, she shuffled down a small incline. There were rocks and a small tree at the bottom which they hid behind. She was temporarily out of sight. She put Owain back in his Bushbaby. He didn't protest. He must have picked up her mood because he was so quiet. Keeping close to the ground with Owain on her back, she half-crawled, half-scrambled through the rocky landscape back to the path. She saw herself as a commando carrying a backpack through enemy territory. It was essential they weren't seen. If caught, they'd be snatched and taken into captivity with the others. As soon as she reached the path back to Barnhill, she stood up and, after adjusting the position of Owain on her back, began the long walk back.

Night was falling. She walked quickly but she still shook with fear. As she walked, the desolation and despair she'd experienced in the early hours of the morning returned. It felt as if she'd become inhabited by an alien force, an unwanted visitor, someone she had little control over. She looked out over to the sea. It was a steely grey. She imagined a black-clad diver appearing out of the waters and that he was climbing up the cliffs to the path to follow her. He'd be one of the thought police. They were everywhere. Hiding, spying, tracking her, everything frightened her. She didn't know what was real and what she was imagining. She looked frequently over her shoulder, trying to reassure herself she was still on her own, that she wasn't being followed.

Owain had become totally silent. He must have dropped off to sleep. It felt as if he'd abandoned her and she was even more alone. She could no longer rely on him as her protector. At the same time she knew that thinking like this was ridiculous. He was a baby and could do nothing.

The wind was picking up. Looking up at the sky, she could see black crows circling high over her head. They made loud, sinister cawing noises. They were following her. They were vultures, not crows, she was sure of that. They were after her because she was carrying Owain on her back. He was vulnerable to their attacking, cruel, black beaks. She tried picking up her pace, to get to the car as quickly as possible, but the rough terrain, the failing light and Owain's weight on her back prevented her moving as quickly as she wanted.

The solitude, the harsh, persistent cawing of the crows and the gloomy light of dusk was progressively unnerving her. She breathed in short tortured gasps. She looked ahead. Barnhill. She could see it now. Silhouetted black against a red, angry, evening sky.

She couldn't move fast enough. Second by second she was becoming more breathless and more tearful. It was almost dark. She was half-running, half-walking when her foot caught under a bramble growing across the path. She stumbled, lurched forward, but managed to regain her balance. She just stopped herself and Owain from falling. She forced herself to slow down. She must get her breath back. Calm yourself, she thought. She took Owain off her back and sat down. She pulled off her boot, massaging her ankle to stop it swelling.

She looked up and stared. In the half-light, picking

her way along the path and some way ahead, was a young woman. She had her back to her and was wearing high heels. Her blond hair was shoulder length and curled under in fifties-style bangs. She was dressed formally, in a smart grey, tight-waisted suit. The woman stopped, turned, looked over her shoulder, and put her hands on her hips. She smiled contemptuously at Flori. Her mouth was like a red gash. She said something but Flori couldn't hear her. The wind had blown her words away. The woman turned, didn't look back and was gone.

Flori sat transfixed. Her mother was here. She tried to make sense of what she'd seen. She struggled to her feet, shouted after her, 'Mummy, don't go.' She screamed and ran, stumbling over the rocks on the path towards where she'd walked, her arms reaching out, calling for her over and over but she didn't return. She was oblivious to her distress.

She sobbed as she spoke, 'Mummy, forgive me. I'm sorry. I tried to help. You know I did. I'll make it alright for you. It's not too late. Don't go, Mummy. Don't leave me again. I haven't told anyone. I promised I wouldn't. I'll be good. Come back.'

Her voice trailed away. Her words were lost. Her mother had gone. Vanished. She stood, twisting her hands round and round. Her mother. How much she'd wanted her, how much she'd tried to please her. But she was the same, the way she'd always been, cruel, playing tricks on her. She knew how to play cruelty to a fine art, how to taunt, how to tantalise, how to torment her. Her mind empty, she put her head in her hands and sat down on the path.

It was almost dark when she heard a baby's cry. She looked up, the baby's cry brought her back to the present. It was the same cry she'd heard this morning when she'd been in the water sliding into unconsciousness. Tids. He was alone. She'd left him in the dark by the side of the path. She ran back, she had to get to him, protect him before her mother arrived. She reached him, he was frantic, his face covered with tears.

She pulled him out of the Bushbaby and gathering him in her arms, tried to calm him.

'I'm here. Tids. Flori is here. I won't leave you. I'm sorry. I didn't forget you. Don't cry.'

He was as distressed as she was and his face was wet with her tears as she stood rocking him in her arms, but sensing someone was standing behind her, she looked up. Standing blocking her path and staring straight at her, was a man with a gun. One she'd seen at the end of the island, a member of the thought police from the bothy. She backed away, still holding the baby in her arms. She'd run if he tried to snatch Owain. She had no fear. Her priority was to protect her baby. She stared unsmilingly at him.

'Are you alright, missee?'

'Don't come near me.'

'You don't seem well.'

'What have you done with her?'

'Who?'

'You know who. My mother. I've seen her.'

The man stared uncomprehendingly. 'There's no one here.'

'Fucking liar. If I didn't have this baby, I'd grab your gun and I'd shoot you. Murderer. All of you. Murderers.'

The man stood staring at her, then he backed away and, avoiding her eyes, he said, 'I need to get past. I'm after rabbits,' and he pushed past her.

Flori stood to one side and waited as he walked away. She held Owain in her arms until she could no longer see him. He walked rapidly, turning round several times to look back at her. She neither knew nor cared what he might be thinking.

Somehow Flori and Owain reached the car. The day's events had disturbed her, leaving her agitated and jumpy, but seeing Rose's car gave her a small, if only a temporary, sense of normality. She put Owain in the car seat, reversed at high speed, and began the drive back to Lagg. She couldn't rid herself of the images of her mother, the man with the gun on the path and seeing the thought police coming and going at the bothy. She wondered if there were more of them concealed in the hedges, whether they were tracking her, or whether someone might jump out in front of the car and be caught in the glare of the headlights.

Seeing her mother walking on the path dressed for going out terrified her. She couldn't understand how and why she was on the island. She remembered how her mother had been when she was a child, and a chill passed through her. That was the past but what now? Had she imagined seeing her mother, was that possible? If she had imagined her that frightened her. It had happened before. It was when her mother had gone into hospital and she'd been taken to stay with her aunt and uncle. They'd said they were going to look after her while her mother wasn't well but one night as she lay in bed she heard the front door bell ring. She heard some people come in and listened from the top of the stairs. It had been her mother's social workers on a late visit, they'd been speaking to her aunt and uncle but she couldn't hear what was said. Eventually, they'd left.

The next day, after breakfast, she'd been told she couldn't go to school because a social worker was coming to see her. She'd asked why but no one would tell her, they just said she must wait. The social worker had been late, but she sensed she was about to hear something bad, because everyone looked so serious. The social worker said her name was May and her aunt had given her a cup of tea and said she'd stay in the room with her, then she'd put her arm round her.

The social worker had looked at her very seriously and then she'd said, 'Flori, I need to tell you something. It's very sad and I'm very sorry, but your mother has passed away.'

She'd pretended not to hear. She'd carried on with her game, hanging the dresses with the little tabs over their shoulders on her paper dolls, lining them up on the table.

She'd asked her aunt, 'Which lady do you like best?'

The social worker had said, 'Flori, I don't think you heard me,' but she had, she just pretended she hadn't. She'd said, 'My favourite is the red dress, the one with the spots. Mummy's got a dress like that. She wears it when she goes out, and with her high heels.'

The social worker had said, 'You know your mummy was unhappy?' and she'd answered, 'Yes, she is sometimes but I can make her laugh. When's she coming to see me?'

'She's passed away.'

She'd said, 'I'm going to my room. I'm late already. I've got to get ready for school.'

Her aunt followed her upstairs, she'd told her to go away, but she wouldn't. She'd asked her what 'passed away' meant, and her aunt had said, 'It means your mother has died.' She'd asked how and she'd said, 'By her own hand.' She hadn't understood that and it took a long time before she understood, because no one ever talked to her about it.

Eventually she worked it out but for a long time she'd felt nothing. When she thought about what the social worker had said, that her mother had been unhappy, she knew that was wrong. Her mother hadn't been unhappy, she was always angry, but she'd kept that to herself, hadn't told anyone.

One day she'd been in the school playground with her best friend and they'd been talking about mothers and Flori asked her if she knew what had happened to her mother. Her friend did know. She said that her mother had been put in a 'nut house' because she was 'bonkers' and that her mother had hanged herself while she was in hospital. Even hearing that didn't really upset her, but after that weird things began to happen.

She began to have visions of her mother. That's what she called them and she started to imagine all kinds of things. Strange dreams, nightmares, flashbacks, they'd come to her especially at night but she kept all this a secret. She didn't want her aunt to know because it wasn't normal. She'd lie in bed waiting for her mother to come to her. She'd imagine she was still alive but this time she'd try to make her mother happy so she wouldn't 'pass away'.

If her mother was in a good mood she'd kiss her. She always wore bright red lipstick and she didn't like that and after she'd gone, she'd rub the lipstick away. She knew her mother wanted to look like a film star because once she'd ask her just before she went out how she looked and when she said, 'Like a film star,' that had made her smile and she'd said, 'When you wake up, I'll be back.'

When she went out her mother always said she had to look after her little brother and that she was responsible for him while she was away. She'd asked where she was going, but she'd just said, 'Ask no questions and hear no lies.' Then she'd laugh. As she'd got older, her mother would shout at her and tell her off for nothing and sometimes she wouldn't speak to her all day but other times she was alright. It all depended and she never knew when and how she'd be. It was just the way she was.

Even so, it was sad that 'she'd died by her own hand'. She asked the social worker why no one had helped her and she'd told her how hard she'd tried to make her happy. She told her how her mother would scream and shout at her for nothing, and blame her for everything going wrong and then she'd refuse to talk to her and push her away whenever she tried to help her.

The social worker didn't seem to know what to say and she said, 'No one could help her,' and that Flori mustn't blame herself. She said she shouldn't worry anyway because it was in the past and it would be best to forget all about it. So that's what she'd tried to do, forget all about it and it had worked. Up until now.

It was being on this island, Jura. It was like the first time, only she was here and if she was on the cliff path, she must still be alive. She looked the same as she'd remembered her. Smart with blonde hair and with that red lipstick which she always wore when she went out. She'd said to her she'd run away next time she was in hospital, so that must be what she'd done. She'd run away from hospital and been in hiding all this time. So everyone had lied to her when they said she'd died by her own hand. She was still alive and this time she'd followed her to Jura.

She'd must have come back to haunt her. She didn't like her caring for the baby and she was going to frighten her all over again with her moods, her tantrums, her demands, as she had years ago. Once she'd said, 'Where ever you are, Flori, I'll always know what you're doing, and I'll find you.' She was capable of anything.

Flori felt a shiver of fear pass through her. She looked in the driver's mirror to check on Owain. He was sitting in his baby seat diagonally across behind her. He was wide awake and staring at her. Their eyes met. His stare made her feel uncomfortable. He was looking at her as if he was accusing her of something. Was it because she'd left him on the path? She knew she'd been wrong leaving him when she ran after her mother, but she hadn't really forgotten him. She would never leave him. It had only been for a few minutes, but she knew even a minute in a little baby's life was an eternity.

She tried waving and smiling at him in the driver's mirror, but he didn't respond and continued staring at her. She was becoming more and more nervous of him. She wondered what he was thinking. Did he hate her? Maybe if she played some music that would help. She bent forward to put on 'The wheels of the bus go round and round'. She began to sing along. In the past, he'd jiggle up and down in time to the music but not tonight. He was totally unresponsive and continued staring at her until they got to Lagg.

She was glad to reach Lagg. She parked the car, got out and stood listening. She wanted to be sure no one was around. There were no lights, not even along the road or across the Sound of Jura that night. The hamlet was as black as a graveyard. A heavy sea mist muffled all sound and anything could happen and no one would know. It felt as if it was just the two of them in the world. She pulled the buggy out of the boot and dragged it along to the croft, returning to the car for Owain. She removed him gently from his car seat and walked the short distance to the croft holding him close, kissing his face, pulling his little fleece hat over his ears, talking to him. His withdrawn mood was passing and he began smiling again, and put his hand forward to touch her face, and when she felt his fingers on her face, she felt happy. He knew nothing of her fears. His world consisted only of her and how she cared for him.

She hesitated before going inside the croft. She never locked the front door but now she regretted it. She opened the door and still holding Owain, she stood for a moment, listening intently for any noise. She was ready to run but she could hear nothing. That didn't mean anything. To be sure they were safe, she'd have to go upstairs. She put him in his buggy while she drew the curtains, one after another, put the lights on and checked through downstairs. There was no one. The croft was empty; unless someone was upstairs. If someone was waiting for her, that's where they'd be.

She'd be stupid to go up without a weapon to protect herself so she looked around for something she could use. It was obvious what she should use. A knife. There were several in the drawer of the dresser in the kitchen. She walked over, pulled out the drawer and looked inside. She chose the meat knife. Probably used for cutting up deer, it was viciously large with a serrated edge. She'd use that if she had to.

She left Owain downstairs and holding the knife at right angles, began climbing the stairs. She stopped on each stair and listened. Silence. Every beat of her heart was magnified and the closer she got to the top, the louder was the sound. She reached the hall landing. Came to a stop. Paused. Ran into the bathroom, her bedroom, Owain's bedroom, looking under each bed, opening each wardrobe, all the time holding tightly onto the knife. She was ready to use it if someone jumped on her.

She pulled back the curtains across the windows. Looked out. It was a still night, the mist blocking the lights from across the mainland. But she sensed someone was out there. She couldn't see who or where, but she felt a malign presence and if they attacked, she was prepared to fight to the death.

She returned downstairs, double locked the front door and did the same with the back door. She put on every light in the house. She pulled the kitchen table by the door and tried to pull the dresser across but it was too heavy. It was made of oak and weighed a ton. She placed the chairs so they leaned against the windows. Although it wouldn't stop anyone, it would make it more difficult to break in. She'd hear them pushing against the furniture when they broke in and that would give her time to use her knife.

The knife. She needed more, she only had one. She looked in every drawer, pulled them out, lined them up in neat rows on the table; meat cleavers, steak knives, bread knives, fruit knives, vegetable knives. She put at least one in every room, but the carving knife she kept with her. It was the one she trusted, the one she'd use that could protect her and Owain if attacked. She whispered, 'No one's getting my baby, not even you. You're not taking him, he's mine now'.

She glanced at Owain. He was crying in his buggy, looking at her resentfully. She hadn't heard him, she'd been so preoccupied. He was holding his arms up to be carried. He wanted to be held by her. She looked at him perplexed. She'd been distracted. He was looking at her as if he wanted something but she didn't know what that was. Was he frightened, too? His cries reminded her that he was a real baby who was hungry and needed feeding.

She was feeling more confused, more disturbed, her thinking increasingly distorted. She looked at him. Who was he? Owain or Tids? She didn't feel real anymore. All she was conscious of was her mother could break in and would try to snatch him off her and she had to stop that.

She went into the kitchen, prepared his milk and began

to feed him. He wasn't interested. He pushed away the bottle and blew the milk in bubbles from his mouth. He wanted to play and he demanded her attention. She tried feeding him again but he pulled at her hair and her nose. He jiggled up and down, kicking his legs and waving his arms. She stared at him, wondering what he was thinking, and what was going on with him. She hadn't known him to be like this before. Usually he loved his food and nothing distracted him from that.

As soon as she put him down, he started to howl. 'What's the matter with you, baby?' she said, and picked him up again but as soon as she did this and held him in her arms, he bounced up and down, and started smiling again. She looked at him and thought how vulnerable he was and how much she loved him. He was so sweet. It seemed as if he was trying to distract her and make her feel better so she gave up trying to feed him and began playing with him.

She picked up his fat giraffe and gave it to him, but he threw it on the floor and when she picked it up, he threw it again, and each time she picked it up, he threw it back down. He seemed to find this game hilarious. So she played 'peek a boo', a game she knew he loved, and then 'this little pig' with his toes, and then 'round and round the garden'. She played with him and tickled him until he became exhausted and quite suddenly fell asleep. Holding him in her arms she crept upstairs with him, but when she got to the top, she hesitated. She wondered if she should keep him in his room, or bring him in with her. She decided she wanted him with her. That way he'd keep her company and she could keep him safe, so after gently putting him in his carrycot, she placed it on the two chairs next to her bed.

She returned downstairs. Owain's games had made her feel better but now he was asleep that horrible and familiar feeling of an imminent threat was coming back. It permeated her body and mind. She could see in her mind's eye a black formless sack creeping across the kitchen floor towards her and when it got to her it would suffocate her. Restless, she didn't know what to do or how to be. She paced round the kitchen. She began thinking of Matt. She played Judie Tzuke singing 'Stay with me till Dawn' but it made her feel worse. The words made her cry because he wasn't there and she wanted and needed him. She switched it off.

When she used to get upset, he'd always made her feel better. He knew what to say, he understood her. She pulled her Gore-Tex jacket down from the hook and searched in the pocket for the white stone from Solva harbour until she found it. Holding it tightly in her hand would make her feel more grounded, maybe she'd ring him, but she'd promised not to contact him and she'd keep that promise, no matter how bad she felt.

She decided to send him thought messages. She'd read somewhere the mind was like a radio. It was both a transmitter and a receiver, so if she thought hard enough, he could pick up what she was thinking even if there was interference in the air. He'd ring her then and she could talk to him. She switched on her mobile but as she did, she realised her mother would know and would also get through so she switched it off.

She whispered, 'Flori, you're in a state tonight. What are we going to do with you?' It was what her aunt used to say to her when she was being looked after and she got upset.

Her gaze fell on the rose in the wine glass. It was the one she'd picked earlier that day after she'd been in the water. That was a long time ago. She stood looking at it. She was puzzled. She was sure she'd put it on the table but now it was on the window sill. It had been moved. Someone had come into the croft and moved things about. They'd come while she and Owain were walking at the end of the island. Someone outside. It must be her mother. She'd followed her from the cliff path.

She was going to scream but then she remembered what her aunt used to say, 'Take deep breaths until you feel calmer, do something ordinary. Doing something ordinary takes your mind off things. Your mind, Flori, it's playing tricks. I know you, now make a cup of tea.'

She forced herself to make a cup of tea and sat down in the lounge. The television stood silently in the corner of the room. Since Rose's visit she hadn't turned it on. She'd put a cloth over the screen. She couldn't look at it. She hated it. She distrusted it. Bad news. *Crime Watch.* She mustn't think about that night weeks ago in West London.

She'd been fine before she'd watched that programme. It all started after that. It transmitted evil thoughts into her, thoughts from her mother. She was out there, hiding in the shadows.

The thought police. They were out there, too. They were everywhere. She'd seen their headquarters at Barnhill and the prisoners held at the bothy at the end of the island, the ones transported by the Argocats. They were the ones who'd been caught for committing a thought crime. She hadn't committed a thought crime, but her mother thought she had. That must be why she was after her but how did the thought police know about her? Her mother must have made a pact with them, they were on the same side but she was prepared for them.

She walked over to the chair, picked up a magazine to try and distract herself. It was one Rose had left and it was an expensive glossy fashion magazine. It must have cost as much as a paperback. She began flicking through the pages. Her attention was caught by a 'shoot' as it was called, on one of the Caribbean islands. The 'shoot' reminded her of guns. Were they there too? The models looked weird. They weren't normal, they seemed elongated in comparison to the ordinary people standing next to them. Flori looked at the scene closely. They'd been positioned to show how elegantly polished, glossy, and long limbed they were and by way of contrast everybody else was stupid, squat, poor and ugly. She turned the magazine sideways on. Had the camera been fixed so the models were seen through some special lens? Or did they really look like that? They were like white female versions of Masai warriors. The clothes were astronomically priced, the equivalent of her salary at Harrods. It was unreal, like everything. Everything was weird. Everything distorted. She looked round the room.

It looked strange, the table, the chairs, the pictures on the wall of deer looked a long way away, and when she walked across the room she felt as if she walked in slow motion. There was a sepia photograph taken a long time ago of people at Lagg standing outside the old post office. The people of Jura, they might look as if they were normal, but you couldn't trust them. Carrying guns and killing people for thought crimes is definitely not normal.

She put the magazine down but she was too agitated to rest. She wasn't sure what to do but then she remembered Rose had said to ring her if she needed help. Anytime, she'd said. Well, she needed help now. Big time. She would ring her. She picked up her mobile, wondered if Rose would answer. She might be out.

7

The phone was ringing. It rang longer than usual and then a man's voice, 'Yes?' It disconcerted her, she'd expected Rose's voice. She asked if she had the wrong number. The man said he didn't know, who was it she wanted? Flori didn't say, didn't know if she could trust him. She asked who he was. His answer, that he was Nigel, confused her further. She asked if Rose was there, told him she had to speak to her. He said they'd been asleep but he'd wake her. There was a long silence before Rose came on.

'How could you, Rose?'

'Could I what?'

'Sleep with a man with the name of Nigel?' She didn't wait for her to answer. 'Rose, I need your help.'

'Flori, are you joking, do you know what time it is?'

'Actually, no, I'm not joking. I haven't looked at the time.'

'It's just turned two am.'

'Early then.'

'I call that late. What do you want, Flori?'

'You're irritated with me, you said if I felt upset, I could ring you.'

'Yes, and?'

'I need to tell you, the people are strange around here. I know who they are. We saw them, didn't we? Up on the mountain and today I walked with Owain to the end of the island and there were loads of them. Going in and out of a bothy. They didn't see us.'

'Who are you talking about?'

'You know, don't pretend you don't. The thought police. I had to hide with Owain. But, I saw my mother. She was ahead of me on the path. She shouted at me, I couldn't hear what she said. I ran after her, but she'd disappeared. They're helping her. She's out to get me. I'm frightened she'll harm Tids. She doesn't like babies. She hates them. Did I ever tell you?'

There was a very long silence. 'Who's Tids?'

'My brother, I told you.'

'Don't you mean Owain? First you said Owain, then Tids.'

'Stop trying to confuse me. I told you Rose, Tids, he's with me.'

She said, 'You're not making this up, are you?'

'No, no, no, it's all true. You said, you said you'd come, if I was upset. I am upset now, Rose, and I need your help, because she could be here tonight. If you were here, I'd be safe. You'd, you'd stand up to her.'

'How do you know she's there?'

'Because she's been here already. In here. I picked a rose, left it in a vase and it's moved. It was moved somewhere else. Who else could it be other than my mother? I already saw her on the cliff path. I told you that already. She's here on Jura and she's following me. She's desperate to find me.'

'But you told me your mother was dead. So how can she be there?'

'You don't believe me, do you? You're humouring me, Rose. I can tell and I don't like it. I'll tell you once more. She's here. I've seen her. She's after me. I thought she was dead, but she's not. Social workers lie. They lied to me. Everyone's lied to me and I want you to come.'

'Social workers. What social workers? Flori, you're overwrought. The isolation is getting to you, you're not thinking straight.'

There was a long silence from Flori. She said, 'So you won't come. If you won't come, then I shall have to take…'

Rose interrupted her. She didn't finish her sentence. 'What? What were you going to say?'

'If you won't come, I'll be forced to go into hiding with Owain. You'll never find us. No one will. I have to protect myself and Tids. I've told you and you're not taking any notice. You should. This is a warning. Things are getting serious, the thought police, that's why I have the knife with me and I'm prepared to use it. I'm ready for them.'

Rose took a deep breath, 'I'll ring you back, Flori. Soon. Give me two minutes.'

Flori sat waiting over the phone. She knew Rose didn't believe her, but she meant what she'd said to her. She had to take her seriously and she would use her knife. She was determined to protect herself and Tids. She couldn't trust anyone anymore, not even Rose, but she needed her. Rose didn't understand how dangerous the situation was but if she came, she'd see for herself.

The phone rang. Flori picked it up immediately.

'I'll be there soon, Flori. I'll let you know when. But take care of yourself and I'll be with you soon.'

Knowing Rose would soon be with her somewhat reassured Flori, but the feeling didn't last. Once she'd put down the phone, and wandered round the room feelings of dread descended on her. She looked at the time. Rose was right, it was late. She hadn't realised the time. She must get to bed. She'd been putting it off.

She hadn't wanted to sleep because once she was asleep she was defenceless. Anything could happen. She went upstairs into her bedroom and checked on Owain. He was sleeping peacefully and as she watched him, she marvelled at how sweet and trusting he was. I was like that once, she thought, but that made her tearful, and she pushed her tears back. She wouldn't allow herself to feel sad, not on her own account. She got into bed, but found she was too wide awake, too jumpy, too alert, to sleep. She lay for over an hour, tossing and turning.

She was thirsty, she should get a drink, but she was too frightened to leave her bedroom. If she went downstairs to the kitchen she'd have to face who or what might be there. She forced herself to get out of bed and stood at the top of the stairs listening. She could hear nothing but the wind blowing through the trees outside. She could go to the bathroom for a drink, but what if a rat had got trapped and had drowned in the water tank? Her mother had told her if that happened the water would be fouled and if she drank it, she'd be poisoned.

Maybe she could get just one drink and taste a tiny bit to make sure it was pure and there was no dead animal rotting and contaminating the water. She couldn't make her mind up, didn't know what was best to do, so she returned to her bed and lay there, her mind drifting. There was about to be a catastrophe. One was imminent, she felt sure of that.

She lay listening to the moaning of the wind, sighing, whining, and weaving through and round the empty crofts. It seemed to be searching, seeking someone with no name who was long gone, as if mourning for the death of someone, its sighs expressing its restless spirit. This thought deeply disturbed her. She entered a twilight world halfway between being awake and being asleep, where images and people from the past floated across her mind's eye.

She sat up. She could hear the child. The voice from the past but she knew who he was. He was calling her name. She recognised the cry. Her brother, Tids, and she could hear him and see him. He was in the bedroom. He was a toddler and he was putting up his arms asking to be picked up. She bent down and gathered him in her arms, holding him so his face was close to her own. His cheeks were soft and she kissed him until he smiled. Then she put him down. She'd made him happy and he ran off to play.

She cried, hot tears falling silently down her face. The pain was great, her grief silent, it came from somewhere deep within herself. She lay sobbing, pressing her face into the pillow, calling for him, over and over, but he couldn't return, he never would, no matter how much she wanted him. He no longer existed, he lived on only in her mind and in her soul. She cried until exhausted, and fell into a fitful sleep.

The loud tick of the clock by her bed woke her. Half-asleep she tried to orientate herself. She didn't know where she was. She half-raised herself to look around, and then she saw something. An apparition. A life-size, black shape slowly, silently moving across the room towards her. It reached her. Stopped. It was bending over her. It was formless with no face. She couldn't move. She was paralysed in her sleep. She could observe but was unable to move. She couldn't speak. She couldn't breathe. It was a living death. A night time terror from which there was no escape. As the shape leaned over to suffocate her with a pillow, she realised she was awake in a nightmare. She struggled to sit up and the figure dissolved, disappearing into the night.

She took a deep breath. Looked round the room. Everything the same. Outside dawn breaking. The cry of the sea gulls. She was still alive. She'd survived. She got up out of bed and walked across to Owain. She was shaking. He lay asleep on his back, one hand curled round the corner of the cot blanket, the other holding his fat giraffe. She pulled the curtains back from the window and looked outside. It was cold, grey, a sombre monotone contrasting with the vivid purple-and-red fuchsia bushes growing outside the empty crofts. The wind was still and had ceased its restless search. She turned to look at Owain again. He was still asleep. They'd survived the terrors of the night.

The words of Rose from last night came back to her. Maybe she was over wrought, but once Rose was here, whether today or tomorrow, she'd help. She went down to the kitchen to make a cup of tea. Everything was the same except for the furniture she'd pushed against the door of the kitchen, and the knives.

The knives. She looked at them, slightly perplexed. She'd leave them where they were. Although the nightmare presence had disappeared, it could come back. She must be prepared. She must keep the carving knife by her at all times. Just in case.

8

It was late evening. Rose had travelled from London and managed to catch the last ferry from Islay to the Island of Jura. She stood watching the boat inch towards the landing stage. She could see Flori already. She was standing waiting for her, holding Owain in her arms. She'd wrapped Owain in a fleece blanket and was adjusting the blanket round him to protect him from the chill winds coming off the grey seas. Rose waved.

It had been a difficult journey. She'd had plenty of time to think about Flori's early morning phone call to her. The seriousness of what they had done in stealing Owain and her collusion with Flori now weighed heavily on her. She wished she'd never met her, that she hadn't got involved with helping her flee to Jura and that she hadn't answered the phone last night, but even worse, for the first time ever, it had crossed her mind that Owain's safety could be at risk. A terrible thought that was devastating to her.

The call from Flori last night was seriously disturbing. She'd sounded deranged. She'd wondered whether she realised how frightening she sounded with her talk of the knife and her threat of disappearing with Owain. After she'd put the phone down, it had crossed her mind that she should call for a doctor but in the end she'd decided against it. She dreaded meeting Flori, knowing how fragile and paranoid she was, and she feared she wouldn't be strong enough to cope with her. She'd even thought not to come and pretend she knew nothing. She could ignore the problem, change her number, walk away from the whole thing and hope that given time Flori would get better without medical intervention. But she recognised the harsh reality; she couldn't do that, no matter how much she wanted to escape from the situation. In the end she'd have to help her. She was her best friend. Flori trusted her and she had no one else.

The ferry was now stationary. Rose walked off and looked closely at Flori as she moved forward to greet her. There was something different about her. It was how she carried herself, how she looked, and as if she was preoccupied with her own thoughts and had removed herself from the moment. She seemed withdrawn and avoided Rose's eyes when Rose bent forward to kiss her in greeting. She'd lost her openness, her warmth, her *joie de vivre*.

Rose put her rucksack in the boot of the car and got into the passenger seat. She surreptitiously glanced across at Flori, observing what was different about her. She certainly didn't look her usual self. Her hair was greasy, her clothes dirty and the colours didn't match. She was wearing a purple top and red bottoms and she looked as if she'd dressed herself with the contents of a charity shop from a particularly poor part of London. Why and how could that be? Rose knew that Flori's wardrobe consisted of many expensive items. Her work in Harrods as a buyer for designer children's clothes meant she was influenced by good design and style and usually she took pride in her appearance but now she looked exhausted, unkempt and as if she hadn't slept for days. It was so unlike Flori that seeing her like this upset Rose.

She turned to say hello to Owain who was sitting behind in his car seat. He stared back at her, solemn and unsmiling, seemingly not recognising her, even though he'd seen her only recently. He, too, like Flori, seemed preoccupied and withdrawn, and not his usual lively, happy self.

As Rose turned away her eye was caught by a carving knife. It was totally incongruous and lay on the back seat next to Owain. Rose fell into a shocked silence. Questions raced through her mind. A knife. Why on earth would Flori be driving around with that? How long had it been there? Was she expecting to be attacked? She felt compelled to speak out. It was too strange to ignore, even if it was an absentminded act. She had to check out what was going on. She forced herself to sound calm. She didn't want to scare Flori, so she spoke as if the question was of mild interest to her.

'Flori, you have a carving knife on the seat by Owain. Did you know it's there?'

Flori didn't answer straightaway but when she did, her response sounded superficially reasonable. 'It's there to keep us safe. Me and Owain.'

'Safe? From whom?'

Flori changed the subject, 'Have you seen Natalya yet?'

'No, but that's a long-term project, Flori. As you know.' Rose was determined to persist in her line of questioning; she wasn't going to be put off. 'Safe from whom?'

'People.'

'People? Which people? Is it something to do with what you told me the other night?'

'I didn't speak to you last night.'

'You know what I mean, Flori. In the early hours, you rang me, you were frightened by what might be going on. I want to know. That's why I've come. To help you.'

'Thank you. I'll tell you when I'm ready.'

Rose realised at that point she'd get no further and continuing to question her would only annoy her so she gave up and instead commented on how well Owain looked, but how solemn he seemed since she'd last seen him.

'You think so?' Flori said, and she laughed briefly but Rose noticed the note of bitterness in her next comment. 'It must be being with me all the time.'

The atmosphere had quickly become tense and they sat

in silence until they reached Craighouse. Rose asked if they should stop to buy food. Flori replied she had everything they'd need. She spoke in such a way that Rose felt more and more constrained from talking, either from commenting on what she'd been doing or from asking Flori about herself. It was clear Flori didn't want to engage in any conversation.

They arrived at Lagg. Rose fully expected Flori to swing off road and onto the track to the croft, but she didn't stop.

'Flori. Did you notice? We just drove past Lagg.'

'Yes, I know.'

'Where are you going then?'

'Barnhill.'

'Barnhill. But why now, it's almost dark.'

'I know, but I thought we could check out what's going on. I prefer to go with you.'

'But it's empty, Flori. No one lives there, and it'll be too dark to see anything.'

'That's what they want us to think, isn't it? If we go when it's dark, we can creep around and not be seen. I'm sure they're holding prisoners there, including my mother. I want to see her. I get thought messages from her.'

Rose looked at Flori incredulously. 'I don't want to go, Flori, and what do you mean "you get thought messages". How does that work? It's not possible. It's in your imagination. Your mother's dead, isn't she? Isn't she? This is madness.'

Flori turned round briefly to look at her, her voice wobbling, her eyes filled with tears. 'How do you know? You never saw her dead, did you? And neither did I. There's things ordinary people don't know about. I thought you were my friend, and I don't like being called mad.'

'But I'm still your friend, that's why I'm saying it, to help you. Besides it's a figure of speech.'

'Well, you're not helping me.'

Rose felt a sense of rising panic. Flori had never spoken like this before. She was no longer open to reason. She turned round again and looked at Owain, almost as if he could help.

116

At least he was some distraction, but when she spoke and tried to make him laugh, he was totally unresponsive and continued staring straight ahead. He'd been jolly and lively when she'd last seen him but now he reflected Flori's moods, so if she was tense, preoccupied and withdrawn, then so was he.

She stared out through her side window. All she could do was wait and see how it was going to play out. It was weird. Flori had changed, but why? If Flori expected her to go with her and prowl around the perimeter, she'd refuse. She didn't want to collude with her craziness and what did she mean when she spoke about the 'thought police' and thought crimes? Was she being metaphorical?

Her mind went back to her last visit and what Flori had said about the deer hunters. It had been bizarre. She knew logically that 'the men with guns' were the 'deer hunters' and Flori had been right, they did seem everywhere, but this after all, was the deer hunting season. They'd seen them before on the mountains and it was likely to be true, that there were more at the far end of the island. She could even see things from her point of view, there was something sinister about the way gun shots ricocheted and echoed around the bracken-covered moors and hills, and how the Argocats carrying the hunters moved relentlessly across the bogs, the streams, and up the hill sides. With their huge wheels, they did look ominous, like military vehicles, or even like tanks, but you'd need an overactive imagination, one out of control, to believe they were actually government agents with their headquarters at Barnhill.

Flori came to a stop. She turned off the engine and looked at Rose. 'Coming?' she asked. Rose looked out. It was almost dark and Barnhill had that familiar air of desolation, which they'd both found so disturbing on their first visit. She'd tried to make sense of it when she was back in London, she'd thought about the atmosphere and how it might have influenced George Orwell, and she'd come to the conclusion his paranoid ideas had permeated Flori's mind, even though Flori had said she'd never read his book.

Rose answered quickly, smiling in what she hoped was a disarming way. 'I'll wait here with Owain while you go. It'll be easier for you on your own.'

Flori looked at her. She was suspicious. 'If I leave you, you might leave, drive off and take Owain with you. You don't trust me and I don't trust you, especially as I know what you think of me.'

'And what's that?'

'You think I'm mad. Well, I'm not. You'll see as soon as we get back to Lagg.'

'Look, Flori, I have no idea what's going on because you're not telling me, and you're talking in code. I'm here because you were upset and asked me to help you.'

She stopped and looked at Flori expectantly but she didn't answer. 'I think it would be a shame to take Owain from a warm car and go out into the night, so I'll sit here with him. You know me well enough to trust me and of course I wouldn't leave you.'

She leant forward and put her arm round her friend briefly but Flori flinched when she touched her.

Flori said, 'Okay. I won't be long. The prisoners may have been moved now but just because it's empty, doesn't mean it's not going on. I've told you. I saw my mother along the path here. Give me the knife.'

'For god's sake, Flori. You don't need that.'

But when she saw Flori's hostility she thought it best not to argue with her. Flori's eyes seemed to bore into her. She picked the knife off the back seat and holding it gingerly, looked apprehensively at Flori, but without passing it to her.

'Give it to me.' Flori glared at her and took it out of her reluctant hand. 'I won't be long but if I hear a car engine start, I know you've left me, and I'll find you, wherever you are.' She stared accusingly at Rose, 'I'm going to have to trust you. Don't let me down.' She slammed the car door shut and walked off into the night.

Despite her aggression, Rose felt upset on her behalf. She

wanted to ask why she was so frightened and why she was behaving in this way, but she knew she wouldn't respond. She wouldn't answer or she'd pretend she hadn't heard. She seemed to have two moods; either taciturn or angry and, like a cornered, wounded animal, was capable only of spitting and clawing at any sign of kindness. She leaned back in the car seat. Usually she'd put on music, but not now, she wasn't in that kind of mood. She spoke to Owain but he didn't respond, so she gave up and waited apprehensively for Flori's return.

She was gone for ten minutes and she was still holding the knife when she emerged from the darkness.

'Well?' said Rose, 'See anything?'

'No. But that means nothing.'

Flori switched on the engine and they drove in silence back to Lagg. With every passing minute, Rose's anxiety was increasing. She comforted herself with the thought she'd taken the precaution of obtaining the ferry times so, if necessary, she could make a quick getaway, but she felt bad thinking of her friend in this way. She couldn't do that. Flori was unwell and she couldn't abandon her. There was also Owain to think about, his well being, his safety. It was all too much. Flori had deteriorated rapidly and Rose felt out of her depth.

They arrived back at the croft. Rose got out the car first, walked into the kitchen and stood and looked. Chaos. The furniture had been moved and was ready to be pushed against the back door. The emulsion that Flori had asked her to bring hadn't been used, and her favourite rug that she'd asked to be brought from her London flat was nowhere to be seen. The sink was piled high with unwashed dishes. Plates were left with the remains of half-eaten food on them, drawers had been pulled out and not pushed back. This was the environment of someone not coping. It was as if a burglar had ransacked the rooms, turned things upside down, and had left in a hurry.

Yet Flori was oblivious to the environment. She turned to look at Rose and said, her voice cold, 'You know where to go, the same bedroom as before.'

Rose picked up her rucksack and slowly walked up the stairs. When she reached the top, she came to a sudden halt. Facing her on the window sill was an arsenal of knives. They lay in a line. She walked into her bedroom. It was the same there. She took a deep breath, walked in to Flori's bedroom to see if there were more. There were. She was frightened now. Flori must believe herself to be under attack. The knives were laid ready for use.

She had no idea how to respond. She wondered whether to say to Flori she didn't need knives, that she was imagining potential attackers. Or whether she should say nothing. Yet to ignore them would mean an acceptance of her craziness.

She put her rucksack on a chair and stood for a moment, uncertain of what she should do. She was tense and exhausted. She felt incapable of coming to any decision. Nothing, it seemed, could be taken for granted and anything could happen. She walked back downstairs.

Flori was standing at the window in the kitchen talking to Owain. She sounded and seemed normal. When she saw Rose she smiled. 'Everything okay?'

Rose paused. She heard herself say, 'No, Flori, it's not. It's not okay. I didn't like you carrying a knife in the car, and I don't want knives in my bedroom. We're not living in a war zone. It's really not on. It's over the top. Who do you think is going to attack us?'

She was half-aware as she spoke that she sounded headmistressy, or like a school matron, but she was trying to be calm, although at the same time she was apprehensive that what she'd just said might be misinterpreted by Flori. She was right. She regretted it. The expression on Flori's face changed. Her eyes narrowed. She placed Owain in his buggy and stared back at her.

'You know nothing. You'll find out. Soon enough. Tonight. That's when she comes. I've seen her.'

'Who? Who have you seen, Flori?'

Flori didn't answer. She said, 'I'm going to put Owain to

120

bed,' and picking Owain out of his buggy, she walked with him towards the door.

'He hasn't been fed yet,' Rose said.

Flori hesitated, then walked back. 'You feed him then, I'm going upstairs,' and with that she pushed Owain into Rose's arms and turning her back on Rose she walked away. When she reached the door she turned round and said, 'You know where his milk and food is, there's a jar in the fridge, give him some from that, and while you're at it, feed yourself.'

'But, Flori. I thought we'd eat together.'

Flori appeared not to hear and left the room.

Rose glanced down at Owain lying in her arms. He looked puzzled. She had had little or no experience of caring for small babies and was taken aback with the responsibility suddenly foisted on her. She began speaking reassuringly, telling him he didn't have long to wait and she'd put him in his buggy while she warmed up his milk and food. But as soon as she put him down, he began to cry. He didn't want Rose, but Flori. He held up his little arms towards the door where Flori had disappeared and for a minute, Rose was unsure what to do. She decided to leave him while she quickly prepared his food.

She hastily removed some baby food from an opened jar left lying on the table. He began to cry. Flori's disappearance and her own presence seemed to anger him, and minute by minute, despite Rose speaking soothingly to him, his cries became louder and more strident. She tried picking him up but he pulled away from her, tears cascading down his cheeks. Clearly it was Flori he wanted and not her.

'What the fuck are you doing?' Flori was standing at the kitchen door. 'Can't you do anything I ask you? Are you totally useless? You sound like you're murdering him.'

Rose felt a flash of anger. 'Well, you look after him. He's your baby. You took him.'

Flori looked at her friend, her eyes cold and hostile. She said, 'Thanks for that really helpful comment.'

She walked across to Owain and picked him up. He

stopped crying straightaway, wrapped his arms round her neck, and buried his head close to hers, sucking his thumb and occasionally staring back over his shoulder at Rose, looking at her as if she'd assaulted him.

Rose continued preparing Owain's food and silently passed it to Flori. She began washing up. She was well aware of the tense atmosphere but her patience was stretched to its limits. She was fed up with placating Flori. She was fed up with trying to make sense of what was going on. She was fed up with not knowing what was going on and that Flori refused to talk to her. The situation was crazy. Something had to change. She stopped washing up, turned round. Flori was now feeding Owain. She seemed aware that her friend was looking at her, and their eyes met. Rose spoke directly to her spontaneously and from her heart.

'Flori, you're not happy. Something's happened to you, what I don't know, but you've changed and not knowing is intolerable to me. I want to know. I want to know who you think is coming tonight, and why you're so frightened, because what you're thinking, is not real. It's in your imagination. I want to know who Tids is, and why sometimes you call Owain, Tids.'

Flori didn't answer. She looked down at Owain to avoid Rose's gaze. Then she said, 'I can't. I can't tell you. I can't. I daren't.'

'You have to. You have to try. If you don't tell me,' she paused, 'I shall go, Flori. I shall have to go.'

'Go where?'

'Home. Back to London or to Oxford, because I'm not staying here. It's not helping you and it upsets me to see you. You're moody, unpredictable, and I'm worried about Owain. You're disconnected from him, he's picking up on your moods and it's not good. I'm going to make a deal with you. Either we talk later, after Owain's in bed, or I go. It's up to you. You decide.'

'That's an ultimatum. I can take it or leave it?'

'That's about it.'

Flori didn't respond. She continued feeding Owain and when he'd finished she left the room taking him with her.

Rose waited, but fifteen minutes later Flori still hadn't appeared. She wondered whether to go upstairs and insist Flori come down, or to wait until she appeared of her own accord. There was no right answer, but she felt relieved she'd given her an ultimatum. She was fed up with being controlled and although she didn't think it deliberate on Flori's part, she found it suffocating.

She stood up. She needed a break. The atmosphere in the croft was oppressive. She hadn't smoked for days but she was under so much pressure she felt she had no choice, she had to have a cigarette otherwise she'd go mad. She kept a packet in her bag in case she ever got stressed and she took them out feeling relieved she hadn't thrown them away as she'd been tempted to do when she thought she'd kicked her nicotine habit.

She shouted upstairs, 'Flori. I'm just popping out. Down to the water. I'll be ten minutes or so.'

She listened for a reply, but there was none. Just total silence. She couldn't even hear Owain, so she assumed and hoped he'd fallen asleep.

She left the croft, slowly wandered down the track towards the sea. It was almost dark but not too dark. She could still see well enough. She looked back towards the croft. There was no light on in Flori's bedroom. Had she gone to sleep? What was she doing? She reached the water's edge, took out a cigarette and lit up, inhaling deeply. She noticed her hands trembling but once the nicotine hit her, she began feeling calmer. The tide was going out and she stood watching the water's slow back and forth movement until it silently moved away, leaving her standing by a line of wet sand. The gentle rhythmic movement of shallow water was soothing. She knelt down and put an imprint of her hand into the sand, and watched the imprint fade slowly into nothing as the sea water absorbed its shape.

She found a thick tussock of grass away from the water's edge and sat down, watching the smoke from her cigarette spiral in the air. There was hardly a breath of a breeze. It was beautifully calm and a contrast to her troubled mind. She sat, letting her mind drift. She knew the next day or two with Flori would be difficult. She had to find out what had happened in the past, no matter what the cost in terms of their friendship. Flori didn't want to talk but she must, because only then would she understand.

Flori wasn't well, that was obvious, but she wanted to know why, and what the cause was. She wished she could speak to her father. It was three years since she'd seen him. He was used to dealing with difficult situations and he always kept calm, no matter what. It wasn't surprising really, as his work required that. He had a presence, an authority, a gravitas, and it was his wisdom and care she craved for at this moment. He wasn't always like that, not when he'd been at home with her mother. Right through childhood she could remember the rows and the vicious insults between him and her mother. Both were articulate, and they hadn't needed things to throw at each other but used words to wound. They were like the two characters from Albee's play *Who's afraid of Virginia Woolf?*.

But now, now she knew she had an illicit half-sister, her mother's anger made sense and was understandable and explained why, over the years, the ferocity of their verbal attacks had increased. At the first opportunity she'd tell her mother she knew about Natalya. She wanted to hear her side.

But what of her father? Had he ever been truly happy in his marriage? What was it about their particular chemistry that made them so volatile and nasty with each other? Perhaps it had been different with Natalya's mother. Her mother on the other hand, was too clingy, she didn't leave him enough space, or herself, for that matter. She was an intelligent woman but she didn't have enough to do and they'd got married too young. They shouldn't have married so soon after uni.

She'd learnt a lesson from their mistakes. There was no danger of that for her; she'd decided a long time ago she'd never get married. Not ever. She finished her cigarette which meant she should go back to the croft and see what Flori was up to. She dreaded it. She had no idea what to say, or how or when to face her but she felt resigned to whatever might happen or what might be said.

She'd play it by ear, that's all she could do. She'd have to respond to whatever Flori threw at her, but she must hold her ground. She walked towards to the croft, glanced up. The light was still off in Flori's bedroom.

She opened the front door, walked into the kitchen. Flori was sitting at the kitchen table facing the door with a large knife in front of her. It looked as if she'd been waiting for her. Rose felt a surge of anger rise within her. She wasn't going to put up with this crap any longer. Flori had to talk. She had to stop this nonsense with the knives and pushing the furniture around as some kind of barricade against her enemies. The enemies were all in her head.

Rose didn't greet her. She sat down opposite. She looked closely at her. It was obvious she was vulnerable and distressed and that she needed urgent help but before she could speak, Flori had said, 'Can you give me a hand to push this stuff against the door? We need a barricade.'

'What for?' Rose said. She couldn't stop herself sounding cold.

'I told you already.'

'No, you haven't. You just said I'd see tonight. What am I supposed to see tonight?' She stared at Flori who didn't answer. 'I need to know, Flori, why you're sitting there with a knife and why you think we have to barricade ourselves in.' Silence. 'Well, are you going to say?'

'I'm going to bed.'

Rose stood up, 'No, you're not.' She walked rapidly over to the kitchen door to block off Flori's exit. 'What's bugging you? I've known you for two years. We're close friends and

I thought I knew you well. But it seems I don't. You're in some kind of strange place, a dream, a nightmare. Yes, a nightmare and I need to know.'

'What, what do you want to know?'

Flori got to her feet so suddenly, her chair fell clattering onto the tiled floor. For a moment there was silence. Neither said a word. They stood facing each other, each eyeballing the other. Rose noticed Flori's eyes. They were cold, hostile.

She gave no warning. She picked up the knife from the table and pointing it at Rose, she walked step by deliberate step towards her. When she was a foot away she stopped. She was breathing hard.

Any fear Rose might have had she pushed away. She was determined to stand up to her. 'Don't threaten me, Flori. I know you're frightened. You don't need to be.' Her voice had become low and controlling.

Another silence. Flori didn't appear to have heard. Her face gave nothing away. Only her eyes. Now empty, glassy, staring.

Rose spoke slowly. 'Put the knife down. Put the knife down. Tell me. Now. Who's Tids?' Her voice was calm. 'He's a baby, isn't he? Are those his clothes in your flat? The one's I've seen. You've dressed Owain in his clothes? Is that why you call him Tids? Where is Tids? Tell me, Flori. I'm waiting.'

They faced each other, watched each other, sized each other up, waiting for the next move, neither trusting the other. Rose noticed Flori look away. She seemed to be thinking. She walked across to the dresser and put the knife down. She began pacing round the tiny kitchen. Up and down. Up and down. Wringing her hands. She reminded Rose of a caged animal. She was trapped. Distraught. Tears coursed slowly down her cheeks.

Without looking at Rose, she said, 'You can never see him. He's dead. He died a long time ago. He's dead. My little brother. Tids is dead.'

It felt to Rose as if someone had punched her in her

stomach when she least expected it. Taking deep breaths, she tried to calm herself and taking hold of Flori's shoulders she stared directly into Flori's eyes.

'When? When did he die?' but then seeing her pain, she said, 'Flori, I'm sorry. I know this is difficult, but you must tell me. Your childhood, what memories do you have? You must tell me What's happened to him?'

Flori avoided her eyes, 'I've told you enough.' She turned away, was silent, but a moment later she moved so close to Rose that she had to take a step backwards away from her. She shouted, 'Enough. Don't you understand? Enough. Haven't I suffered enough with you? I can't bear the sight of you. You always want something. You remind me of your father with all your mithering. Leave me alone. Go away. Leave me in peace.'

She began sobbing and, turning away from Rose, ran to the corner of the room and stood with her back to her.

Rose had no idea how to respond. But an image of her father came to her. How he'd calm her mother with his quiet response when she became distraught. She'd do the same. In a slow, calm voice, she said, 'Who are you talking to, Flori, because the words you used don't apply to me. I'm Rose, your best friend.'

Flori continued sobbing, pressing her hands for support against the wall. Rose walked over to her, and standing beside her, speaking softly, she said, 'Flori, I don't want to frighten you any more than you are already, but I'm here for you.'

Flori didn't move or respond but kept her back to Rose.

'I can see how upset you are, and I'm wondering if it's because of losing Tids. I'm thinking how much you loved him and how sad you feel he's no longer here. Sometimes you imagine he's not dead. You want to speak with him and hold him. You loved him. He was your little brother and he didn't deserve to die. No tiny baby deserves to die.'

Flori was listening. She turned round, stared at her. Rose returned her gaze. 'How do you know? How do you know?'

'I was guessing, I didn't know for sure, but am I right?'

Flori nodded.

Rose said, 'Come, Flori, come and sit with me at the table.'

Flori picked up a cushion and, holding it close against her body, as if it gave her comfort and protection, moved across to the table and sat down opposite Rose. The storm had passed. They sat quietly, Flori hugging her cushion, gently rocking, her gaze lowered to avoid Rose's eyes. Rose waited to find the right words to say more. She was drawing on her own experience as a child when she was sent to a therapist. Mrs Ehrenburg always knew the right thing to say when she'd become upset. Now she had to find out about Flori's past, before she retreated again to sitting behind her arsenal of weapons, a place where she wasn't open to reason.

'Why was your brother called Tids? It's unusual. What did it mean?'

'Tids? It was my pet name for him. I called him that. I chose it. It was short for Tiddler,' Flori smiled, 'because that's what he was. a little tiddler.'

'You loved him.'

She nodded. She put the cushion down and looked down at her hands, spreading her fingers out as if to inspect them.

'How did he die?'

The question had touched a raw nerve in Flori. Rose watched as she closed up. She reminded her of a sea anemone. If she got close too quickly or said the wrong thing, she turned in on herself. She was withdrawing from her. Her mouth tightening, her eyes blank, she'd disappeared out of the room and into her head. It was as if Rose and the present were no longer real. She didn't answer and although Rose waited, she said nothing.

Rose asked again, 'How did he die?' Flori remained silent. 'You must tell me. How did he die, Flori?'

'No. I can't. I can't tell you. It's too dangerous. No. No one must know. I can't, I can't say, I mustn't. It would be a thought crime. Not allowed.' She was mumbling, looking down at the floor.

'But you're innocent of any crime, I know that. You loved him.'

'Yes. I did, but she didn't.'

'Who? Your mother?'

Flori's eyes bored into her. 'Don't say that. Don't ever, ever, ever say anything like that again.'

'What? About your mother?'

'My mother. She did it. A hate crime. I knew. It's too late. She got him. She's following me. She knows everything. She can hear us. She can see us.' She stood up, walked over to the window, slowly pulled across a corner of the curtain and looked out into the night, then turned and stared at Rose. Her eyes wild, almost crazed. Her voice low, sinister, threatening. 'She's here, outside. Aren't you frightened?'

'I'm not. No. I'm not frightened. It's all in the past. The memory tortures you, but Flori, it's in your head. It's past. Now you remember it as a hate crime. What is it? Tell me. Tell me.'

Flori didn't answer. She moved to the front door, stood blocking it, then said, 'I'm tired, Rose. Leave me alone.' She was twisting her fingers, her face contorted with anxiety.

Rose watched her, calculating when and whether she should push her further. She spoke quietly and intensely. 'I'm tired too, Flori. Okay, maybe we should leave it, but I want you to trust me like you used to. We were happy once and we used to have fun. Remember the party in Earls Court? That room with all the food and how we stuffed ourselves and danced around the table. Mutiny on the bounty, that's what you called it. I ate so much I thought I'd be sick.'

Rose laughed. But one look at Flori's face and she realised she'd made a terrible mistake. She'd inadvertently reminded her of the night she'd taken the baby. Flori wasn't laughing. Instead she was staring at her. She moved back close to Rose and stood facing her. Her eyes were filled with hatred.

Rose waited. Appalled. She'd assumed she could make Flori laugh, but instead she'd come across as if she didn't understand and was making light of everything Flori had told her and experienced. Rose felt sick in the pit of her stomach. Christ. How insensitive she'd been. She'd seriously misjudged Flori's mood. She tried to back pedal, retrieve the situation. She apologised. 'I'm sorry, Flori.'

'Sorry? Sorry for what? It's too late. He's dead, but Owain? He's not dead and I'm not going to let him die. He's not going to. He won't die. I've told you, no one's taking him from me. That includes you, and if you or anyone tries, we go together.'

Her voice like ice, she moved with speed across the kitchen, snatched the knife from the dresser and walked slowly towards Rose. She pointed the knife at her, jerked her head towards the outside door. 'Go. Go. I don't want you here. Get out. Now.'

Rose stood up. Transfixed with terror, she couldn't believe what she'd just heard and seen. Flori had changed so quickly. Her breathing almost stopped, and a nervous tic started in one of her eyelids. She was about to obey, when a protective rage surged through her.

'Don't. Don't talk to me like that. I'm not going. I'm staying here with you. You're frightening me. But I've had enough. I'm not going to let you frighten me anymore. Put the knife down, Flori. Do what I say.'

They stood face on, confronting each other. Rose shouted. 'Go on, you heard. Put the knife down. Now.'

Somehow she trusted Flori wouldn't harm her. She knew her too well. Rose stood close and without backing away, she said, 'Give it to me.' She put her hand out. 'Give me the knife.' Her voice was slow and emphatic.

Flori did nothing. Rose leant towards her and took the knife from her. 'You don't need that. Now tell me. Tell me, Flori. Tell me because I have to know. What did you just mean? You just made a threat. You said, we'll go together.

That's a threat, a threat to his life. He's done nothing. He's a tiny baby who's grown to love you. You feed him. You wash him. You care for him. He's dependent on you. You love him. You're a mother to him. How could you, Flori, how could you, how could you make a threat against his life? Even as a joke, it's horrible.'

'Joking? You think I'm joking? I wouldn't do that. You don't understand. You don't understand.'

'No. No, I don't understand. Tell me. For god's sake. Tell me. Who killed your baby brother, Tids?'

Flori sank down to her knees. She put her head in her hands. Sobbed uncontrollably.

'Don't cry. For fuck's sake, stop it. Get up. Just tell me, tell me, I want to help but if you don't talk, I can't. Do you hear me? I want to help you.'

There was a long silence.

Flori called out, 'My mother. It was my mother. She killed him.'

'Your mother! How? How?'

'She smothered him. She smothered him with a pillow. After she'd rowed with his father. She'd always hated him. She told me. She told me she never wanted him. Even when she was pregnant she tried to get rid of him. She said he made her ill. She said she hated the sight of him. She left him with me. I looked after him.'

She was crying uncontrollably.

'One night she went out. I'd lit a candle to show Tids. I forgot about it. I left it. There was a fire. I knew I had to call for the fire engines. They saw I was alone with a tiny baby. They put me in care. My aunt and uncle, they brought me here. To Jura. They said they'd help her, but they didn't because, while I was here, she killed him. She held a pillow over his face until he couldn't breathe. I shouldn't have left him. She was put into hospital and then she killed herself.'

Rose was silent. Unable to take in the horror of her story, she stared at Flori. Incapable of responding.

'I have bad dreams now, Rose. All the time. It's being here. Brings it all back. She told me never to tell anyone that she did it. She's coming now. Because I've broken the promise I made, that I'd never tell anyone. Nobody knew, but I did and I've told you now. She will come.'

'You were brought here? To Jura? Who brought you?'

'Them. My aunt and uncle. When I was in care.'

'They were foster parents?'

'Yes. They said it would be a holiday, while my mum was being looked after, but I've hated it here. I worry about Tids, because she can't look after him. She'll harm him. I know her.'

'Flori, Tids is dead.' Rose raised her voice. She took hold of Flori's shoulders and facing her, spoke emphatically, 'Your mother is dead. It happened a long time ago.' Rose looked her in the eye. 'Isn't she? Flori, she's dead, you don't need to be frightened. Not anymore.'

'I don't believe you. I'd rather kill him myself than let her have him. It would be kinder if I did.'

'Kill who?'

'Tids.'

Rose's breathing stopped. Who was she talking about? Tids or Owain?

'Where's Tids now?'

'Upstairs, asleep. As long as he's with me, I know he's safe, but she might come tonight.'

Rose thought fast, said, 'I'll stay with you tonight. If we're all together...' She didn't finish her sentence.

'In the spare bed? In my room?'

'Yes. I'll keep you safe.'

'I'd like that.'

Flori visibly relaxed, smiled, but inwardly Rose was terrified. What Flori had just said was chilling. She understood her now. Her unpredictability. She was moving in and out of a different time frame, confusing the past with the present, believing Owain was Tids. It was too much. Rose felt exhausted and yearned to sleep. She calculated that for the moment Owain would be safe. The crisis had passed, but she had no idea how long it would last.

She made a cup of tea for them, told Flori she needed a rest and dragged herself to her bedroom. She closed the door, lay on her bed, curled up like a child and cried. She cried for Flori and for herself. Flori's story had horrified her. She felt totally and utterly alone.

9

Rose was exhausted. She'd hardly slept. What Flori had told her, it was indescribably horrific and Flori's last comment, that she'd rather kill the baby than let her mother have him, filled her with fear. She could hear Flori downstairs. She lay for a moment listening. She was singing 'Rock-a-by Baby', as if everything was normal. Her voice was pure and clear and she sang in tune, but she was singing the same nursery rhyme over and over. There was something chilling in the words, 'Down will come baby, cradle and all'.

How could she protect Owain? Could she bundle him into the car when Flori's attention was elsewhere and drive off? But she'd have to get him off the island and he'd cry for Flori and she didn't know how to look after him. Even if she made it to the mainland it might be miles before she found a police station. Not only that she had no time to pack his food and nappies.

She realised the situation was desperate, and that her thinking was the result of extreme tiredness. The whole night had been fractured with Flori's restlessness. Three times she'd been woken by Flori and each time as she'd come into consciousness she could hear Flori padding round the croft. She was like a caged animal. She didn't seem to need sleep. No wonder she was thin and dishevelled. She'd lost interest in how she looked. Her hair was uncombed, the original style lost. She flung on the nearest clothes to hand. She looked what she was, mad.

The first time Flori disturbed her, she could see Flori standing over Owain. He was sleeping peacefully in his crib under the window and she was staring at him blankly, as if she didn't recognise him, didn't know who he was, or what he was doing there. Her blank expression had unnerved her. She'd watched and waited from her bed but decided not to go to her. Eventually Flori got back into bed, but it had taken Rose a long time to get back to sleep.

The second time she woke, she could hear Flori downstairs. She was moving the furniture around, probably, she thought, to barricade them in and her mother out. She'd felt that familiar flash of irritation. For god's sake, she'd thought, give me a break but she hadn't got up. She'd left her to it until the noise stopped and Flori had come back to her bed.

The third time she heard her, she couldn't bear listening. Flori had crept out of bed and she could hear her downstairs crying. Her cries were sad and plaintive, as if she was a child and alone in the world. Rose had gone to her. She'd have to have a heart of stone not to be affected by her sadness. She wanted to comfort her and as soon as Flori had seen her she'd clung to her. She couldn't say why she was crying, except she was desolate. It had taken all Rose's self-control not to cry herself.

It had been a long night, the longest night she'd ever known. The situation she found herself in was totally bewildering and she recognised she had a grave responsibility towards Flori. As for Owain, whenever she thought of him, her heart contracted. It was unbearable to think he might be harmed by Flori. She'd never, ever have thought that possible, but observing Flori's gradual breakdown, a persistent and horrific image had come into her mind. It was of Flori holding a pillow over Owain's head.

Rose was now racked with guilt. She went through how she'd helped Flori escape with Owain and she hated herself for it. If Flori harmed Owain and it came out that she, Rose, knew about her state of mind but had done nothing about it, she also would be responsible for his death. True, she'd had no way of knowing when it all started that Flori had a horrific childhood history and that this would make her vulnerable to a breakdown, but that wouldn't exonerate her in a court of law. Stealing a baby, for whatever reason, she now realised, had been a crazy thing to do, and she was complicit in the abduction.

The burden of responsibility was too much to bear. She had to get away, do something, get help from a professional, contact someone. She dragged herself out of bed, got dressed, took several deep breaths, and went downstairs.

Flori was sitting on the floor surrounded with toys, playing with Owain. Everything looked and sounded totally normal. She smiled brightly at Rose, asked if she'd like breakfast and offered to come and sit with her. The awfulness of the previous night had been forgotten, or so it seemed. Yet not making any reference to what had been said, pretending all was well, made her feel disorientated but she thought it better to hide how she felt. She said she would like a coffee.

She watched as Flori put Owain in his buggy, hang his bright red, blue and yellow duck mobile in front of him and then wheel him into the kitchen. She'd already washed up, shifted the furniture back, pulled the curtains back from the window, put the knives away. The kitchen looked as it used to look. That was, until she saw the meat knife partly hidden behind the bread bin.

Rose had never felt fear like this before in her life. It came in waves; the shortage of breath, the contraction of stomach muscles, the paranoia, the inability to think, to sort out what was real from the imagined. So Flori still felt under attack. This meant, Rose now knew, she also had the potential *to* attack. Yet she feared confronting her in her present state of mind, so she said nothing, knowing Flori's apparent good mood was a cover for something more sinister. Flori might be smiling, but she didn't trust her. She could tell by her eyes that she was concealing something.

'What about coming to Barnhill with me today?' Flori said.

The comment made her feel sick in the pit of her stomach. 'I have to get back, Flori, to work for my finals. I have to write up my research, as you know, and I want to do well. But, what about you and Owain coming back with me? We could travel together to London.'

Rose's tone sounded reasonable and friendly. It betrayed nothing of her anxiety.

A shadow passed across Flori's face. 'Me? Back with you? What for? Are you mad? I'd be caught. I like it here. I'm staying.' Her voice was sharp. She smiled brightly. It was another of her brittle smiles. 'And Owain likes it too, we want to stay.'

'That's not what you said last night.'

'Really? Well, you got it wrong. I want to bring Owain up here. Didn't I say that? It's where we belong and also my mother's here. I have things to sort out.'

Rose looked at her in disbelief. She wasn't sure whether Flori really thought that her mother was on the island, but she felt so exhausted she decided not to contradict her.

'Fine. If that's what you want. I have the ferry times, and there's one leaving in the late afternoon. Will you drive me there?'

'But what about Barnhill?'

'Maybe you can go later. After you've dropped me off, if you will.'

It was a statement rather than a question. She hoped Flori hadn't noticed the relief in her voice. She didn't know for sure why Flori wanted to visit Barnhill but she could guess. To track down her mother. She still believed she was alive and that she could rescue her mother from the thought police. It was grim. She feared she'd go mad herself if she didn't get away soon. It crossed her mind to wonder whether madness was catching, but then she realised, thinking in this way was crazy. Madness wasn't like measles or flu. But of one thing she was sure, that while she remained with Flori it was impossible to think clearly.

She had hoped Flori would come back with her, and that somehow she'd get her to see a psychiatrist, but she wasn't surprised that Flori refused. It was a forlorn hope. She looked up. Flori was staring at her intensely as if she was trying to read her mind. It made her feel uncomfortable. She felt as if her thoughts were transparent and accessible. She looked away from her penetrating eyes and made an attempt to normalise the conversation.

'So is that okay, Flori? That you drive me there?'

'Of course, Rose. Yes. I'll go later to Barnhill, after I've dropped you off.'

Flori was artificially polite, but Rose didn't care anymore. She just wanted to leave and sort her head out. She went upstairs, packed her things, told Flori that she had a long journey ahead and would go for a walk first. She wanted to get away from her so she headed up the track into the hills. She returned hours later.

Flori watched Rose as she walked away from the car towards the ferry. As soon as she saw she was on the ferry she drove off. She wanted to get away. Rose had changed. She was unpredictable. It was how she looked and how she spoke to her. She was guarded, she was hiding something and she couldn't trust her. She didn't like thinking about her in this way, but she had to protect herself from Rose's lying.

She knew Rose thought she was mad and she wanted to get away from her as soon as she could. She was certain of that. She regretted now that she'd told her about her mother and Tids. She'd vowed to herself that she'd never tell anyone about what she knew, but she'd broken that promise and if the police got to know, her mother would be charged, even after all these years. There's no time limit for murder, that's what she'd heard.

When Rose said to her that she was imagining things

138

and it was in all in the past, that undermined her. She was no longer sure what was true and what was false, but she comforted herself with the thought she still had Owain. He was her baby and when he smiled and looked at her with those big, innocent eyes and clung to her like a little koala bear, he reminded her of Tids. But one thing she did know, whatever had happened or whatever had been said, nobody could bring Tids back. He was gone forever

She turned round quickly to look at Owain. He was in his car seat and half asleep. His head had fallen to one side onto his shoulder and a little line of dribble from his mouth curved down his chin. His eyes kept closing. He didn't want to sleep, but he couldn't keep awake. She smiled and thought how lucky she was to have him.

Now Rose had gone, she planned to go back to Barnhill, hopefully for one last time. She wanted to see if her mother was there. She didn't understand why she was so drawn to the place. Perhaps her mother had cast a spell on her when she'd seen her on the path. She had shouted out something but she hadn't heard it. If she saw her again and spoke to her, maybe she'd come back and it would be like it used to be when there was the three of them; Mum, her and Tids. She'd drive her back to Lagg and they'd be together again and she'd look after them and they'd be safe for ever.

First though, she'd call in at the croft. Owain needed feeding. She pulled off the road, drove down the track, stopped by the croft and gently removed him from the car seat to take him into the kitchen. He was sleepy. He seemed to have lost his appetite. He refused to eat. He's not hungry, she thought but there was no rush so she took her time. She went upstairs to tidy up and strip Rose's bed, then decided to put Owain's nightclothes on there and then. That way, he'd be ready for bed when they returned. She wrapped him with his fat giraffe in his fleece blanket and put him back in his car seat.

He loved car journeys, but darkness was falling and there was little for him to see through the windows. He fell asleep straightaway. There were no street lights but by then she knew the way so well she could have driven it blindfolded. They passed only one vehicle, a Land Rover travelling in the opposite direction. The driver flashed his lights at her in greeting but she didn't flash back. She didn't know who he was, and he could be a thought policeman pretending to shoot deer or rabbits. She knew their game now, what they got up to; they didn't fool her.

There was a half moon that night and Barnhill stood isolated and in almost total darkness when she arrived. She got out from the car and stood listening. She wasn't frightened. She had to go through with it. She knew what she might have to face. She could hear the call of a lone owl and the sound of the wind blowing. It was eerie, the sky was clear and black and looking up she could see the milky way and the pinpoints of a million stars. The sea was close but she couldn't hear it unless there was a storm, and even then it was difficult from where she stood to hear the waves crashing against the cliffs.

She paused, wondering whether to leave Tids in the car. She could lock the door, he was asleep and she'd be quicker without him, but if he woke and saw she wasn't there, he'd be frightened and cry for her. She picked him out from the car seat, and decided to carry him in her arms. Her plan was to walk round the house and look in all the windows. She had to check if her mother was inside and if she was, she'd try and free her.

She hadn't got far before Tids' weight slowed her down. She tried readjusting how she was carrying him but it was just the same. He was getting too heavy for her. She began imagining the thought police werc hiding in the bushes. She tried to reassure herself that it was all in her mind. It worked until she looked through one of the windows. The window was at the end of the building and the glass was covered with grime and sea salt which she rubbed away. She peered in. She could see something black lying on the floor.

As soon as she saw it, she began to lose control and panic. It was here now, what she'd seen in her nightmare. The black sack, the thing that had moved across the floor towards her. Somehow it had got here and it was about to suffocate her. She felt she couldn't breathe and she was going to pass out. She had to run. Get back to the car. She couldn't carry Tids a moment longer.

A scream. She heard a scream. Piercing, cutting through the fabric of the night like a knife. Memories of her mother flooded back. She used to scream when she had nightmares. She'd wake her. Want to get into her bed with her. She'd frighten her. Her mother muttering, tossing and turning next to her. Stopping her sleeping. Was it her screaming?

A fox ran in front of her. Holding a rabbit's writhing, bloody body in its mouth, it disappeared into rough grass. Foxes were evil, they didn't kill for food but for cruelty. The fox was an omen of the devil, her mother had said that. And it was here, close by her. It was horrible. She was sick with fear. She wanted to hide. She pushed hard against one of the outbuilding's doors, but inside what she saw was far worse – hanging from the rafters naked dead bodies – skinned alive, tortured and left to die.

She screamed. She couldn't stop herself. It was a loud piercing scream that woke Tids. He'd been dozing on her shoulder but she'd frightened him so much, he wrapped his arms round her throat. He was strangling her, his grip as powerful as a grown man's. She screamed again, pulling his arms from round her neck. He'd terrified her, but she was brought to her senses. She glanced up again. They weren't bodies, but dead deer. With their fur stripped off they looked like naked bodies.

She was seeing things. She tried calming herself, breathing slowly and deeply. She began talking to Owain, comforting him, reassuring him they'd be alright, that she'd be strong and look after him. She ran. She had to get back to the car quickly. She was holding him tightly, she feared she'd drop him as she ran. When she reached the car, she bundled him back in his car seat. She felt she was going crazy. Tears were falling down her face. She was in a total panic, her heart racing, out of breath, panting.

She turned the key in the ignition, accelerated backwards at speed towards the road. She hated the place. She'd never go back, even if her mother was there. But as she drove off, doubt crept into her mind. Perhaps Rose was right, her fears her mother was alive were in her imagination. How could she know? Maybe she was, maybe she wasn't. Wherever, whatever, she didn't care anymore. Over the years she'd suffered enough for her. A monumental anger came over her but it was an anger that felt good. She'd had enough. Her mother could go to hell.

But she did care about Tids. She was sorry she'd frightened him.

As she drove away, she became aware that the further from Barnhill she got, the less frightened she felt. An overwhelming sense of calmness and peacefulness seemed to descend from the sky and envelop her. She began thinking, questioning herself, wondering why she'd gone to Barnhill. Why, when the place and the atmosphere terrified her and gave her nightmares, had she returned to it? The place persecuted her but she would bear it no longer. It was horrible, sickening, disgusting, full of death, pain and nightmares. It had driven her almost insane.

Something was changing within her. A conflict, a trouble, an uncertainty, was becoming resolved. An end was in sight. The change felt apocalyptic. It was big, unknown, and she felt calm even though she knew in reality nothing had changed. She felt capable of anything and would die to achieve it even though she had no idea what it was.

She arrived back at Lagg. She got out of the car. The place looked the same as when she'd left it, a tiny hamlet in darkness and quiet as a Sunday in the City. She stood, aware of a sadness. Suddenly she yearned for the real and what she had known, for the streetlights of London and the big stores round Oxford Street, and the tiny restaurants, and the coffee shops of Soho, and its people. She wanted its people so much. She wanted Londoners with their quick irreverent wit, the kind of people who ran the tubes and the buses, the 'jack the lad' builders who stood with their arms crossed while they made some outrageous observation, and the fast-talking market traders, and the clever irony of the black cab drivers. The ordinary people of London, the ones who'd used to make her laugh. Once she had laughed, but that was a long time ago and now she felt such a profound loneliness and weariness reaching in her soul, she had to sleep.

She gathered Tids lovingly into her arms and, keeping him by her bed, lay down. She was relieved he fell asleep quickly. He seemed to have recovered quickly from the shock of her screaming. As she fell asleep she wondered where Rose was, and whether she was near home, and why she hadn't been in touch. That was what she used to do after they parted, and she missed her. But her silence puzzled her and the distrust she'd felt as she'd watched her leave on the ferry was growing.

10

The skies were leaden and along Pall Mall the roofs of the official buildings were shrouded in mist. A heavy downpour sent rivulets of filthy water gushing along the gutters down into the drains and flowing from there into the sewers.

Rose stepped out of the black cab and looked up at the impressive façade of her father's club. She was early. She was nervous. She'd never been here before, but she knew her father was a frequent visitor whenever he returned to the UK. She gripped the handle of the umbrella hard, then loosening her grip turned to pay the cabbie. He winked at her, 'Alright love?' No, she thought, actually not, but she said nothing, smiled wanly and made her way up the stone steps into the imposing entrance. Inside a heavy smell of brass and furniture polish assailed her nostrils. Everything had been polished until it gleamed.

A middle-aged man in a neat dark grey uniform decorated with red piping came from behind a large mahogany table to meet her. Rose noticed his excessively shiny black shoes. She could almost see her face in them. Probably ex-army, she thought, that's the kind of thing they were trained to do, polish shoes. His grey hair was cut close to his scalp. It wasn't flattering. He smiled but it was a smile that revealed nothing. It was an official smile and it was servile. He didn't know her, but neither did he have the slightest interest in her. Any warmth he might have would be reserved for the familiar, his own sort, and any conversation he was capable of would be perfunctory, bland and opaque. His role was to welcome those who were members of the club and restrict those who weren't, and control them in such a way the quiet, warm, predictable ambience of the club would be maintained. What did he do at night when he wasn't working, did he come alive? Did he have a personality? It was hard to imagine.

'Can I help you?'

'I've come to meet my father.'

'And his name?' He was coldly polite, looking down his nose at her.

'Nicholas. Nicholas Anselm. He said to wait for him in the library.'

'Ah. Mr Anselm. Yes. And your name?'

'Rose, Rose Anselm, I'm his daughter.'

'The library is straight ahead. Turn right when you reach the swing doors.'

She walked towards where he pointed, pushed open the doors, walked along a short corridor and sat down. She was relieved to see she had the place to herself. She picked up a copy of *The Times* but after an attempt to read it she put it down. She couldn't settle. She was too agitated, a jumble of thoughts stopping her concentrating. Her mind was still with Flori and Owain and what Flori had told her about her childhood. She knew it was the last visit she'd ever make to Jura. She'd reached the point where there was no going back. She walked across to a window and stood looking out, preoccupied with what she'd gone through.

The drive to Feolin had been awkward, but the timing right and she'd been relieved to see the ferry was docking as they'd driven up. It meant she didn't have to wait with Flori, make awkward conversation and could leave Jura immediately. They'd given each other a perfunctory kiss on the cheek, and she'd noticed as she'd leant forward to give Owain a hug that he'd seemed oblivious to all that was going on. He'd looked puzzled but he hadn't cried. He so rarely cried, it was strange. He didn't seem normal and she'd thought fleetingly he'd grown up quickly, before his time. He looked older than he actually was but she wasn't sure whether this was good or bad. She had so little experience of babies but still she felt for him and was concerned both for his physical safety and his emotional well being. But there was also Flori to think about. She cared for her, too.

Just as she'd stepped onto the ferry, she'd said, 'Flori, I'll ring you when I get back. Take care of yourself and Owain, won't you?'

But Flori hadn't answered and despite her promise, she hadn't rung her. She looked at her coldly and she'd known then with regret and sadness, a gulf had developed between them and their friendship had changed. It was now based on a mutual suspicion and mistrust. She'd wondered what the future held for them and as she had stood on the tiny ferry and looked back to the road, she saw Flori had already left. She hadn't even waited to wave her off. Her eyes had filled with tears. Something was about to change, but what that was, she didn't know. She'd felt low and very alone as she watched the mountains of Jura fade into the mist.

She'd stood looking over the guard rail of the ferry as it ploughed across to Islay. She'd watched the churning grey water disappear under the boat's hull and felt an almost unbearable pressure. She knew now for sure something was seriously wrong with Flori. She recognised that she was imagining things, perhaps distorting memories and incidents from her childhood past that had disturbed her, but whatever the truth was, she could no longer walk away as she had before and hope things would get better. What Flori had told her had deeply shocked her and that she'd lived with such a terrible burden and hadn't told anyone for all those years, was unimaginable to her.

She didn't know what she should do and had thought, albeit with some bitterness, it was time for her to grow up.

What she'd heard from Flori would mark her. It was almost like the mark of the stigmata, one that wasn't physical, but emotional, but like an actual stigmata it would last forever.

Flori had had no control over her childhood and what had happened to her, but this terrible event had now impacted upon her. It had changed their friendship and it would further change her life, but in ways she couldn't yet envisage. As she'd watched the island of Jura fade in to distance, the lines from one of Dylan Thomas' poems had come to her. 'Now as I was young and easy under the apple boughs/About the lilting house and happy as the grass was green.' She'd always loved that poem with it's beautiful imagery of the past, but those times had gone and as she'd thought that her tears had flowed hot against the coolness of her skin.

It was then she'd decided she had to talk to someone, share with them her burden, but whom? As she'd thought of each of her friends she'd rejected them, one by one. Ben? Still a boy. Charlotte? Anna? Two of her closest friends, fellow students at Oxford, but they were too young, too immature, their lives gilded and privileged, compared with Flori's. Up for a laugh, but not much more. Competitive and confident, their thoughts were on bright futures. She'd been like that once, but no longer. What did they know about life? Very little. They'd been protected and cocooned in their safe, complacent, predictable, affluent lives. They wouldn't know how to help, how to respond, and neither would they have the right words. She felt a flash of anger course through her like a line of searing lava, even though she knew her judgements were harsh.

But what of her friendship with Flori? She was contemplating the betrayal of her closest friend and what she should say and must say could land them both, she now realised, in prison because she also had been part of Flori's madness. She'd been complicit but it was time to bring it to a halt, for the sake of both Owain and Flori. What she must face now was the hardest decision of her life.

It had been a short ferry crossing over to Islay and as soon as she'd arrived she'd walked off and made her way to the waiting taxis at the ferry terminal. She'd told one of the drivers it was essential that she got to London that day. She'd spoken as if she was drugged, barely able to think straight, she'd felt so disconnected from reality.

He picked up her urgency. 'I'll take you to the airport. It's only a short drive and there's a plane leaving the island in two hours. It's going to Glasgow and once you get there, you can fly on to London.'

She'd got into the back seat of his car and lit up another cigarette, inhaling the nicotine deeply into her lungs. Neither spoke but when she caught the driver's eye in the rear mirror she saw he was observing her closely and that he was irritable. 'Dinna you notice, there's a "no smoking" sign?'

'No. Sorry,' she said, and she'd opened the window and thrown her cigarette out. 'My mind, it's elsewhere.'

She'd bought her ticket for the plane, another packet of cigarettes and sat and waited in the small terminal. She was chain smoking. She'd finish one cigarette, stub it out, start another. She made no attempt to restrain herself. Her smoking calmed her. She wasn't sure what she was going to do, or who she needed to speak to, but the longer she sat there, the more doubtful she felt. Looking around the tiny airport where everything was normal and orderly, the contrast had made her think that perhaps she was over-dramatising events. How could she be sure she'd got it right, that Flori was capable of harming Owain in a moment of madness? But even to think this was a terrible burden and one she couldn't live with on her own. She felt bad about leaving him with her, but she had no choice. She had to get away to get help.

She'd thought about contacting Matt, but she didn't know how. She didn't have his number. It was true he sounded decent and he cared about Flori, even if he was a bit messed up. How else could it be explained, that, as soon as he and Flori split up, he'd got someone pregnant, a Japanese girl at that. As if relationships weren't difficult enough, without adding cultural issues to them, but he wasn't mad, that much was clear from what Flori had told her. If she had asked her, Flori would never have given her his number. She'd want to know why she wanted to speak to him and without doubt her paranoia would increase and she might then go on the run, taking Owain with her.

It had been at that point she'd decided to contact her father. It had been a desperate decision and she'd felt reluctant but she'd been driven by how frightened she was. She hadn't spoken to him or seen him for three years, not since they'd had that row. She'd just been going up to Oxford and he'd wanted to speak with her. He'd been critical of what he called her careless life style and her friends. He'd told her she was immature, spoilt and it developed into a major argument. What he'd said deeply wounded her. She'd shouted at him, told him he was old, a snob and she never wanted to see him again and she didn't want his money. She'd said she had her own money and she'd pay her fees from the money her grandmother had left her.

To her astonishment he'd ignored her anger and continued paying her grant into her bank account on a monthly basis and he'd sent her birthday cards, even though she'd never replied or thanked him. Thinking about it now, she felt bad about her lack of response. She hadn't known how to make amends and eventually he must have accepted the estrangement because he hadn't been in touch for so long. Maybe, she'd thought, in some strange way, this could be an opportunity for a reconciliation. She'd regretted how angry she'd been but she would get in touch. She'd no idea what she'd say, but he might help. He had experience of the world. He was no monk, for sure, but that made him more human.

Now standing in his club, waiting for him, she thought grimly about her mother's letter, the one she'd found this summer. She wasn't sure whether she'd bring it up. Perhaps she wouldn't. It was too painful and there was already the

149

nightmare she had to tell him about. But she could remember the letter by heart, every single word. She could also remember one of her father's favourite sayings. He'd said to her once, 'First you live, then you philosophise.' Well, he should know. When she'd first heard it she'd liked it, and later, when she made mistakes in her life, and they usually concerned men, the phrase would come back to her.

She'd concluded as fathers go, he was kind, a stickler for duty, but with his work, he needed to be. She remembered with a smile the smell of his favourite jacket. No wonder they were called 'smoking jackets', his jackets always smelt of nicotine. But when he went to one of his functions, he'd discard it for an expensive suit, one that smelt of an expensive male fragrance. To attract the women, she now thought. It was Dior's Eau Savage, or something equally sophisticated and subtle, but whatever it was, it had been too expensive for her to buy as a young teenager. Her mother had offered to buy it on her behalf, but she'd refused. She'd wanted to buy it with her own money, or not at all. She'd liked his choice of fragrance and used to tease him about it , call him a 'ladies man', and he certainly was a 'ladies man', but then maybe the same could be said of her, only in reverse. She liked men. Perhaps she was similar to him. She smiled to herself. She'd missed him and she wanted to see him.

Her thoughts returned again to Jura, to when she'd waited for the plane to take her to Glasgow. She'd sat hunched, mindlessly watching people pass to and fro in front of her. She'd smoked cigarette after cigarette. It was as if she wanted to smoke herself to death and for what? To avoid the decision she must take? She'd known she had to go through with it and her father could help, put her on the right track. She could think things through with him and the worst that could happen was he wouldn't understand, or he'd be rude and reject her, but she knew him well enough to know that was unlikely. She'd lose nothing by contacting him just to see what he'd say.

She'd picked up her mobile and rang the Foreign Office. She'd asked to be put through to Mrs Booth, Nicholas Anselm's secretary. She'd picked up straightway. It seemed he still had the same secretary.

She'd said, 'Hello, I'm Rose Anselm. Is it possible to speak to my father?' She could tell Mrs Booth recognised her, that she was surprised to hear her, but true to diplomatic form, she'd made no comment other than to say he was in a meeting. She said as soon as he came out, she'd tell him. He'd be about half an hour, she'd said. He rung in fifteen minutes, just before she was due to board the plane for Glasgow.

'It's Rose,' she'd said, 'your daughter.'

'Yes,' he'd said, 'I know who you are,' but she could tell by the tone of his voice he was pleased to hear her. She was direct and to the point. There was no time for polite preliminaries.

'Daddy, I have a problem, a big problem.' She'd taken a deep breath. 'I'm sorry to spring this on you, especially after all this time. But it's urgent. I'd like to talk things over with you. Would you be able to meet tomorrow? I know it's really short notice, but I'd really appreciate it, if it's possible.'

She'd felt and sounded like a child. There was a long pause. He'd asked her to wait, and she could hear him talking to Mrs Booth. Rose heard her say, 'Well, I'll reschedule it, Nicholas. Shouldn't be too much of a problem.'

He came back to the phone. 'I can do 2.15 pm tomorrow for a late lunch. It would be at my club, if that's alright?'

'The one in the Mall?'

'Yes, the one in the Mall. My schedule is tight over the next twenty-four hours, but if it's important you can ring tonight.'

'No. I need to speak with you. Face to face. I want to see you. I'll wait until tomorrow. Thank you. Thank you so much.'

'Good. If you get there first, go to the library and wait for me there. I'll come and look for you. I may be a little late, you know how meetings can be unpredictable. Oh, and Rose.'

'Yes.'

'I'm pleased you've contacted me. I'm looking forward to seeing you.'

'Yes,' she'd said, but because she couldn't think of any more to say, she'd said, 'Well, okay then, see you soon.'

She'd felt embarrassed. She'd switched off her mobile and stubbed out her cigarette. It had been so long since they'd met and she wanted to give him a present. She thought she'd just about have time to buy a bottle of Isle of Jura Whisky from the airport shop. She'd waited impatiently while it was wrapped before racing for the plane. They were closing the gates as she arrived but they let her through. It was about to take off. She'd fastened her seat belt and looked out of the window as the plane took off. It had been a clear day, but evening was approaching, the light falling and as the plane banked over on its flight towards the mainland, she could still make out the three Paps of Jura. She'd wondered what Flori was doing, but guessed; for sure she'd be driving obsessively towards Barnhill with Owain.

She looked at her watch. He was late. Waiting for her father after not having seen him for three years made her nervous. She was apprehensive, wondering what his reaction might be to what she was about to tell him. He, on the other hand, would innocently expect some sort of reconciliation. The whole situation was too ghastly for words. She hoped he wouldn't be too long; waiting was making her edgy and she couldn't even smoke to calm herself.

She walked back towards the table with the newspapers. They were unread, arranged neatly in lines. Maybe it was too early for members of the club to be here. She again picked up *The Times* but still she couldn't concentrate. She was reading but with no idea what she'd read. Her mind returned again to Flori and the baby. How would her father react when she told him about taking the baby? One thing she knew. She'd been drawn into a madness, and for that she couldn't blame Flori. She had to take responsibility for herself.

How it would end she had no idea. She looked at her watch, half an hour had passed, and he still wasn't there. And all the time Owain was at risk. Perhaps she should go to the police now, not wait any longer. She was in two minds, wondering what to do, whether to stay or whether to leave. The meeting would be difficult. She felt like leaving. She didn't know if she could cope with what might be said. Maybe she'd ring Mrs Booth, find out where he was and how much longer he'd be. She wandered over to the window. It had started raining again. She began biting her nails, something she hadn't done since a child.

She heard him before she saw him. Her father's voice. It was loud. It was posh. He'd always slightly exaggerated the 'o' in her name making his accent sound even more upper class than it already was. 'Rose.'

She turned round. Her father swinging through the library door, making his way towards her. He'd always looked confident and he'd always had presence. He was opening his arms in greeting to hug her and for a split second Rose was cringingly embarrassed. His gesture reminded her of when he and her mother used to visit her at school. Her father had always been effusive compared with her mother's coolness but she'd found it difficult to respond naturally to them. Neither way had suited her, both of them had always seemed like strangers. She felt herself blush, but she allowed her father to hug her, aware how stiff and formal she felt.

'Hello,' she said. She paused, and in a small voice said hesitantly, 'It's good to see you.' It wasn't really true. Not in these circumstances.

'Is it, Rose?' He must have picked up she was ill at ease. He'd always been a good judge of character. 'You know I've missed you. It's been three years. What have you been up to?'

He pronounced each sentence and each word precisely, clipping the ends, as if talking to an idiot or a foreigner with a poor grasp of English. It had been a long time and she'd forgotten how posh he was. She mixed with a different crowd now, but it was his way, and he'd always done it his way, just like the Frank Sinatra song he liked so much. She glanced quickly at him. Had he really meant what he'd just said? He was looking straight at her, his eyes warm and direct. She smiled. Despite herself, she couldn't fail to respond to his openness and his total disregard for her wariness. He did have charm and he knew how to use it. She didn't answer.

'I have a present for you. Here.' She handed him the bag.

He looked taken aback, but took it from her. 'Shall I open it?'

'Yes, do. I hope you like it.'

He sat down on one of the library chairs and carefully took the box from the bag. He read aloud, 'Isle of Jura Single Malt Whisky, matured ten years,' looked across at her and then back to her present. 'How thoughtful. A wonderful choice. Do you know I've never tried this whisky, but I've always wanted to. Jura. Isn't that off the west coast of Scotland and isn't it a Hebridean island.?'

'I believe there's some controversy about that, whether it's Hebridean or not. But it's an island and off the west coast, as you say. I thought you might like it.'

'Thank you so much. Your gift means a lot...more than you'll ever know.'

'Well, good. You said, you said, you missed me. Did you mean it?'

He didn't answer, not directly but said, 'Rose, Rose, Rose. Let me get you a drink, or would you prefer lunch now?'

He was friendly, exuding attentiveness. No wonder women found him attractive.

'Lunch, please. I haven't got long.'

She sounded rude but she couldn't help herself. She was nervous and was always sharp when nervous, she became like her mother.

'Come with me,' he said.

He placed his arm round her shoulder and steered her towards the door. She felt herself stiffen at his touch. He removed his arm and they made their way to the dining room. Her father was taller than herself, and he seemed to have developed a slight stoop since they'd last met. He wore a dark, expensive-looking suit and a colourful tie with an abstract design. Probably a Miro design from Liberty's, she thought; that was the type of thing they sold and the type of thing he would buy.

He glanced down at her. 'Well, do I pass muster?' It was almost as if he'd known what she'd been thinking.

Rose laughed. She felt playful, for that brief moment forgetting why she was there and the purpose for meeting him. 'Yes, you do. You cut the mustard, but are we going to have lunch swapping ridiculous phrases?'

He didn't answer, but smiled again at her. He'd always had a good sense of humour. She felt herself slowly responding to him. He was genuine and warm, and however ill at ease she felt, she could see that he didn't feel the same way, but then, he would have no idea what she was going to tell him. She felt her stomach tighten in a knot at what lay ahead.

The head waiter led them to their table. It was laid for two in a quiet area at the side of the large dining room and next to one of the large windows overlooking the street outside. They sat down. Her father gestured to a waiter and asked for the wine list. Rose picked up the menu, glanced quickly at what was on offer and immediately put it to one side. She really didn't care what she ate, she'd chosen the first thing she'd noticed.

'I'll have the fish special,' she said.

She looked around her curiously. The place exuded history, class, privilege, status. She noticed the hushed restrained conversation of the other diners. An image of the croft on Jura came to her. The island was a world away and in contrast to here, Flori's croft would fit into this dining room. What would Flori and Owain be doing now? Probably, she thought bitterly, driving to Barnhill. She dragged her attention back to her surroundings.

It was oak panelled with extraordinary high ceilings, the walls hung with huge oil portraits of the club's eminent and famous members, the politicians, the judges, the captains of industry. They'd all made their mark in one way or another but now they were dead and mostly forgotten. The side windows ran almost from floor to ceiling, and the massive navy-and-gold tapestry curtains hanging from brass poles, were half pulled back, giving a mysteriously warm half-light to the room. Placed around the plush ruby-red carpeted dining room were variously sized dining tables covered with freshly laundered white damask cloths and then these were overlaid with smaller diagonally placed red cloths. The cutlery shone, the white napkins were carefully folded and the wine glasses on each table sparkled under the light of the chandeliers. Rose picked up a glass and held it against the light.

'I wonder if they're cut glass,' she said. She was thinking out loud.

'What?' Her father looked up from the wine list, peering at her over his half-glasses.

'I was wondering if the wine glasses were cut glass.' She slightly raised her voice thinking he must have become a little deaf.

He glanced at them, said, 'I expect so, but don't test them.' He smiled. 'What about this wine if you're having fish?' He pointed to a wine. 'It's a Sauvignon Blanc from Cloudy Bay in New Zealand. I've had it before. It's excellent.'

Rose looked down the list of wines. As with the food, she couldn't have cared less what she drank, as long as it was alcoholic. It was irrelevant compared with the problems she faced. 'Whatever' she thought, her mind distracted.

'It's expensive. Nice name though. Have it, if that's what you want.'

For her, 'Cloudy Bay' put in mind the beach at Lagg and Flori and Owain, but then everything and everywhere was a reminder of them. It had taken root in her mind. As a distraction she returned to observing her father's club and smiled inwardly. Maybe she could research 'the anthropology of state savants at play' for her dissertation, but she didn't tell him that. It would sound rude. She was ill at ease with the club's formality. It made her feel jumpy, rebellious, delinquent. She looked at her father, noticed he was observing her closely.

'I recommend it and I think I'll join you with the fish. Looks good.' He paused and then said, 'Look, I want to make things up with you, Rose. It's been a long time and it's not every day I take you out. I'd like to treat you. That is, if you'll allow me?' He smiled again and looking directly at her he said, 'So what have you been up to?'

She didn't answer. She wasn't ready to speak and was saved with the appearance of the sommelier. Her father ordered the wine and Rose was silent while he tasted it.

'Fine,' he said, nodding to the waiter. 'Please, go ahead.'

The waiter poured a tiny amount into her glass and her father watched her as she took her first sip. 'Will that do?'

She nodded and smiled. 'So,' he said and paused, as if she was about to speak. She noticed that he hadn't asked directly why she needed help and what lay behind the dramatic phone call she'd made yesterday. Very diplomatic, she thought. But now she was here and sitting in front of him, she wasn't sure how to begin. She felt awkward in his presence so she played for time. She told him about her anthropology course, how much she enjoyed it, how she planned to do her Masters, her plans for a doctorate. Her academic studies were a safe topic and she had his attention. She could tell he was listening with interest, genuine interest, by the occasional question he asked.

'What about yourself?' she said. 'What have you been up to and where have you been posted since I last saw you?'

He talked readily and easily about his travels to Eastern Europe, how he was called on to advise the various trade delegations visiting Russia and the newly emergent Balkan states. But when he mentioned Russia, Rose for a moment forgot about Flori and Owain. Unwittingly his talk of Russia reminded her of the existence of her half-sister, Natalya and she became distracted. He'd made no direct mention of Natalya, but then he wouldn't, he wouldn't know she knew about her existence.

Rose stared at him, as a series of question ran through her head; she was wondering whether he ever thought about Natalya and whether she was important to him? He paid maintenance to her mother but did that represent the sum total of his interest and responsibility for her? Was it a kind of pay off, to ensure the silence of all three; her mother, Natalya and her mother and his ex-lover? Did he feel about her, Rose, as he did Natalya? That was, out of sight, out of mind? Or was that only in her imagination? She didn't know.

She felt sorry for Natalya. They were connected through a father who, she thought, saw his responsibility only in financial terms. Although she recognised her judgement was harsh, she was still resentful of his many absences throughout her childhood, and how he'd disappointed her, and how despite his claim it was work commitments, she'd never really believed him. With good reason, as it turned out.

Yet she wanted to understand him, and paradoxically, she wanted to like him and be closer to him. She watched as he talked, studying his face carefully. She didn't know what made him tick. She hardly knew him, not as a father. She noticed the warmth in his smile, the bags under his eyes, and the laughter lines that ran from his nose to the corner of his mouth. But as he talked, she sensed the loneliness. It was in his eyes. All that travelling, the different countries, the different cultures, different customs, different languages, listening, adapting, negotiating, always having to be polite, patient, urbane, understanding.

Could she understand, ever forgive his unfaithfulness? She looked at him, and for the first time ever, she felt some love for him. But she had to look away. A shared glance now would be too intimate, too sudden. She wanted to avoid his eyes. He might see himself as she saw him, through her eyes and she didn't want that. She felt she didn't want him to know her and how she saw him.

The wine waiter was pouring out her third glass of wine and her father's fourth when she spoke. She surprised herself. She'd taken a sip of her wine and she'd put the glass down. She hadn't planned it. It wasn't the way she'd envisaged it would happen, but she felt compelled and spoke without thinking. She looked directly at him.

'I know about Natalya.'

His fork was halfway to his mouth. It stayed there for a split second longer than expected after she'd spoken. She could see him staring at her, but his face was expressionless. He looked away, put his fork down on the plate. It still had fish on it. He leant over the wine in the ice bucket, pulled the bottle out. It was empty.

'Same again? Or something different?' he said, as if he hadn't heard what she'd said, or what she'd said was normal, and the reference to her half-sister hadn't broken a family taboo. He was avoiding the intensity of her gaze and playing for time. She knew she'd shocked him, but she wanted a reaction.

'Your choice,' she replied, playing his game for a while longer.

He called the wine waiter over, ordered another bottle, returned to the abandoned fork with the fish and placed it in his mouth. He sat, continued eating, chewing slowly and thoughtfully. Evidently, he was finding it difficult to meet her eyes. He was keeping his head down.

After two or three minutes, Rose said, 'Aren't you going to say anything?' Her tone was neutrally patient.

'I'm thinking, Rose. Give me time. I need to collect my thoughts.'

He sighed, looked across the room, leant sideways on the table, resting his head on one of his cupped hands. He was, she knew, acutely embarrassed, but she was indifferent to how he might feel, she had to know more. When he spoke,

159

it was difficult to know from his tone what his thoughts were.
'Is this why you wanted to meet?'

'No. No, it isn't. There's something else. But it was when
you were talking about Russia, you reminded me. Of Natalya.'

Her voice trailed away. Her mobile was ringing;
intrusively, loudly, rhythmically and it had disturbed the
tranquillity of the dining room. The ringtone was Fontella
Bass singing 'Rescue Me'. Her voice was insistent, petulant,
disturbing the quiet, measured atmosphere of the dining
room. The diners sitting nearby looked across disapprovingly.
Rose had downloaded it a couple of months ago when Flori
had rescued the baby. At the time she thought it funny, but
not now. Nobody smiled. It was a sick joke.

She picked up her mobile, glanced at the name. Flori.
Her stomach churned. She'd lost count how many times Flori
had rung her over the last two days. Each time she hadn't
answered. She couldn't bear to speak to her. She hated her,
she wanted to pretend she never knew her but she didn't like
feeling like that. Not for Flori. What timing, she thought, she
must have a sixth sense. She felt like getting up from the table
and running. From the club, from London, from her father.
It was all too much. Why now, of all times, did she ring and
why had she brought up her half-sister, when she had this to
confront?

She looked at her father. He was looking closely at her.
He must have noticed the change in her manner, but if he
wondered why she hadn't answered, he said nothing. She
switched off her mobile, but the action distressed her. It was
almost physical, as if she'd pushed Flori away. Turned her
back on her. She caught her father's eye. It wasn't the right
time. It was bad timing, bringing up Natalya, out of the blue.
Inappropriate.

She looked down at her food. She couldn't finish it. She
understood now. She'd avoided confronting her own fears
for Owain's safety by referring to Natalya and indirectly,
her father's infidelity. She wanted to get under his skin, too,

irritate him in the way Flori did herself, and sidestep her own problems. But having raised it, she'd have to see it through. It wasn't fair on her father.

'I'm sorry, springing that on you. I hadn't realised I was going to say anything. But I know about her. I found out.'

'How long have you known? Was it your mother, did she tell you?'

'No. I found a letter from her. It was the letter she sent you when she found out about your affair. You'd rowed. She wanted a divorce, she'd put a copy in a drawer but I found the key. She doesn't know I know and I didn't know when or if I was going to speak to you about it, but it doesn't matter, not now. I've got the copy, you can read it again, if you've forgotten. It's years old now.'

She took the neatly folded letter from out of her bag and passed it across the table. 'Here. Do you remember it?'

He took the letter from her. She thought he might refuse, but he didn't. She watch as his eyes scanned each line. He read slowly, his face impassive. He passed the letter back and glanced at her, his eyes full of pain. It hadn't occurred to her how humiliating it would have been for him, that she knew now about his affair.

He paused before speaking. 'How could I forget? I'm sorry. It's all so sordid, and so long ago, but you're old enough Rose, to know about the problems between your mother and I. At some point I was going to tell you. About Natalya.'

'When?' She sounded challenging.

'I don't know. Some time, when it seemed right, though it can never be right. I'm sorry. Rose, it's been hard over the years, but I make no excuses, I've let you and your mother down, and it's unforgivable. I've been weak.'

'Weak?'

'Yes, I can say this now, you're old enough. We should have separated years ago. But I think you know that.' He looked away from her and sighed.

'Well, why didn't you? Separate?'

'Appearances. It wouldn't have looked good, not with my work. It's always been work. The Foreign Office, my reputation, my appearance, my duty. I've put these before everything, including my family. It's the code of conduct. I've conformed, but I hate myself for it. As for Natalya. She doesn't know me and I don't know her. But being away so much, I'm to blame for the family breakdown.'

Rose was momentarily taken aback. He was so open, honest even, but his guilt. She hadn't thought about that, that he'd feel guilt and sadness. Perhaps that was to do with regret at a wasted, loveless marriage.

'I don't feel like that, and I don't blame you, not anymore. Everybody makes mistakes. I understand that. I've grown up. I've had to.'

She started moving the salt, the pepper, the water glasses into a straight line, as if in a battle and she was about to barricade herself in. 'I need to tell you something. Why I'm here and why I contacted you. It's not good.'

'You don't have to, Rose.'

'I do. I have to. You're the only one I can trust, and I need your opinion.'

'It sounds serious.'

'Serious? Worse. But I need to get my head straight first. I'm going to the loo. I'll be back soon.'

Her father's eyes widened. He was visibly concerned, but before he could say anything more she stood up and walked quickly across the floor towards the door. Once outside the dining room she made her way to the ladies. Tentatively pushed open the door. Thank god. She was alone. There was no one there. She stared at herself in the mirror. She looked strange, intense, standing in her straight black dress with her pale skin and red hair. She looked as if she was about to cry. She distracted herself by reapplying her lipstick and eyeliner, all the time her mind replaying the scene when she'd confronted Flori in the croft. She leant against the wall, clasping her hands, willing herself to go through with it. She must return to the dining room, sit down opposite her father. Tell him. She had to. That's why she was here.

Taking a deep breath she walked back along the corridor to the dining room. Avoiding the eyes of the other diners, their attention caught perhaps by her good looks or the intensity of her gaze, she focused on reaching the table where her father sat waiting. She sat down, but continued with the previous conversation, just as if everything was normal. Still she couldn't bring herself to face him with her truth.

'Your work, what you were saying about it, it's true, you've always conformed, done the right thing, been so proper, but I think you'd have liked to have cut free of all those rules and expectations.'

He looked surprised, but said nothing. Their eyes met.

'I want to meet Natalya. Where is she? Does she know about me?'

He looked at her intently. She knew he was calculating how much he could tell her, whether it was the right time, whether he could trust her. 'Why? Why do you want to meet her?'

'Because, because, isn't it obvious, she's my half-sister. I've always dreamt of having a sister, and to think, for all these years, I have one. Does she look like me?' Her eyes filled with tears. 'Where does she live?'

He took her hand across the table, held it for a moment. She didn't remove it. He stroked her hand thoughtfully, said, 'I will tell you, but there's your mother's feelings, too. I have to think of her, but you have a right to know, because, as you say, she's your half-sister.'

He looked intently at her, his head on one side. 'I've only ever seen photos of her. It was better that way for all concerned, but looking at you, I see there is a slight family resemblance. It's in the shape of your mouth, but her eyes, they're diffcrent. Hers are blue and deep sct.'

'Where does she live?'

'With her mother, a half-brother and a stepfather in Moscow.'

'Does she know about me?'

'No, at least, I don't think so, but maybe she does. I've had no direct contact with her mother for years.'

'But you pay maintenance?'

'Yes, that's the least I can do.'

'Did you love her mother?'

He looked at her, then looked away quickly. He didn't answer straightaway, then he said, 'I did or I thought I did.'

'Why didn't you have another child with my mother?'

There was a pause. 'I think you know the answer to that.'

There was a long silence. 'But you wanted to tell me something?'

So he hadn't forgotten why she'd contacted him so urgently. 'Yes.' She took a deep breath, it was now or never. 'That call on my mobile, it was from Flori, my best friend. At least that's how I used to think of her. She was like an adopted sister, but I don't think that anymore. I've changed how I think about her. We used to have fun, and we'd have done anything for each other, but, something's happened, something terrible. I'm out of my depth. I don't know what to do. It's terrible.'

'What do you mean? What's terrible?'

'It's why – why I wanted to see you, I need your help. We're in serious trouble...and there's a baby.' The room seemed to go quiet. She looked round, wishing she get up and run away but no one was looking. She heard her father say, 'Carry on.' She didn't answer immediately.

'You said a baby? Does your friend have a baby?'

She took a deep breath and she said the words she dreaded repeating. 'Yes, and I'm frightened that she'll hurt him.'

The waiter came over, cleared the plates away and asked if they wanted the dessert menu. Her father waved him away. The expression on his face was intensely serious. He folded his arms, leant on the table, moved his face closer towards her. He spoke quietly so only she could hear. 'Tell me. Tell me. Everything.'

'It all started this summer. I've known Flori for two years and our friendship has always been intense. We'd gone to a party in Earls Court. I left early. Flori fell asleep in the garden but when she woke up, everyone had left. She was trapped. She climbed into a flat, through the windows, she thought she'd get to the street that way, but when she left...she took their baby. They were asleep. She said he wasn't loved. She wanted to look after him, she asked me to help. She's been in hiding since. But...'

She never finished her sentence because her father cut across her. Deeply shocked, the colour drained out of his face, his lips had become tight and he was pressing his hands together so hard the knuckles were white. He spoke coldly. 'I've heard about this. It's been in the news. I've read about it. It's the baby snatched in Earls Court. Isn't it?'

He stared at her but Rose couldn't face him. She looked down, avoiding his eyes.

'That you're involved. It's hardly believable. My own daughter. That you could do this.' He put his head in his hands as if needing support, then looked up. 'Where is the baby?'

'Scotland. On an island with Flori.'

'My god. This is awful. Awful. The baby. Has she harmed him already?'

'No, but that's what, that's what I'm terrified about, that she might. That she might harm him. She's had a breakdown. I've seen her. I've been with her. She's confused, frightened, making threats, about herself and the baby. She thinks her mother is alive. She isn't, she's dead, but she thinks she's there on the island and that she's going to steal the baby from her. I don't know anymore what's true and what's not. She's not coping. She's unpredictable, paranoid. I'd just left her with the baby when I rang you. I've come for help. She could hurt him. She's not in her right mind. I don't know what's best to do.'

Her father looked at her. He was silent, his expression grave before he spoke. 'Rose, let's be blunt about this. From what you're saying, the baby's life is at risk. She could kill him, and if that happens, you'll never forgive yourself.'

He sat up very straight, called the waiter over and ordered a double whisky. He said nothing until it arrived, then warming it in his hands, he downed it in one. He looked at her, the expression on his face hard, 'You know what you have to do. You needn't ask. There are no choices. You know what to do. Do it now, and quickly.' His face taut with anxiety, he emphasised and repeated every word to make sure she understood.

'Should I go to the police?'

'Precisely. Immediately.'

'But what if she gets better or she's not as bad as I fear? I'm confused. Maybe it's not as bad as I think.'

'That's not for you to say. Go to the police, Rose.'

'But our friendship, she'll never forgive me'.

He raised his voice, but still spoke quietly. 'Rose, you must take responsibility for what you've done. You're implicated. Do it for the baby. Go to the police.' She was staring at him, as if she couldn't believe what she was hearing. 'You'll need a good solicitor. I know one. Shall I come with you?'

'To do what?' She looked defensive.

'Look. The situation is dangerous. You know that. Time is short. A baby's life is at risk. I'll pay the bill, contact the solicitor, accompany you to the nearest police station. Now. We're going now.'

'I don't want you with me, I don't want your help, I don't want your solicitor, I don't want you taking over. You've never been around, have you? You're only thinking of yourself and what others will say. I'm a criminal. Leave me alone, like you always do.'

She stood up from the table, glowered at him, unaware that the tension between them was attracting the attention of other diners. A red flash of anger crossed his face, but his voice remained well modulated. He was used to keeping his temper in public. His look was intense, but he held her angry gaze. He wasn't intimidated. He'd entered some other space, a professional space where he was absolutely clear about her moral duty and he was going to make sure she followed it. There were no ifs and no buts. Not anymore.

He spoke slowly, 'This is no time for recriminations. Tell me, promise me you're immediately going to the police. Tell them where the baby is. You must. You know that. You have no choice. You're part of a madness and the sooner you act, the better you'll feel. Think of your friend. She must be frightened. Terrified. Do it for her, too. She needs help. And you can give her that help. Rose, I trust you.'

'I might be sent to prison.'

'I doubt it. You can do the right thing. Now. You must. Please. Go.'

Rose stood for a second, an image of Flori's face contorted with anxiety flashed across her mind. He was right. She had to go. 'I'm going'.

'Well done. Call me. I'll be waiting for you. Go.'

She hesitated, and then she said, 'I'm going to phone Crime Stoppers. I prefer anonymous in the first instance.'

'Fine. Go ahead. Just go.' He repeated. 'Now.'

She walked out of the dining room, and after a moment's hesitation, he followed. She was standing alone, along the corridor, out of sight of the diners. She looked desolate. He put his arms round her, 'Rose,' he said, 'you're not alone. I'll stand by you. You're my daughter.'

She didn't pull away. She needed him. Looking straight ahead, she walked away, past the reception area, down the steps of the building and into the street. She was shaking, feeling she was about to faint. Her father's emphatic response had increased her fear, her sense of responsibility and she knew now she had to act fast, but it had to be in her own way. She didn't want to use her mobile. She looked for a public phone, but couldn't see one along the street. A cab pulled up.

'The nearest phone box,' she said.

It was only two streets away, it wasn't far. She paid the

cabbie, jumped out, pulled open the door, entered the phone box. She was keenly aware that what she was about to do would have consequences that she'd like to avoid but she forced herself to go through with it, hoping the phone would be out of order. It wasn't. It worked.

She looked in her bag for the Crime Stoppers' number. It wasn't there. A moment of panic. She'd left the number inside the croft. It would be still there, stuck inside her copy of *Vogue*, where she'd hidden it after they'd watched *Crime Watch*. For a split second, she stopped breathing, desperate, hoping that Flori wouldn't find it, that her lack of interest in high fashion meant she wouldn't read the magazine.

But if she had, she'd know then, that she, Rose, had intended to betray her. She stood racking her brains for the number until it came to her. She dialled the number. She listened to the recorded message, all calls are anonymous and no caller would be traced, it said. Could that be true? She didn't care. She had to go through with it. A moment's hesitation. She put the phone down. She knew what she was going to do would be the end of her friendship with Flori. She stood thinking about what Flori had been through, what Flori had told her about her mother, the knives, the threats, baby Owain, his dependency on Flori, his sweet, innocent, trusting face. She had to do something. The baby had to be protected. This was more important than anything.

Again she picked up the phone, waited for the recorded message to finish and this time she heard a real voice. A woman.

'Hello. Crime Stoppers. Can I help you?

Rose didn't answer. She was so transfixed with fear, and held the handset so tightly she thought it would break. It was impossible for her to continue. The woman's voice continued. She tried reassuring her that what she said would remain anonymous. Rose listened but still couldn't speak. All she could think about was that she was about to betray Flori. An image of Flori's face came to her. Crying. When she told her about the death of Tids. She didn't want Owain to die, too.

She heard herself say, 'You don't understand. I'm guilty, too.'

Her voice shaking with fear, she replaced the receiver. She could go no further and stood inside the phone box. She couldn't move. Someone was tapping on the window of the phone box. She opened the door. A man spoke to her in a language she didn't understand.

She left the phone box, walked down the street. She needed time. She took out a cigarette. The words of her father came back to her. 'Do the right thing' and 'You're implicated, too'. It seemed another age when he'd said that. She'd been living in a nightmare for the past two months. It was as simple and as complex as that.

She had to go through with it. It was the hardest thing she'd ever done in her life. She paced up and down smoking. She promised herself when she'd finished her cigarette she'd go through with it. She returned to the phone box. It was empty. She stubbed her cigarette out. No more excuses. She dialled the number, listened again to the recorded message until the woman came on, then she spoke. Urgently and slowly, emphasising the danger.

'Are you listening? Listen carefully. The baby stolen from Earls Court in July. He's with someone called Flori on Jura. Scotland. Be quick. He's in danger.'

She slammed down the phone. Walked away. She'd done it. She felt her tears flow. They wouldn't stop. She called her father. Sat and waited for him. He came within fifteen minutes, took her back to his house, made her tea, wrapped her in a blanket and said when she was ready, to tell him all that she wanted him to know. It was hard for her. She sat for a long time, thinking. Then she began, she told him everything, her voice shaking, her hands plucking at the blanket, her eyes fixed on a picture on the wall. An internal journey, she was trying to make sense of her life and her friendship with Flori. Her father listened intently, barely speaking, interrupting her only occasionally.

*

'She'd called me, it was after a party we'd gone to and early Saturday morning. She said she was looking after a neighbour's baby but she had no nappies and she wanted me to get them. That was the first I heard of it. I walked into her flat and saw a baby lying asleep on a table surrounded with cushions. His head was surrounded with five red carnations. It looked so weird, I almost laughed, except Flori's face put me off. She looked deadly serious. The scene reminded me of an old master's painting, almost as if the baby was a tiny Eastern potentate about to be worshipped. There was a strong fragrance coming from two burning candles and I could hear Indian Raga music in the background. The whole scene was ridiculous, if not bizarre.

'I walked over to the baby and stood looking at him. He was in a deep sleep and breathing steadily. He looked contented and as if he hadn't a care in the world. I said, "He's beautiful." He had so much hair. He was adorable with a tiny mouth like a rosebud, round cheeks, and little hands and fingers. To me he looked like a little cherub from heaven. I'd have been so proud if I was his mother. It was the first time I'd been so close to a newborn and I asked Flori how old he was and what his name was.

'It was from then on I realised there was something going on that made me uneasy. She switched off the music and stood looking at me so I said, "I've got the nappies here. Are they okay?" She looked out of it, but she thanked me, and then she said, "I'm not sure how old he is, I need to find out. His name's Owain. But, Rose, I need to tell you something, something important, but I'll get you a coffee first. Sit down. I won't be long."

'She went to the kitchen and it was then I noticed there was no crib or baby buggy in the room. Surely, I thought, a mother would have one of those? Not only that, she was looking after someone's baby but she didn't know his age. Weird. Nothing stacked up and the more I thought about it all, the more uneasy I felt.

'When Flori reappeared, she put a mug on the table and sat down opposite me. I could tell she was nervous, she was watching me intently, turning her coffee round and round in her hands. She was quiet at first, as if she was thinking about what she should say and how she should say it. She asked me first about Dave, the guy I'd met the previous night at the party. I could tell she wasn't really interested, so I just told her I liked him and it was a shame he'd gone to Greece. I waited. I knew she was going to tell me something important but she couldn't bring herself to say it.

'The atmosphere was tense, and she was just sitting there staring at me, so in the end I said, "Flori, let's cut to the chase. Tell me what you want to say. I want to know because something's up and you're looking evasive."

'I'll never forget how she looked when I said that. It was if she was terrified. She couldn't look me in the face for longer than a second. When she did speak, her voice was wobbling. I thought she was about to cry. She looked and sounded like a little girl.

'She said, "Rose, I need your support. Don't let me down. You're all I've got. There is no neighbour." She took a deep breath, said, "I've taken the baby from a flat, his parents don't know, I had to do it because if I hadn't, he would have died. I have to keep him safe. He's only got me, and I'm the only one who knows how much his life is at risk."

'She cried then. I couldn't take in what she was saying. I felt I was awake in a nightmare. I could hear the words, but none of them made sense. She told me how it happened. The parents were rowing and she thought the baby would be murdered by them and it was up to her to save him. I won't ever forget how she put it. It was so vivid. What she overheard. She was hiding while the row was going on. She said his parents hated each other and the baby and that he was treated like a thing, as if he was deaf. They were having a slanging match and she didn't like the fact the baby would hear and he'd be frightened and wouldn't understand. She said it was hellish and the experience terrified her. Before she left, she went to see him, she wanted to see what he looked like and that's when she stole him. But she called it rescuing. She picked him up out of his crib and left, holding him in her arms. It was all on an impulse.

'I asked her what she was doing inside the flat. She said she'd got trapped in the garden after the party and planned to get back onto the street through the flat. Apparently a window had been left open in this flat and that's how she got in.

'After she'd told me, I had no idea what to say. Both of us sat for several minutes without saying a word. It was too much to take in. Almost unbearable. I was upset not only by what she'd said, but what she'd done. At the time, I didn't think she was mad. I admired her. It was the type of thing only Flori would do. I glanced at her but she seemed to have disappeared into another world. I struggled to make sense of it, but something weird happened then. I felt as if I was turning into Flori and I was the one hidden behind the curtains, and I could hear the couple shouting.

'I felt the same anger as she'd had. The fury was flooding through my body just the same as Flori. I was thinking they shouldn't have had that baby, not if they couldn't look after it. But before I could say any more, Flori spoke. She said, "He's my little baby now. I love him and I've named him Owain. But, Rose" she said, "I'm desperate. I need your help to hide him. He mustn't be found. He mustn't go back."

'I looked at Flori and at the tiny baby still lying asleep on the cushions in the middle of the table but I had no idea what the best thing would be to do. I did suggest we contact Social Services. I knew she wouldn't agree.

'I said, "What about Social Services. Will you tell them about what you heard and why you rescued the baby? Don't you think we should?"

She almost shouted at me. "No, absolutely not, no, no. He's mine now. He's my baby, and nobody else's. I don't want social workers poking their nose in our business. They'll take him away, do an assessment and he'll be put back with those horrible parents, and we, or at least I, will be in trouble. I want to foster him. Foster him unofficially. I can look after him."

'Then she looked at me in that way she has and said, "Don't tell on me, you won't will you, because if you do, that's the end."

'She sounded threatening and I asked what she meant and she just said our friendship. I didn't like the sound of that, but I put it down to how upset she was. The baby needed rescuing and although I'd never have had Flori's courage to do what she did, I thought she'd done the right thing and her heart was in the right place. I knew she loved babies and cruelty of any sort upset her.

'I said, "Well, I'm only asking but don't worry, I'm with you all the way. But we need to plan. Everyone will be looking for him and we'll have to keep a low profile."

'I was having trouble taking stuff in and I asked if Owain was his real name…her answer was weird. She said, "I called him Owain because he looks like an Owain, don't you think? At his Naming Ceremony I had a vision of him as a Welsh warrior. I held it before you came but I wish I'd waited for you. You could have been his official Pagan God Mother, but I didn't know whether you'd support me." She said again, "You won't let me down, will you?"

'I'd never known her to be interested in myths. It was then it crossed my mind she was mad, because this was a side of Flori I'd never seen before so I didn't contradict her. With hindsight, that was the moment of no return. I really wanted her as my friend and I was swept along with her crazy fantasy. The baby fascinated me, too. I remember I walked over to him. He was just waking up. I spoke to him, said I was Rose and shook his hand. It was so tiny. His face crumpled as if he was about to cry, and he stared up at me. He looked puzzled. He didn't recognise me, I hid my face behind a cushion, and went "boo" and as I showed my face again, he laughed. He was so sweet.

'We talked about what to do, how to look after him,

where we should go, and that was when she referred to the baby clothes. I'd seen them in the flat before. They'd been hidden. She'd gone out to pick up some milk and I hadn't known her long then.

'I said, "Flori, we must draw up and prioritise a list of things we have to do," and that's when she said, "I've got baby clothes and toys already. All we need is a buggy."

'Like I said, I'd seen them before but I hadn't asked why they were there and I didn't this time either. I couldn't. Things were weird enough already. I decided to keep my mouth shut and wait until she told me, as there was more than enough to take in. We planned what we were going to do. We had to explain Flori's absence from work. Her ingenuity was endless. She conjured up a relative living in the States, supposedly a single parent with children. She'd become ill and I was to say she was flying out to help her. My role was to call Human Resources and tell them. Of course, I agreed.

'Later in the morning, I suggested we watch the news, to see what was going on and what the police were up to, but it freaked Flori. I'd switched on the TV to watch BBC 'News Twenty Four Hours' There was an opening shot of the Mansion Flats where Flori had taken the baby. The flats were taped off and police were standing outside holding back groups of bystanders.

The newsreader read out, "In the early hours of this morning a baby aged two months old was snatched from his cot in one of these flats. His parents were asleep in the next room. Police say the mother is too distressed to be interviewed, and a specially trained police liaison officer is caring for her. Police are examining nearby CCTV. They urge who ever took the baby to give herself up. She is in urgent need of medical attention. Further news will follow as we receive it."

'When she heard that, Flori sprang up. She shouted, "I am not in urgent need of medical attention. It's them, the parents who need urgent medical attention, they'd know that if they'd been there."

'I told her to take no notice, it was a standard response, but she was furious. She stomped over to the television and switched it off. "Fuck them," she said, "They're not getting Owain. They can fuck themselves. We'll get away, as soon as possible. I'll sort that out, Rose. Don't you worry!"

'But watching the news clip made me feel awful. Seeing the flats where we'd been to the party. Hearing about the baby's mother. The police search. It was serious. Not exciting. What she'd done was a crime, whatever the reason Flori had for snatching a baby. It made me feel tense. I glanced at her. I could see she was defiant. She had no intention of giving up. I knew then I was well and truly compromised. The situation was frightening. Little by little I was becoming as implicated as Flori. I was intimidated by her angry determination to keep Owain but the thought of breaking away from her felt impossible. We were best friends and although Flori had gone beyond normal behaviour, I was part of that, as if we were conjoined twins.

'I sat thinking about it for a while. I said, "Look something has just occurred to me, where are you and Owain going to live? You can't stay round here, can you? I know no one knows you but it's too near to where he lived and any single mother with a tiny baby is going to attract the police's attention. We've got to get out of London. Do you think you were seen on CCTV anywhere?"

'She said, "No, I'm sure I wasn't. I took care to avoid the cameras, that's why I didn't go by tube, or get a black cab. But you're right, we're going to have to think where we can go. I'll have to get out of London, or go abroad. There's too many people around here."

'I said, "But how? How are we going to spirit away Owain without being seen? It's difficult enough to leave London now it's made the news, and it'll be even more difficult to leave the country. Owain needs a passport and you've no documents and obtaining one would be almost impossible. It requires contacts with the criminal underworld, and I don't have those contacts, do you? We're trapped."

'She said she'd think of something, or somewhere, but she needed time. She began pacing up and down, then she stopped, and what she said, I'll never forget although then I didn't know its significance.

'She stood in front of me and she said, "I know where we can go, it's an island, a really remote island, off the coast of Scotland. I've been there before, when I was six. Jura, it's called. An island in the Hebrides. It's magical, beautiful. I remember it, how the mist rose from the sea and drift towards the hills and there's three mountains in the middle and more deer than people." Then she laughed and said, "And deer don't talk, so we'll be safe, because hardly anyone lives there. We could live at the end of the island, away from Craighouse, that's the only village and no one will know we're there. I'll wait until the fuss has died down, and Owain is bigger, then we'll come back."

'I didn't say anything. It sounded too good to be true and I wondered again if she'd made it up. Then she said, "But I'll need your help, there's no buses, no black cabs, no mini-cabs, there's only one shop, so I'll need your help."

'She was looking at me in such a forlorn way, I couldn't say no. I said, "Flori, of course I'll help. You can use my car, we'll drive up together and I'll leave it with you and I'll organise a place for you to stay. I'll say you're a writer with a baby and need total solitude. Don't worry."

'She stood up and gave me a hug. Her eyes were filled with tears. She walked over to the window and stared out. She said, "It's scary, isn't it, Rose? I'm frightened I'll get caught."

'I tried to reassure her that everything would be alright once she was in hiding. I told her I'd find the best route to get there, but when I looked I could see how difficult it would be to get there, whichever way you went, and all the time the police would be watching, on the lookout for a woman alone with a baby.

'In the end I said, "I've been thinking about the route. It's hellishly long, and I don't think we should go together

176

because we'll attract attention. Two women with a baby, one an accomplice. Looks pretty obvious, doesn't it? Can you make it on your own?"

'She said she couldn't, that she had to have someone with her. Eventually she got there with the help of a guy she told me she'd been in love with, and from what Flori said, he sounded decent enough. I've never met him. She didn't want me to, said it was to protect both of us, so the plan was after a week or so, I'd drive the car up and leave it with her. I can't remember the exact dates. Everything merges together. It's all so horrible.

'Things were alright at first. She doted on Owain, but just before I was due to leave Jura, she became very strange. I thought at first it was because she didn't want me to go, but I don't think it was as straightforward as that. She'd become suspicious of me, especially after we'd watched *Crime Watch*. It had upset her and from then on our friendship began to deteriorate. Flori accused me of intending to "grass" on her, that was the word she used. She said I was only interested in the cash reward and that's why I was helping her. That was so out of character, she frightened me. After that I copied out the number of Crime Stoppers, just in case.

'The terrible thing was I have told on her, but not for money, but to save Owain's life.

'When she became ill, I tried reassuring her but I couldn't get through. I could see she'd lost trust in me. When she looked at me, she was full of hostility, if not hate although I don't want to exaggerate. I said I'd visit again if she needed help. I'd only been back in London a few days when she phoned me. She was in a state. I've known her long enough to know she wasn't herself. She was paranoid. Thinking her mother was on the island following her and the deer hunters were tracking her. Worst of all, she was mixing up Owain with her baby brother Tids. She threatened me. Said if I didn't come she had a knife and she'd take Owain and disappear. What could I do? I had to go. I went the next day to Jura.

177

'I was shocked when I saw her, how she looked, what she was saying, how she behaved. There was a confrontation. I made her tell me what had happened when she was a child. I asked about her brother and her mother. What she told me was awful. It disturbed me so much, I felt as if I was going to go mad. I just didn't know what to do, who to contact for help. I was frightened of her by then and what she might do. She wasn't in her right mind. You just don't know, not with her background. I didn't know what was real and what was made up. She was unpredictable, potentially violent. I got in such a state, I was torn in two, it was like the baby or her, and time was running out. Minute by minute the clock ticking.

'Yet, all the time there was this bond between us. I didn't want to betray her, let her down. I felt for her but I knew I had to do something.'

Her father said, 'What was it, what did she tell you?'

She stopped. There was a loud banging at the door. She didn't finish her sentence. The bell rang. It was loud, insistent. A pause. A shout. 'Police. Open up.' She looked at her father. He was looking grim. She was too frightened to speak.

Her father stood up. 'Prepare yourself, Rose. We know who it is.' He walked out of the room, down the hall. She heard him open the front door, silence, and then a quiet conversation. He was gone for five minutes. She couldn't hear what was said but when he returned he was with three police officers.

One of them spoke immediately. He sounded friendly, 'Rose, you're going to have to come the station. It's about the abduction of the infant on July 23rd from 14 Albemarle Mansions. I think you'll be able to help us.'

Rose looked at her father. Distraught, her eyes filled with tears, she was in a state of shock. She behaved like an automaton. She hardly heard her father say, 'You must tell them everything that you've told me, Rose. I'll come with you and call for my solicitor.'

She was led to the police car and sat in the back with her father, her mind blank, waiting for the inevitable interrogation.

11

For three days Flori and Owain stayed inside in the croft. Sometimes she had cabin fever and they'd go down to the water's edge to watch the movement of the tides. She was becoming a world expert on tidal movements and the cry of the birds, most of which she didn't know the names of, except for the ubiquitous seagulls with their shrill calls to each other as they soared and swung on the winds above them. It was a time of reprieve but she knew it wouldn't last. She felt she was psychologically preparing for something, waiting for the right moment, but this would occur only when she could psychically confront it.

On the third night she had a dream. It was strange, like all the dreams she had on Jura. In the dream was a remote lane and at the beginning of the lane, a yellow-and-black road sign which said 'Narrow Road with Passing Places'. Along this lane a deer pulled a baby's black buggy. The buggy was a tiny open coffin. It seemed to be wrapped in light and as it passed along thousands of people stood silently watching. The sky was a brilliant blue. Red carnations, fell like shooting stars onto the coffin. She'd tried to reach the coffin, see who was inside, but the crowds stopped her, they made it impossible.

When she woke, she lay awake thinking about the dream until she understood its meaning. Inside the coffin

179

was the tiny body of her baby brother, Tids. When he died, she'd been stopped from going to Tids' funeral, because they thought it would upset her. At the time she'd been left feeling desolate, even though his death had occurred many years ago. The dream carried a message: Tids was dead and the red carnations falling from the sky were a symbol of her love for him. Only now could she accept it. Only now was it possible to resolve her grief. Once she understood, she began feeling at peace.

But time was passing and with every hour she was becoming more conscious that Rose hadn't been in touch. She'd tried to phone her on her mobile but it seemed permanently switched off. Normally Rose would ring her back, but she hadn't done so. She'd tried texting her, but there was still no response. She finally had to accept that Rose was avoiding her but she'd try once more. She had to stock up with food from Craighouse and while there, she'd email Rose from the hotel. She hadn't brought her laptop from London, primarily on the grounds she wanted to cut herself off. She'd done that alright, but now she had to contact Rose.

She put Owain in the car and drove to Craighouse and parked by the water. No one spoke or showed any interest in them, so after she'd shopped and before they went to the hotel, she sat on the jetty with Owain on her knee watching the sea. She loved the view from Craighouse across the waters to the mainland. It soothed her soul. The two of them sat together for an hour, Owain as quiet and still as Flori. The hotel was close by and after pushing Owain in his pushchair inside the hotel foyer, she asked the receptionist for half an hour on the computer.

The receptionist barely looked at her as she took her money. She was busy with new arrivals, most of whom looked like red-faced, whisky-sodden carnivores, the type to be hunters. It crossed Flori's mind to wonder if they were really the hunting, shooting, fishing type, or whether they were the thought police in disguise, but she came to the conclusion she no longer cared and could therefore ignore that thought.

She logged onto her web mail, first working her way through the thousands of stupid spammy emails which took time to delete but once she'd finished, she wasn't sure what she should say. The message needed to be short. She wrote eventually that she was writing from the hotel and as she hadn't heard from her, she was worried and wanted to know what was going on. She asked Rose to contact her on her mobile as soon as she could. She didn't feel hopeful she'd respond but she'd just have to wait and see.

She had ten minutes left. She opened the BBC's news website. She wasn't a big news fan, and since she'd been on Jura she hadn't thought about the events going on in the world outside. But sure enough it was the same as when she left London. Wars, disasters, famines, coups, fight, they all continued. The destructive forces of nature matched only by the destructive forces of human nature. The BBC was streaming the news, and as Flori watched, the newsreader picked up a piece of paper that was passed to him.

His face was impassive as he read, 'Police report they have received an anonymous tip-off concerning the missing baby snatched from the West London luxury flat in July of this year. A young woman is said to be in hiding with the baby on a remote Scottish island. No further information has been given.'

Flori sat in shock. She couldn't think. Her mind blank, she was in a state of total disbelief. She looked at Owain. She'd never give him up. He'd fallen asleep. She felt as if she was about to collapse. Who could it be, who on this island knew and had told on them? She looked around the ornate room. No one was looking at her. They assumed she was a tourist. She had to get out but without being noticed. If she ran out suddenly, pushing a baby in a buggy, it would surely attract attention. Difficult though it was, she stood up and walked slowly through the reception area, bending down, pretending to fuss over Owain. Once outside she walked purposively back to the car.

In that short space of time, everything had changed. It was irrelevant now that Rose hadn't contacted her. She and Owain were in danger. The realisation that the police were searching for her was a terrible blow. She became totally preoccupied with who might have told them, her mind ranging over various possibilities. She couldn't understand how it had got out. She'd deliberately kept herself to herself as Matt had advised. She could count the number of people on one hand she'd spoken to, but people gossiped. This happened everywhere and Jura was no exception. Had someone watched the television programme and put two and two together?

Then it came to her in a flash. Rose. It could only be Rose. It was after they'd watched *Crime Watch* and they'd quarrelled and she remembered afterwards noticing a copy of *Vogue*, the magazine Rose had brought with her. She'd flicked through the pages and a tiny piece of paper had fluttered out and fallen to the floor. She'd picked it up and noticed the number for Crime Stoppers had been copied out. She'd been preoccupied at the time and thought no more about it but now she understood its meaning; it was confirmation of her betrayal.

At first, she took it calmly, wondering how much time she had and whether Rose had already told Crime Stoppers they were on Jura. She remembered the woman on *Crime Watch* said that all calls to Crime Stoppers were anonymous, but she guessed that depended on the call and if someone's life was in danger and how much they told, and she had no idea what Rose would have said. For a brief moment she hated her and wished she'd plunged the knife into her when she had the chance, but she remembered then the many good times they'd shared and in some bizarre way, she knew she loved her like a sister. She remained important to her whatever she'd done. Yet it felt unbearable to know it was Rose who'd betrayed her.

But it could only be her and it would explain why she hadn't answered her calls and why she hadn't contacted her.

She was avoiding her because she felt guilty about betraying her and she couldn't face her.

She drove back to Lagg in a daze, silently fed Owain and put him to bed for the night. Her mood had plummeted. She felt lost. It was obvious she could no longer rely on Rose, and this was devastating to her. She opened a bottle of wine and sat through the night at the kitchen table, drinking, thinking, wondering what to do. It was a long night.

But she knew with every minute time was slipping away, and the police could be getting nearer. She thought about everything she'd been through; her mother, the death of Tids, stealing Owain, running away to Jura, her dreams, her nightmares, imagining her mother was still alive. She was beginning to understood now why she'd stolen Owain; he was a replacement for Tids and she'd wanted to love him and protect him, as she'd tried but failed to do with Tids. But Owain wasn't Tids and the reality was they couldn't live in secret forever. It was impossible, not unless she aligned herself with the criminal underworld and she wasn't prepared to do that. She began formulating a plan. One which would get her out of the trap she'd created. It was a momentous decision.

12

Monday, 30th August

It was evening. The light had almost gone and the sky was a beautiful colour of indigo, but darkness was approaching like the black ravens circling like vultures over Barnhill. The atmosphere was strangely quiet and eerie. Carrying Owain in her arms, Flori walked along the rough track towards the sea. When she reached the shoreline, she stopped and stood looking across to the mainland. The tide was on the turn with its own slow rhythm. There was no wind, just the imperceptible surface movement of the dark waters. Her mind quietened. She must say goodbye.

She looked down at him. He was awake, staring at her, his eyes bright and fixed on her face. He'd been with her for two months, almost half his life of four months, and she'd loved him and cared for him as if he were her own. She turned away and holding him close, walked back to the croft. Together they visited each room. It would be the last time. But Owain sensed something bad was about to happen. Whimpering, he wrapped his arms tightly round her neck, his tears falling as he looked into her eyes. She brought him close to her, feeling such a savage grief she didn't know whether she could go through with her plan. But for them both she must, even if it was unbearable.

She put him in his buggy. It was time to feed him, wash him, change him. They had so little time left together, but there was something else she should do. She'd brought a baby sedative with her from London in case Owain ever suffered with teething troubles, but she'd never imagined these would be the circumstances she'd use it. She broke the seal on the bottle, carefully placed the pink liquid on a spoon, and gave him slightly more than the recommended dose. It must have been sweet because he took it so readily but the way he'd fixed his eyes on her and looked at her, made her feel bad. It felt like she'd betrayed his trust.

He was quiet watching her with his big eyes. She'd become so withdrawn. She wasn't playing with him, or singing to him or making him laugh. She placed him where he could see her as she prepared for their departure. Then she told him she wouldn't be long, she had to go outside but she could hear him crying so she returned, wrapped him a blanket and took him with her, pushing his buggy through the long grass to a hollow among the bracken at the back of the crofts.

Inside the hollow she'd piled up the papers and documents that would incriminate her. She held a match to them until they caught fire. The flames lit up the tiny hamlet and she stayed and watched until they'd burnt into nothing and the red glow had disappeared. She kicked the ashes around, and finally poured a pan of water over them. Nothing must be left, no evidence that could be used to track her down. She turned and stood, looking back at the croft, her mind returning to the night she and Matt first arrived.

She remembered stepping off the boat, walking up the track, opening the door into the croft and the deathly atmosphere. She'd felt someone had lived there years ago, a woman who'd been unhappy. A lost soul who'd once existed. She hadn't been imagined. She was the spirit of the place, she was everywhere. Perhaps it had been the woman she saw on the coast path. Maybe she was watching her now as she prepared to leave, but thinking this frightened her and she pushed it away. She'd vowed since that last visit to Barnhill not to think like this anymore. She'd had enough of nightmares.

She made a promise to herself that when and if she got away from Jura, she'd go back to Wales and visit Newgale and Solva, the two places she loved and where she'd first met Matt. She took the white stone from her pocket, the one he'd given her when he left and holding it tight, waited until his voice and his words came back to her. He'd loved her, made her happy and she was going to need his strength.

She looked down at Owain, who'd fallen asleep. She pushed him back to the croft. She had to wake him so she could dress him for going outside. She put on his baby fleece, the one with the hat and the big ears. By now his limbs were floppy, he was easy to dress. She returned upstairs, pulled her walking gear out from the wardrobe, and dressed as if the weather was going to be wet, cold and windy. She packed some fruit, and four high-energy food bars in her rucksack and finally attached her water bottle and a head torch to the clips on the outside. She put her boots on.

Then, carrying Owain to the car, she settled him in his car seat, placed an unopened pack of nappies, some milk and baby food on the seat next to him and returned to the croft. She locked the door behind her. It was the first and last time she'd do that. She put the key under the flower pot, the same one it had been under when she first arrived and walked back to the car. Owain was still asleep in the back. She sat in the driving seat, turned the key in the ignition and without pausing drove off, bumping over the grass and the heather until she reached the road. A wave of exultation passed over her.

She drove along the road until she came to the place where she and Rose had first parked weeks ago. It was the day they'd walked into the mountains and when they'd seen the deer hunters, but they wouldn't be around now. It was too dark. She passed no other cars on the road and when she reached the exact same place where they'd parked, she pulled off the road and switched off the lights. She was exhausted and an overwhelming urge to sleep came over her, but she couldn't sleep here parked on the verge. She'd be too easily seen. She drove further up the track, well away from the road and then switched off the engine.

The deep silence of the night surrounded her. She could hear nothing. Nothing at all. Not a voice, not an animal, not a bird, not the sound of the sea, nor the sound of the wind. They were totally alone. She got out of the driver's seat, opened the back door and sat by Owain. She wanted to be close to him before she left. She sat watching him.

Their last night back at the croft, she'd copied out in her best handwriting, Pablo Neruda's seventeenth love sonnet. She'd read it out aloud to him, just as she had many times before. It was her favourite poem. The same one she'd whispered to him when she'd named him. It was the poem that had inspired the dream of the carnations falling from the sky. And it seemed right, that now their time was coming to an end, that she should read it to him again. It marked the moment of her deliverance of Owain and she hoped when he got older he'd understand that she'd loved him and would always love him.

When she spoke, his eyes had opened, and he'd watched her with his big serious eyes, listening, totally quiet and still, his eyes never leaving her face. Every now and again she'd paused and look to see if he was listening, but when she got to the line, 'I love you as certain dark things are to be loved/ in secret, between the shadow and the soul,' she felt as if she was fragmenting like the vase her mother once threw at the wall. The pieces had scattered into tiny shards of glass. It had been irreparable.

Now they were parting she'd leave the poem for him. It was her gift to him and she wanted whoever found him to keep it for him. She wrote 'For Owain' on the envelope, sealed it, and pushed it in the back pocket of his buggy.

He was deeply asleep and was snoring gently in the way small babies do, but it wasn't a natural sleep, it was the medication she'd given him. She felt bad about that, but she had to do it, she didn't want him to wake and cry for her as she walked away.

187

She couldn't bear what she was about to do, but she had no choice. She didn't want to be caught. Whatever happened, now or in the future, at some point he'd be taken off her, and rather than give him up herself, or have him screaming for her as he was forcibly removed from her arms by the police, she was about to leave him.

Her mind returned to that time when she'd taken him. She was back there; she couldn't and probably never would rid herself of the memories of that summer night. The party, the garden, the flat. Scene by scene she replayed it, the sights, the sounds, the smells. It had been the beginning, the start of it all. She remembered it exactly as it happened, everything, the building, the windows with the white voile curtains, the bedroom, the lounge with the street light shining outside, the moth, the screaming, the sobs, the baby, her adorable, beautiful baby. The baby she'd taken but she was now giving up.

She felt emotionally exhausted. She had to sleep. She pulled the fleece blanket over herself and Owain and drifted off but the images of the past months returned to disturb her. She was restless, turning, shifting her position constantly. When she woke, she didn't know where she was. The darkness of the mountain surrounded her. Owain was by her side. She looked at him for the last time. Seeing his sweet innocent face and listening to the rise and fall of his gentle breathing and knowing his trusting dependency touched her so much. She hated herself for what she was about to do. She stared through the window into the night, listened to the wind rushing through the pines, but nothing she did or thought could comfort her. She was about to abandon him, leave him on this lonely road on a remote Scottish island at the foot of a mountain, all to save her own skin.

Yet, the alternative, turning herself in, was too dreadful to contemplate. She could imagine it. The press. She'd be pushed, pulled, screamed at. Her name would be called, 'Flori, Flori, look this way.' They'd take pictures of her crying,

Owain screaming as the police and Social Services dragged him out of her arms.

It would be like before. Her childhood. The past. All those memories. It had been unbearable. She couldn't live through that again. She must block those memories. She refused to think of them and she must go now. While he was asleep. If he was awake and saw her walking away into the dark, never to return, it would traumatise him. It would be his eyes. His eyes would follow her as she walked away. They'd enter her dreams forever, become nightmares.

After she'd got away and the police had picked him up, would he be returned to his parents? Would they care for him in the way she had? Would they have learnt a lesson? Over and over she'd considered every possibility, but each time she'd returned to the same decision. She had to leave him, even though she loved him as her own. The situation she found herself in, and Rose's betrayal, made it impossible to stay. She wasn't strong enough.

She took a deep breath, opened the front door of the car, got into the driver's seat, switched on the engine and reversed back along the track to the road. She parked the car in the road where there was no passing place. It was deliberate; she wanted to block the road. Anyone coming along would have to stop. But there was one last thing she must do. She'd almost forgotten, she had to leave instructions for Owain's care. She'd written the note while she was in Lagg and she read it once more before she tucked it inside the pocket of his fleece.

Reading it, upset her again. It said:

To whoever finds baby Owain,
Please look after my baby. He loves his food but please
don't give him meat because he's a vegetarian baby . His
favourite dessert is organic apple puree with custard. I've
left some jars for him on the back seat.
He likes going out, either being pushed in his buggy
or in a car. He likes it if you sing to him. His loves his fat

189

giraffe and on no account must this be lost. It's his only possession and has been with him forever. It's precious to him.

In the pocket at the back of his buggy, I've left a poem for him. I'd be grateful if this is kept safe. I used to read it to him often so I would think he knows it. It must never be lost. It's my present for him and although I didn't write it, it doesn't matter because I might have written it if I could write like that.

Will you tell him I love him and always will and I'm sorry for all the trouble I've caused everybody, and I especially want Rose to know that.

Flori with all my love to Owain

She looked for the last time at Owain. He was still asleep. She put the car sidelights on, left the keys in the ignition, and got out, quietly closing the door. Without looking back, she ran back up the track and into the mountains. When she reached a clump of fir trees, she stopped and hid among them so she could still see the car on the road. The lights were faint from where she stood, the car looking tiny. She'd watch and would stay until someone stopped and found him. Then she'd go. It was the 30th of August 9.15pm when she left him.

It was two hours before any one came along the road. They were driving towards Craighouse and when they saw the car they came to a halt. At first no one got out. Maybe they assumed someone was reading a map or there were two lovers inside the car and they were talking to each other, but whatever was passing through their minds, for a while they did nothing. Not like London, Flori thought, where in a split second people would lose it and start honking and shouting. Up here it was different. Eventually a man did get out and he walked to the car. He was a way off but as he passed the headlights of his car, he was lit up and she could see he was dressed in a kilt. He must have been to some function at the other end of the island.

190

He walked to the front of her car, saw there was no one in the driver's seat, bent down, and looked in the back. He must have been looking at Owain. She hoped he was still asleep, otherwise he'd be scared seeing a strange man peering through the windows in the dark. Usually he slept through the night but to be sure she had given him the sedative.

The man stood up and looked all round him. Flori felt she could read his mind. He was concerned or wondering whether someone had been taken short and gone into the woods, or had broken down. As she thought this, a flash of her dark humour re-established itself. He'd be right if he thought that. She had broken down, but that had been a long time ago. He walked back to his car over to the passenger's side and stood on the road talking to whoever was sitting in his car. They evidently didn't know what to do.

Flori was fascinated. It was like watching a mimed play. Another car drove up and stopped. The driver, a woman, got out. She also was dressed up. Maybe they'd been to the same function. The female passenger from the first car joined them so it became like a mini traffic jam and they all stood talking in a group in front of the car's headlights, looking round them as if expecting someone to emerge from the darkness. They'd left Owain in the car so she guessed he was peacefully asleep, oblivious to what was going on. Eventually the man took out his mobile and rang someone. Maybe the police. She didn't think there was a police presence on Jura, so they'd have to come from the mainland but at that point she thought she'd leave and not wait any longer to find out.

She put on her head torch and wrenched herself away. It was a significant moment. It was unlikely she'd see Owain for a long time, possibly ever and despite resolving not to get upset, tears streamed down her face as she followed the rough track up and into the mountain. It began to rain lightly, the wind picked up and the temperature dropped the higher she climbed. The words of Matt came back to her. It was when she'd told him she'd taken Owain. How angry he'd been. He'd tried to persuade her to give him up. He'd said, why don't you leave him somewhere, somewhere safe, that way you could avoid getting arrested, but I wouldn't advise it. At the time she'd ignored that advice, but that's what she was doing now; she was giving him up but she hated herself for it.

She continued climbing, picking her way over the rough track, occasionally looking up at the thin clouds drifting across the night sky. Luck was on her side, because once she was clear of the forest, between the light of the moon and her head torch, she could see the path well enough. She missed Owain but she'd never have made it carrying him on her back. His weight would have slowed her down and for speed she had to travel light. She wished she'd got a photo of him. When Rose had visited she'd taken some and maybe she'd give them to her, when and if they ever met again. But right now she had to get off the island without being caught.

She was heading for the mountain bothy, the one she and Rose never reached. She planned to stop and sleep there for the night. She prayed to God it would be empty, but she had a story prepared if there were walkers already there. She'd tell them she was walking from one side of the island to the other and she'd got lost in the dark on the mountains.

She kept to the rough path and after an hour or two she saw the bothy ahead. It was white washed and conspicuous in the clearing, seeming to shine in the moonlight. She'd made it. It was just past midnight. She stood close by for a few minutes, waiting to see if there were any signs of walkers, but there were none. She moved slowly towards the bothy. The place was in darkness. It had a small porch. The bothy would have no electricity, any lighting would be by candles, but there were no flickering lights coming from the inside. She walked all round. There were no curtains across the tiny windows so she shone her torch through to the rooms inside. It was primitive, simply furnished: two rooms, one with bunks, the other a sitting area with benches and a table. Both rooms were empty. She quietly opened the front door and went inside. This was her refuge for the night.

She looked around. The open fire place with its neatly stacked logs smelling of wood smoke had a welcoming, friendly feel. Four empty wine bottles with candles stuck in their neck tops were placed neatly along the roughly hewn table and on a shelf along the wall were placed a few tins of baked beans, a tin opener, a badly washed saucepan with black scorch marks, a kettle filled with water, and that was it. There was a visitors' book, but she didn't open it. She was too tired. She took off her Gore-Tex jacket, drank some water from her water bottle, ate one of her energy bars, lay on a bunk without undressing and fell asleep within five minutes.

13

Tuesday, 31st August

She was woken by the deafening sound of a helicopter circling just above the bothy. She sprang up, looked at the time. It was 8.25 am and her first thought was for Owain and that he was no longer with her. Already they were hunting for her so he must have been found. She stood listening to the engine noise, her pulse rate increasing as she waited expectantly for it to get louder, to cut out, knowing if that happened, it would have landed. She wanted to look out but she didn't dare. She'd be seen.

She stood thinking, working out what was going on. She felt calm, her mind clear, with luck she might be back in London in three days. The helicopter must be the Mountain Rescue Police looking for a place to land. They had a base across the Sound on the mainland. She hoped the steep scree down the side of the mountain and the wooded terrain would make it too dangerous to land, but it could hover, drop a man. She'd seen them winch rescuers down from the helicopters to reach inaccessible areas, and they could do the same here. Only this wasn't a mountain rescue, they were searching for her.

She remembered in the croft someone had left copies of the Annual Reports of the Oban Mountain Rescue Team and she'd read them all. She knew they had heat-seeking equipment to detect fallen and injured climbers and walkers, but she also knew heat-seeking rays didn't work through buildings so as long as she stayed inside and waited until it flew off, she was safe. If she heard someone being winched down, she'd have to run. They might know the terrain, but she was young, fast and her adrenaline was up and she was confident she could outrun them.

She sat waiting until, five minutes later, to her relief, the helicopter flew off. She forced herself to stay inside a while longer and while she waited she ate some of the fruit and the high-energy bars she'd brought with her. She had no coffee so she drank water, and thought about what she should do next. She was more excited than frightened. It was her against them, but now, because of the helicopter, she had to change her route.

She had planned to walk back along the road towards Lagg and from there phone for a boat to collect her from Tayvallich. It had been from Tayvallich Matt had taken her across the Sound of Jura to Lagg weeks ago. She would say she was a walker and had to get home quickly, but that was impossible now. Not after the helicopter. Probably the police had already searched through the stuff she'd left behind at Lagg. She hadn't had the time or been able to burn everything and it was possible some might still have personal information. They'd know from her clothes how tall she was, and Rose might have told them what she was likely to be wearing. She might even have given them a photo of her. It was likely that by now Jura would be swarming with the police from the mainland all looking for her.

She'd have to get back to the mainland some other way and different to the one she'd followed last night. To retrace that route would lead straight back to the car where she'd left Owain. She looked around for a map. She found an OS map left behind on one of the shelves, opened it and laid it flat on the table.

She wasn't an experienced map reader but she could see there was another way off the mountains. It was convoluted, in parts difficult, and the route meant going down scree. She'd been down scree before on a school trip and she hated it. It was tiring, required maximum effort to keep upright and not to cascade on the loose stones and be propelled down the mountain. Walking on scree was like walking down a slope of marbles, but she had to do it. Once she'd got over that part, the track led straight to the road and from there she could walk to Craighouse where there were regular boats across the Sound. That had been her initial thought.

But then she remembered. There was another problem. The ferries. When she was sitting by the water with Owain two days ago, she'd noticed the boat service had been suspended temporarily and visitors were advised to use the Feolin ferry at the end of the island. But if she was to go there, the police would be waiting. Whatever, she thought, she had to leave and now. Time was passing and it was too dangerous to remain any longer, wondering how and where to get off the island. Maybe, while she was walking, an alternative plan would come to her.

She picked up her rucksack, swung it onto her back, pulled the door shut and left. She looked briefly over her shoulder as she walked away. She regretted she hadn't had time to sit outside on the bench in the morning sun. It had stopped raining and there was a beautiful fresh feel to the morning. Perhaps some other time, she thought. First though, she'd have to find the path and one which would hide her descent. She saw one immediately. It was a path leading away from the bothy and was easily visible. It passed through the trees and had probably been used many times by other walkers. Once she'd found it, she was able to move rapidly under cover of the trees growing each side of the brook.

She noticed their tortured shape as they bent double towards the water. It made her think about what Rose had told her. About the winds on mountains, and how once up, their ferocity made it difficult to keep upright. For a moment she felt alarmed. She'd also told her about the wind-chill factor, but today wasn't like that. She'd be fine, the weather was holding, the setting sublime.

It occurred to her as she passed through the trees they'd become like the David Smith sculpture she and Rose had once seen in an exhibition at the Tate. Their stark skeletal outline revealed the history of the landscape, and walking here, even though it had an austere remote beauty, gradually soothed her. As she walked she thought about Owain, wondered how he was getting on. She went again through all the possible options, but whatever she might have done or could have done, she knew in her heart nothing would have worked. It was an impossible situation and one she now recognised, had been created by herself. She hoped he'd forgive her one day and understand why she'd left him. Perhaps when he was older she might even meet him, explain why and what had driven her.

She continued picking her way through the numerous extruding tree roots, bushes, rocks, but as she got lower down, the general uneven terrain along the water's edge slowed her and her lack of speed made her more anxious. It was tough and time was passing. Looking across the hazy low mountains of the mainland, lying below the vivid blue of the sky, and running parallel to the sea, she could see a long winding road. She stopped for a moment to look across to the Sound. She could see Lowlandman's Bay. It was a lonely place, standing on the coast, and roughly halfway between Lagg and Craighouse. Only a rough track from the main road led to it.

She noticed the two boats moored in its waters and it crossed her mind that maybe she could temporarily borrow a boat to get across the Sound, but a moment's further reflection made her realise she couldn't do that. She didn't know how to sail or how to operate a boat engine. She remembered also Matt telling her that the Sound contained sandbanks at low tide, a fast current, and that skerries caused problems for the inattentive or inexperienced sailor.

There was nothing for it, other than to hire a boat to get

across to the mainland. For this she'd have to ring Tayvallich and ask for one to pick her up from the bay. She'd have to chance it, that they wouldn't know about what was going on on Jura. With any luck one would be waiting for her by the time she arrived.

She continued walking until she saw a ridge ahead. According to the map, beyond the ridge was the scree, and sure enough when she reached the crest, there was the scree-strewn slope. It fell away from beneath her feet for at least one hundred metres. She stood looking at it. She knew going down this steep, unstable terrain would be risky, but she had to do it. She was a solitary figure, conspicuous in her bright red jacket as she descended. But she couldn't stop herself skidding and sliding and that made her more and more nervous. If anyone came along the road and looked up, they'd see her.

She was halfway down when she heard the high-pitched hee-haw and whine of sirens. Three police Land Rovers came into view. Lights flashing, they were racing at high speed down along the road below and towards Lagg. She threw herself flat on the stony ground. She'd never seen the police on Jura before, but they passed, didn't stop so they couldn't have noticed. Seeing them meant she'd have to move faster and get out of sight of the road but increasing her speed meant a greater risk, an increase in the momentum of the stones, which already were slewing away from under her feet.

As she descended, she felt more and more out of control and feared she'd fall. She had visions of being propelled down the mountainside so by the time she reached the bottom of the scree, she was panting and hot. She waited to get her breath back before she rang for a boat from Tayvallich.

She took out her mobile and phoned. The ferry service picked up straightaway. She said she was a lone walker travelling along the west coast of Jura but she'd got lost and had to get back to England quickly and needed a boat to get her across to the mainland. She asked if she could be met at Lowlandman's Bay in about three hours. She added that at Tayvallich she'd need a taxi to the nearest station. Could that also be organised? She was nervous, aware the sooner she got off the island, the safer she'd feel.

The woman was helpful, but asked for her name. She was immediately suspicious but perhaps it was a reasonable request. She gave her a false name, one straight off the top of her head. She said she was Lydia Tregarron. It was suitably Celtic. The woman wanted a payment before she was picked up. She realised if she wanted a card the name wouldn't match with her card number, so she said quickly she had cash and would pay her when she got to Tayvallich. She said she'd be waiting for the boat on the foreshore and she'd be easily recognised because she was carrying a large rucksack and wearing a red Gore-Tex.

Jura no longer felt safe but more like a prison but after that call she felt more relaxed and with any luck she could be back in London in a couple of days. She was so cheered by the end being in sight that she was able to increase her pace and when she came to a deer track leading down to the road, she followed along it, walking rhythmically and making rapid headway to the sea, reaching the bay in just over two hours. She still had an hour to wait.

She had the place to herself, there wasn't a soul in sight. She sat down, ate the remainder of her food, drank some water, and looked idly at the lighthouse on one of the low-lying islands in the bay. Her mind was calm. She was thinking how, when she returned to London, she could pick up her old life. She thought of Owain, of Rose, of Matt and wondered what each of them was doing while she sat there.

The weather was beautiful, the sun was out, the wind was minimal and the bay so remote, it felt safe enough to go to sleep. She walked over to an old, rotting carcase of a clinker boat, sat down and leant against it with her face to the sun. The boat smelt of tar and seaweed, the wood was warmed by the sun and gradually she drifted off to sleep.

She dreamt that the three of them, Owain, Rose and

herself were making their way to the bothy. Matt was waiting inside and he'd made a meal for them. As she sat down to eat, she heard the distant sound of a helicopter. Matt said they must hide in the boat but first they'd have to upturn it to make it into a shelter. The dream and her waking thoughts merged into one. It was the second time that day she'd heard a helicopter and she watched it dip over her, shading her eyes against the late afternoon sun. It seemed to fall into the sea. It was bright red and it flew so close she could read Royal Navy Rescue written on its side. The noise of the engine and of the rotor blades became deafening, but suddenly it banked steeply, flew low over the foreshore, and landed some distance away on firm ground. She stood up and saw three figures climb out, two men and a woman. They were running towards her.

She watched them as they got closer. She stood up, began to walk in the opposite direction. She could hear them calling her name, 'Hey, Florianne. You're gonna have to stop. We have to speak to you,' but she ignored that and didn't stop. She carried on walking. She was calm. Matt would rescue her. They were shouting now, louder and louder but she felt oblivious to that. She was still in a dream, believing if she carried on and reached the bothy, they'd disappear and she'd wake up.

Two of the men caught up with her. They looked like police officers and the woman was following close behind. She heard the rise and fall of a whining police siren. A police Land Rover appeared from the opposite direction. It must have come off the road and was being driven so fast along the track, it skidded to a halt in front of her. Another two police officers got out, one male and one female. She looked at them, then back to the helicopter. There were five police officers now, three behind and two in front. She was surrounded. It was real, not a dream.

They'd stopped shouting. It had gone quiet, deadly quiet. She heard a sea gull scream overhead. No one said anything. She waited until they were all there. There was no point running.

All five stood round her. She was surrounded, standing in the middle of them. She felt nothing. Nothing at all.

One of them stepped forward. She heard him say she was being arrested under Section 3 of the Child Abduction Act 1984 for the abduction of an infant on June 26th from Flat 14 Albemarle Mansions, London SW5. He said she didn't have to say anything. There were more words but she could take little in, although she did hear, 'anything you say might be used as evidence in court.' It was the kind of thing they said on television, but it was meaningless to her.

She asked after Owain and whether he was missing her, but no one replied. She looked at each of them carefully.

One of the police officers had deep brown eyes, bright red hair, and a very pale complexion without freckles. She smiled at him. He didn't smile back.

The woman was young with short very curly fair hair.

The other man was older, with a beer gut and was going bald.

The fourth was like a thug and looked as if he was into body building.

The other woman must have been in her mid to late forties. She was plumpish and looked slightly care worn. She was studying her closely. She was the only one without a uniform.

She said, 'That's not my name. Florianne. What you called me back there, it's not my name. My name is Flori. That's what I'm called,' and she turned away and began to walk past the Land Rover.

The one who looked like a thug caught hold of her by the arm and said, 'Just a minute, you're not going anywhere, Florianne.'

His grip hurt her and he pulled her back roughly. She spat at him. In the face. He looked disconcerted. He hadn't expected that. He wiped his face. He raised his hand as if to strike her. She heard him call her a bitch, but someone told him to cool it. He got out his handcuffs and moved forward to snap them on her wrists, but the two women called out, both at the same time, 'Leave her.'

She turned and continued walking away. The older woman spoke to the others, said she was going to talk to her, and she began to walk by her side as if they were friends. She said her name was Helen and she was a doctor. Flori glanced at her. She could hear her speaking as if from a long way off. She was saying Flori was in a lot of trouble and she wanted to help her. She carried on talking but Flori didn't hear what she was saying; instead she was listening to the musicality and intonation of her speech. She had a low, quiet voice and spoke with a soft Scottish accent. She found it soothing. At some point she said, and it caught Flori's attention because she called her by her right name, she would have to go back to London.

'You have face up to things,' she said.

Flori said, 'What things?'

'You know what things, Flori.'

'I don't. I've done nothing wrong. What do you mean?'

She didn't answer and said, 'Come, Flori,' took her by the arm and led her back to where the others were. Then she said, 'I have to go back to the base station and leave you. You'll be taken to London now.'

Flori said, 'You know I thought my mother was imprisoned at Barnhill but she never was there. She's dead. She is dead, isn't she?'

Helen looked at her without speaking.

Flori said, 'I have a terrible secret,' and looked closely at Helen to see how she'd react.

Helen looked intensely into Flori's eyes. 'Yes, I know,' she said, but she didn't say anymore.

There was a long silence, then Flori spoke, 'Was it Rose? Was it Rose who told you about my mum?'

Helen looked straight back at Flori and Flori knew by that look it was Rose who'd told the police and that was why the police were here and how they already knew her mother killed Tids, and she'd stolen Owain.

She watched Helen nod at the fair-haired woman officer. She put her arm round Flori and told her she had to sit in the back of the Land Rover because she was going back to London. She asked her to behave herself, as if she were a child.

Flori said she would but she was tired and she wanted to sleep. She took out the white stone from her pocket, the one from Solva harbour, the beautiful stone that Matt had given her, the stone like an abstract sculpture. She held it tight in her hand. It was the most beautiful thing she'd ever owned. She climbed into the Land Rover, pulled the hood of her Gore-Tex over her head, lay down across the seat, and fell asleep, still holding it.

14

Matt stood watching the sun rise lazily over the morning surfers at Newgale. The air was fresh, the light pure; it was going to be a beautiful day. He'd just delivered a batch of sea water samples to the labs in Haverfordwest and the rest of the day was his own. He turned away, climbed back into his Land Rover and drove along the St David's Road, his mind wandering aimlessly.

A petrol station came into view. He slowed down, pulled onto the forecourt, jumped out, filled the tank with petrol, pulled the door shut behind him. He picked up the *Guardian* newspaper from the rack outside. His eye was caught by the bunches of red carnations stuffed into a large, green, plastic container. He hesitated, caught unawares, a mixture of feelings swept through him – nostalgia, regret, and sadness. They reminded him of Flori. He'd given her carnations when he'd first met her. He still remembered the moment.

Her tentative smile. How upset she seemed. She said it was the first time anyone had given her flowers. He'd found that hard to believe. She was attractive and he couldn't be the only one who'd noticed that. She'd had something about her. She was pretty, fun to be with and different from the girls he usually met, so he hadn't cared if it was true or not. He paid for the petrol and the paper and climbed back into his Land Rover. It was getting on for eleven and he'd already been up hours and needed a break. He decided to stop in Solva on the way home for a pint and a sandwich. He put the paper flat on the passenger seat and glanced at the newspaper's headlines.

He couldn't miss the headline: 'Police close in on Baby Snatcher' in large typeface. His mind went blank. He had to read it twice before he could take it in. He skimmed the article, then sat staring through the windscreen trying to make sense of what he'd just read. So if they knew about Flori they might now know about him. They knew she was in hiding on Jura, the small island off the main coast of Scotland, the place he'd taken her to go into hiding with Owain.

Someone had rung Crime Stoppers and told on her. The police might already be on the island and for all he knew she could be in custody and the baby removed from her care. But would they know about his involvement? Had she told on him? There was no reference to him in the report. That didn't necessarily mean anything. The police always played their cards close to their chest, releasing information only when it would benefit them.

A car hooted behind him. He was blocking the forecourt. He threw the paper down, drove off and pulled into the first lay-by he came across and sat thinking, wondering what, if anything he could do. She'd be distraught. She'd need him, but despite his concerns for her, he couldn't help but wonder again how much she'd tell the police. She'd always said she'd never tell on him, but if the police put pressure on her she could crack.

He hoped to god she'd the strength to withstand police questioning, but he couldn't contact her. Every call to her mobile would now be traced. Maybe it was time to turn himself in. Tell them straight he'd helped her. That would take some of the pressure off her, but he couldn't do it. He had others to think about. He was in the middle of a major undercover project and to go to the police now would blow everything apart. All he could do was sit tight and keep cool.

Who would have betrayed her? Jura was remote. There

were no neighbours in Lagg, so it had to be someone who knew her well. The only person it could possibly be was Rose. It had to be her. He'd never met her but he'd always thought of her as a potential weak link. He knew of her only through what Flori had told him, that she came from an extremely privileged background and he'd thought when he heard this, it was an odd friendship. He'd wondered what they'd had in common, but he'd never said anything. They were clearly close friends but if he was right and it was her, Flori would be devastated by her betrayal.

But why? Why had she done it? Had there been a new development, had something happened, which had made Rose change her mind about supporting Flori? Something must have changed to make her contact the police. In a way he wasn't surprised. He'd never approved of Flori taking the baby and it was obvious that at some point it would come to an end, however worthy she thought her motives. From his point of view her action was mad, and he'd told her that, but it had been like talking to the deaf. She'd been adamant and nothing he'd said dissuaded her.

He could do nothing, other than wait and see what happened. He turned on the engine, opened the windows of the Land Rover and drove off towards Solva. As he drove past their old haunts, memories of their relationship and the happy times they'd shared flooded back. It had been short and intense love affair but Flori had always had a hold on him. It had been the afternoon of a hot summer's day when he'd first met her. He'd been driving fast when he'd seen her sitting on a grass verge and thumbing a lift. She looked fed up. He'd braked and reversed at speed, thinking she must need help. He'd always been a sucker for damsels in distress.

She told him she was heading for Newgale and since he was driving in the same direction, she climbed in. She smiled and thanked him for stopping. He immediately noticed her smile. It was sweet and direct. She'd been shopping, she said, and missed the bus back. From the start he was attracted to her.

It was her physical presence. She sat close to him, so close he could smell the sea on her and as he changed gear, he glanced down and noticed a white film of salt on her bare legs and feet. Her hair was streaked blonde, naturally it seemed as if she spent her days in the sun and by the sea. She entranced him. She told him she was on her own and staying in a cheap caravan at Newgale for the summer, using it as a base for surfing.

The attraction between them had been immediate. It was obvious to him she'd picked up on his attraction for her. She smiled frequently, and he noticed her glancing at him as he drove. He was about to drop her off, when he asked whether she'd like a coffee and if so, where would she like to go. Yes, she said, she would, but she didn't want to go to the café at Newgale, it was too dreary so they'd driven on to Solva. He reassured her he'd drive her back later.

They both knew Solva. It was a tiny village, a coastal inlet where the sea curled like a ribbon into the dip of the valley. The main street was lined with pretty, pastel-coloured cottages and small Edwardian villas with narrow front gardens protected from the road by ornate art nouveau iron work railings. He'd stopped in the car park by the sea, and they'd sat outside the pub, the one by the harbour, drinking coffee until the tide had gone out. It had been sunny that day and they'd walked barefoot on the wet sands, picking their way around the marooned tilting boats waiting for the sea to float them upright again.

Flori's playfulness had surprised him. She suggested they play a game, one she'd made up and which she called 'let's pretend I've won the lottery'. She offered to buy him any boat he wanted, but he had to choose one. He pretended to take her seriously, inspecting each boat, knowledgeably and amusingly commentating on their pros and cons. That game had led to another, her version of 'hide and seek' where he was to hide, throw a stone into a pool to catch her attention and she'd run to find him. As the afternoon passed, they became more and more like children.

He liked that about her, that she was fun to be with, but he was aware of his strong sexual attraction to her and the more time they spent together, the more sure he was that it was mutual. It was the way she looked at him and how she laughed at his jokes.

They stayed the rest of the day together, talking, it seemed, for hours. Flori was a good listener. She picked up on his Scottish accent and wanted to know where he'd been brought up. He told her about his upbringing, that he'd been brought up in Fraserburgh on the East Coast of Scotland, and that his family's involvement with the sea went back through the generations of his family, and how, as a young boy, he'd accompanied his father on fishing trips just as his father had before him. His father, he said, had lived for the sea and knew all its moods, but with the collapse of the fishing industry, his health had deteriorated. He'd needed the challenge of going out to sea in all weathers for the fish, but even his voluntary work on the Fraserburgh life boat was unable to replace his lost sense of pride and his identity.

Time passed unnoticed that day. Beer and wine replaced the coffee but neither he nor Flori noticed the sudden build up of squally weather until it was closing time and Flori reminded him she had to get back to Newgale.

He knew it well. It had long, wide, bleak sands, topped with the banks of large rounded pebbles that rolled and curved noisily around each other under the onslaught of the tides. The high pebbles protected the road from the forces of the sea, but not the ferocity of the winds coming off the grey Atlantic sea.

He drove her back as he'd promised. He chose the back country lanes until they reached the main road which swept around Newgale and at the end of the bay he'd turned off towards the caravan site. By then a storm was blowing and it was raining with such fury the wipers were barely able to keep the front windscreen clear. He was forced to drive close to where the wind whipped long spray off the waves and the high spring tide surged over the low, grassy bank, as it ran across the narrow road.

He parked the Land Rover as near to the caravan as he could. Then they ran, but the wind was so strong it was difficult to keep upright and as they ran their words were snatched away from their mouths. Inside the caravan, he held her. He could feel the tension in her body. She was nervous. He suggested he stay the night. He said it as if he was indifferent and he was doing her a favour and she replied similarly, thanking him, saying because of the bad weather and how much he'd drunk that it was better he stayed, that it would be risky to drive safely back.

That was the beginning of their love affair. The first night they'd slept as if children, their arms wrapped around each other for warmth and comfort, until the calm, quiet light of the early morning sun flooded into the caravan. The rest of that summer she accompanied him and they grew to love each other, their intimacy as much to do with their shared passion for the sea as for each other. Their need for each other became intense but perhaps, because of this, they began to argue. The rows had become so vicious he couldn't bear the pain of her anger any longer and eventually he decided he had to leave. He walked out, but it had been with regrets.

He missed her at first. But he'd been determined to push these feelings away. Then he met Amami and quickly become involved with her. It had been a distraction, on the rebound and too fast, but realising that had come too late. When she became pregnant, he knew he had a responsibility for her and the baby, but his love for Flori remained. He still yearned for her. She'd been different, playful and funny. Amami was serious, focused, academic, and like himself, was a scientist. At first, he'd found her qualities attractive but his interest in her hadn't lasted. He'd missed Flori's quirkiness, her passion, her tempestuousness, her occasional black moods. She was wild, her moods like the sea, and he'd loved her intensely in a way he'd never love Amami.

Their relationship was difficult, they could be tetchy with each other and they frequently quarrelled. Amami was jealous of Flori, and complained he was often distracted and that he gave the baby Nami more attention than her. He knew what she said was true but he didn't know how to respond.

One day following one of their typical spats, he'd had to visit Newgale and found himself near the caravan site where Flori had stayed when he'd first met her. Memories of their love affair had come flooding back. He was angry and hurt following the row with Amami and he'd contacted Flori. She'd sent him a card with her mobile and landline number when she moved to London but he hadn't responded to that. Now he rang her.

It was a gesture of defiance to prove to himself Amami's complaints were irrelevant. Flori hadn't picked up straightaway and he'd had to phone three times but when she'd answered he knew immediately something was up. She'd wanted to see him but she wouldn't say why. She'd said she'd only tell him when she saw him but it was urgent.

He'd felt he had to go and what was more, he wanted to see her. He hadn't thought through the consequences and by the time he did, it was too late. He told Amami he had a meeting in London and within a few hours he'd left for London. It had been a major error of judgement.

Their meeting had been bittersweet. He'd arrived at midnight and as she'd opened the door all the old feelings for her returned. She was dressed the way he'd remembered. Baggy jeans with a leather belt and a tight navy blue tee shirt showing the curve of her breasts. She wore a shell necklace round her neck. Her hair was shoulder length and glossy, one side falling over her eyes. He'd felt awkward at first. It had been so long since they'd seen each other.

'You haven't changed,' she'd said and smiled. 'You still have that quizzical, humorous look. But your hair! What's happened to it? What's happened to your hair? It's too short.' She'd paused, 'I liked it the way it was.'

He hadn't told her the truth, that Amami had insisted he had his hair cut. As far as he knew, Flori didn't know about her.

'I had it cut. I didn't like the way it was. It had got too long, but I'm the same. It's only hair. It can grow back.' He'd given her a half-smile. He'd felt uncertain. He hadn't been sure how she'd respond to him. There was a long silence. She was studying him, her gaze intense and direct. Spontaneously he'd pulled her close towards him, but she'd immediately pulled away as if she wanted to keep a physical distance between them.

'Don't. Don't do that. I don't want you to touch me.'

He'd made a gesture of surrender with his hands. 'Okay. Okay. It's okay. I'm sorry, Flori. It's no problem. I'll back off.'

He'd asked if he could sit down, and he'd sat on the sofa at right angles to where she sat. Initially they'd been ill at ease but he'd glanced at her sideways on. It was the same moment she glanced at him and they'd caught each other's eye and in that moment he knew for certain his feelings for her were the same, whatever had happened, and how ever much time had passed since that final row.

'It's good to see you, Flori. I was nervous, in case things have changed. They haven't. Not for me anyway.'

He'd thought then he should tell her about his relationship. It had to be soon. She didn't know about Amami and their baby now a toddler. He'd felt apprehensive, and had put it off, waiting for the right moment. But she'd spoken first. She was looking wary. He noticed she'd taken a deep breath and then said, 'I have to tell you something. You may be shocked. I haven't hurt anybody, but I'm in trouble and I need your help. You rang me at the right time.'

He'd been silent, her directness taking him aback. He hadn't answered. His mind was still on his own problems and she'd caught him off guard. He hadn't expected this as soon as he arrived; that she might have her own problems. He'd

211

been thinking on the train what and how he might tell her about Amami and that he was now the father of a little girl, but now, sitting in front of her he didn't know what to say. How could he tell Flori of his ambivalence about his present relationship? It wasn't fair on her, it was his problem. What could she do about it and what did he want of her? Was it a return to the carefree and wild past which once they'd shared, or was this only in his imagination, an escape from his responsibilities?

'Matt. You're not here with me. I don't think you heard me. I'm in a mess. Big time.'

This got through to him. 'In a mess? What's going on?' He pulled his attention back to her, focused his mind on what she'd just said, but she'd picked up on something about him. She was no fool.

'I think you're in trouble, too. Is it work, are the police on to you?'

He said, 'No, not work. It's personal and it can wait. What you're going to tell me sounds more important.' She'd looked at him, gauging what might be going on, but he wouldn't give anything away. Not yet. He said again, 'I can wait.'

'I want to know, you're hiding something.'

Still he said nothing. They sat in silence, Flori staring intently at him. 'It's important. You come all this way to see me, but you're withholding something. I know you too well. Tell me.'

'Why's it so important to you?'

'Because it's important to you. What is it? Until you tell me...' She'd paused, left her sentence hanging mid-air. 'Would you like a drink?'

'Problems. I have them and right now the world seems full of them. Just water, thanks, that'll do.'

She stood up, went to the fridge, got some chilled water. When she returned, she'd sat down and looking at him directly had said, 'You're in another relationship, aren't you? And it's not going well.'

'How did you guess? Yes.' He'd sighed. 'We have a daughter.'

He looked at her, waiting for a reaction, but her face was impassive. She hadn't responded, not straightaway. She watched him drink the water and then she asked him to come with her. She led him into her second bedroom. Not for a moment could he have predicted what he was about to see. In the corner of the room was an expensive buggy and the indefinable milky smell of a young baby permeating the atmosphere. He recognised the smell but initially he'd said nothing. He silently walked over to the buggy and bent down and looked. Inside was a sleeping baby. He'd straightened up. For some unfathomable reason, he'd felt angry. He'd walked back into the sitting room. Flori had followed him and they'd sat down. They were facing each other.

'So, this is what it's about. You've had a baby, but you'd never told me. Shocking, you say. Hardly. It happens. You don't waste much time, do you?'

'Nor you for that matter, and you don't own me.'

That stopped him in his tracks. She was right. He'd fathered a child with a partner he felt ambivalent about, but he'd put that out of his mind now he was with her. He'd thought, hoped, perhaps arrogantly, perhaps childishly, she'd always love him, no matter what, even though he'd walked away from her. He looked at her. His expression challenging, waiting for her response.

She said, 'You've got it wrong. I didn't give birth to him. But he's mine.'

He'd been taken aback. Confused, he'd said, 'What do you mean? Have you adopted him?'

'No. Not exactly. I've taken him.'

He'd struggled to take in what she'd said. He'd stared at her, incapable of taking in the implications. 'What's that mean? You've taken him. What do you mean, Flori?'

She'd started talking. At first slowly, nervously, but then as she became more anxious, her words came out fast with no pauses, describing second by second what she'd overheard and what she'd thought to the moment when she'd taken the baby.

He hadn't answered straightaway. He'd felt stunned. It was unbelievable, he'd never have thought she could do something so crazy. It was insane. When he spoke, he hadn't held back. He'd raised his voice.

'You're mad, and I mean it. Mad. You must be to do something like that. I'm shocked. I have no idea what to say to you. But you have to give him back. You know that, don't you? You have to give him back. He's not your baby.'

He'd stood up, begun pacing back and forth, averting his eyes from her. He'd glanced once at her, saw she looked defiant. He'd seen that expression on her face before, but only occasionally. She looked calculating, determined, her eyes hard, her mouth set in a tight line. Only her eyes gave her away, they were full of tears.

'I'm not giving him back. No. I'm not giving him back, whatever you say, he's mine now. I've told you. My baby, he's mine, mine, mine. Don't you understand?'

She turned away from him. He'd stared at her but instead of feeling angry, and because he'd loved her, he'd felt a wave of compassion, sensing that despite her defiance, she was upset, frightened and she needed his help.

He'd spoken gently. 'Flori, you must return the baby. You have no choice, you must. Think how the parents feel. Think how they'll miss him. It's not too late. It's cruel to take him, even if you did hear them argue. Everybody argues. We argued and we didn't hate each other.'

It was the wrong thing to say. She'd spat back, 'Yes and look what happened. You walked out.'

She turned away, picked up a book, began flicking over the pages. She wasn't open to reason. It was as if he spoke in some alien language. He'd become more forceful.

'It's illegal, Flori. It's against the law. You know that. You can't just take other people's babies, for whatever reason, it's not allowed. If you're frightened of returning him, leave him somewhere where he'll be found, but if you do that, make sure he's safe.' Then he'd paused, said, 'But even talking like this. It's mad. You're making me feel mad. Please, Flori, please return him.'

She'd ignored him. She put the book down and stood facing him. She responded to his comments as if it was an academic debate. She spoke reasonably, and as if to a rather slow and stupid child. 'Look, I'm not stealing him. I'm rescuing him. Can't you understand? You rescue dolphins, whales, seals, because they're at risk from pollution and from hunters killing for profit. You told me about it, and I agreed with you. This is just the same. My baby was at risk. His life was in danger from his parents and I had to take him. For his protection.'

He'd listened with astonishment. He could see she wasn't open to rational argument, but again he'd tried. 'For Christ's sake, Flori, they're different. Animals and humans. Surely you can see that?'

'They're not, humans are mammals, you used to say that, don't you remember? We're all connected, you said, and we're all part of the natural world, and we all need to care about each other. That's what you used to say.'

He was silent. Was he to blame for what she'd done? After that final row and he'd walked out, was it his absence that had driven her to such an act of desperation? He hadn't seen her for over two years and hadn't contacted her because he'd feared her response. But he'd never have thought she was capable of this. It was crazy.

He heard her say, 'What's it to you, anyway? Why should you care?'

'Because babies become attached to their parents, they're hardwired that way, which means you can't remove them as if they're a commodity on a supermarket shelf. He could be grieving. He can't speak, so how would you know?'

'Grieving for them? I don't think so. He seems happy enough to me. He's smiling and I love him, why wouldn't he be happy?'

He'd ignored this. There was no point in arguing, he could see that. He was exasperated, but also angry at being drawn into her madness.

'Well, now you've told me, you've just made me part of the crime. Have you thought of that? It sounds harsh but what do you expect me to do?'

She walked across to the window and looked out onto the street. She also was angry. She'd said, 'You know, I'm not surprised you got involved with someone else so quickly after we split up. It's what blokes do, isn't it? I thought you were different, but no, you conformed in the end to stereotype. One mummy goes and there's always another round the corner, just like the proverbial bus. How old is your baby?'

She was attacking him, but he refused the bait. The stakes were too high. He gave a reasonable answer. 'Fifteen months.' He waited for the explosion but none came.

'And what of the mother? Who is she?'

He said, 'What about her?' He'd paused then said, 'You want to hurt me.' He looked directly at her but she still had that hard look.

'What of it? Do I know her?'

She sounded up for a fight, but he was determined not to get drawn in.

'No, but so what? Whether you know her or not, I wasn't two timing. I met her after we split up. In Taiji. The dolphin campaign. She's Japanese.'

'Actually you're right, it's of no consequence, who she is or where she's from. I couldn't care less what nationality she is or where you met her. Not now. Because I have my own baby.'

She sounded triumphant, out of touch with reality and he'd watched as she'd got up, walked out the room to check on the baby. She'd stayed for a couple of minutes, then returned and sat down opposite him. He waited, wondering what was coming next, noticing she had an expression on her face he couldn't read.

'I'm not interested in her or your baby, but what I am interested in and what I don't understand is why you've come to see me. It doesn't make sense. Shouldn't you be there, with your little family?'

He noticed the sarcasm in her question but ignored it. He said, 'I don't know Flori and that's the truth. I don't know. I've missed you. It's all been so complicated, it happened too soon after we split up, meeting Amami, but you've been on my mind. You probably don't believe me and why should you?'

Their eyes had met, and he continued with, 'And what about you, why did you speak to me when I rang because you're still so angry with me? Aren't you?''

They were psychically dancing round each other and neither was giving anything anyway. Flori held his gaze.

'I wouldn't have spoken to you if I'd known you were in a relationship, but I loved you once and I admired your courage, and I thought perhaps we could try again. Now I know that's not possible. You're an outlaw, Matt, but you're a walking contradiction, you're an outlaw with strong principles, and you're the only person apart from Rose, my best mate, I can trust.'

She was silent and then she said, 'I need your help. I have to get out of London and I need help to get out.'

He didn't answer. He avoided her eyes, stared straight ahead.

Flori continued, 'All I'm asking is for you to get me and the baby out of London. I won't contact you again, and I'll never tell anybody, and you know I keep my word. Will you? For the sake of what we had?'

She was sitting opposite him, leaning over, her arms wrapped round her knees, smiling uncertainly at him. It was a powerful appeal. He glanced quickly at her, wondering again about the strong chemistry between them. It was like a kind of animal magnetism. Their eyes met, and he was aware then how much he desired her, despite everything. He stood up, reminding himself of Amami and their baby, and moved away from Flori and across the room to distract himself. He stared at the framed poster on the wall. It was a vintage photograph of couples jitterbugging by the River Seine and they seemed full of energy, life and love. He needed time to think. He could see the logic of rescuing the baby, twisted though it was, but she'd gone about it the wrong way. Underneath she was distressed and he felt for her, but the outcome was inevitable. She'd be found eventually and it would be awful. She'd be humiliated. The press would be intrusive. The police would crawl all over her flat, and she wouldn't be left alone. He knew from his campaigning work how tough one had to be, and Flori wasn't tough. She desperately needed his help and support. Two weeks later after telling Amami he had a project on that would last a week, he took her to Jura.

Looking back, he should have gone to the police then, explained, become an advocate on her behalf, but he couldn't do it. It would have been an act of betrayal even if, logically, it would have been the right thing to do. She'd never have forgiven him and it would be the end of them. Forever. He hadn't been able to go through with it. He'd known then that he still loved her but he was torn between what he should do and wanting to help her.

Their relationship had been intense, fiery even, and she'd always made demands on him but he'd also made demands of her and now, thinking about what she'd asked of him, he'd found it impossible to say no. He'd decided he'd do what he could. She was in a mess and he owed her. He owed her because he'd abandoned her, and because he'd become involved in another relationship. It had been too soon and he was racked with guilt. She'd given her heart to him and he'd walked out on her, betrayed her love and become involved with someone else and worse, was now a father. It saddened him remembering this and knowing that with the police hunting her she was in an even bigger mess.

He'd reached Solva. He drove down the tiny main street

towards the harbour to the same place where he and Flori had parked when they first met. He felt low, at a loose end and climbed out of the Land Rover and watched three boys building a dam with large stones they'd found in the stream running under the bridge. He was tempted to help but in the end, he didn't. An elderly couple walked past talking in Welsh. They seemed irritated, perhaps because of the large numbers of visitors sitting drinking outside the pub. He went inside. It was busy and there was a warm, dark fug compared with the brightness of the harbour outside. He had to wait to get his order, a pint of his favourite beer, the Rev. James, and a crab sandwich. When they arrived he went outside. He wanted a seat away from the tourists but there were none and as the tide was out, he walked further along the sands until he found a wall to sit on. No one came near. He had the place to himself. He took a bite out of his sandwich and began thinking again of Flori and of the time spent together in London.

He realised now how guilty he'd felt about leaving her and that with hindsight, it could have been predicted that when she'd asked for help, he'd agree. At one point he'd asked, 'Have you changed, Flori? Since we were together?' and she'd said, 'What do you think? Yes, of course, I have. But maybe not for the better.'

She smiled then but he could see she was vulnerable, and he'd caught hold of her by the shoulders and looked at her, face on. It was a proprietorial, affectionate gesture, almost of ownership. The kind of gesture that a lover might make where there was already an assumption of a shared understanding, but she'd pulled away and gone to check Owain. When she returned, she'd said she was hungry and took a peach from the fridge, offered half to him, but he refused and said he didn't feel like eating.

She'd sat down, holding the peach in her cupped hands. It was pale pink, glowing yellow, succulent looking, with a velvet skin and looked as if it had ripened naturally in the sun somewhere far off. He'd watched fascinated as she held the peach and turned it round in her hands. He imagined it was delicately fragrant and he was reminded of the summer days they'd spent on the Welsh coast, when they'd surfed in the high, wild waves, and then dried off in the sun among the lonely, hot sand dunes. They'd been happy then.

His mind had been taken with this memory, but his attention was further caught when she began stroking the soft skin of the peach. She'd bit into its soft flesh, raised her eyes and gazed straight at him. Had she been aware how provocative she was? He'd looked at her, wanted her, but she must have become aware of how he felt, because she looked away and when she'd finished eating, she'd told him she was going to bed.

She'd said, 'Help yourself to food, there's stuff in the fridge and if Owain wakes up and cries, I'll see to him, you don't have to do anything.'

Her words had jarred. She'd disappeared into her bedroom and he'd lain on the sofa and pulled the duvet she'd provided over him, but it was impossible to sleep. He lay, tossing and turning, replaying their earlier conversation, keenly aware of her physical presence and of the sexual charge between them. He remembered conversations from the past, and wondered if they might still have a future. His mind became like a fragmented kaleidoscope, with thoughts, events, and images from their past spinning round. Hours later, he was still awake, he couldn't settle, couldn't sleep.

He'd sat up, thinking he must be mad to have been persuaded by her to help. It was almost dawn when she'd opened her door. She'd looked taken aback when she saw him; perhaps she'd forgotten he was there.

She spoke formally as if they didn't know each other. 'I'm just getting a drink,' she said, 'sorry to disturb you.'

'No problem,' he'd said. She was standing in the semi-darkness wearing a short, white, thin nightdress, staring at him, seemingly transfixed.

'Something wrong?' he'd said.

She'd smiled then. 'I thought you'd be asleep. It's been so long, I forgot, you know, what you're like. I've missed you. I can't sleep.'

He'd put out his hand and gently pulled her towards him. She hadn't resisted. He'd put his arm round her, drawing her closer, caressing her, feeling the warmth and shape of her breasts under her nightdress. They'd made love and again thinking back to that meeting after their two years separation, perhaps it had been inevitable they'd end up in bed together. But he'd felt bad about it and when he'd returned to Amami, she noticed straightaway something was different about him.

'You've been with a woman, haven't you?' He hadn't answered and avoided her gaze but they both knew what the silence was about. He couldn't tell her. Not about Flori, and the strength of the sexual attraction between them. It would have been cruel.

The long journey to Scotland firstly up the M1 and then the M6, through Glasgow and round the lochs had given him plenty of time to reflect on his motivations. They'd hardly left London when Flori confronted him about their past. She'd been playing music on his CD player and one song with a haunting tone caught his attention. It raised his curiosity. He'd fallen straight into it.

'Who's the singer?' he'd asked.

'Judie Tzuke. The song, 'Stay with me till Dawn'. I love it because it reminds me of Newgale and when we first met. We'd spent most of the day in Solva and you'd taken me back to the caravan. There was a storm outside. It was our first night and I was scared. I fell asleep in your arms and by the morning it had died down and we made love as the sun rose. It was really early, we fell asleep again and woke late. I didn't want you to go, but you said you had to work. I thought I'd never see you again, but you came back. Remember?'

221

He'd looked at her and their eyes met briefly and intensely. But he hadn't answered.

'Why don't you answer?' Flori had said.

'Because I don't know what to say.'

There was a long silence. She'd turned the music down, and then came the question he'd hoped he could avoid. 'Why did we break up?'

'You know why.'

'I regret it.'

'Yes.'

'You do, too?'

'Yes.'

'Well, it's too late now. Isn't it?' She was testing him.

'Probably.'

Another long silence and then she'd said, 'I want to know about you and Amami. I know nothing.'

'What do you want to know?'

'How you met. Stuff like that. Why you got involved with her so quickly. You didn't give me time. Time to sort things out in my head, get my priorities right.'

He struggled. He hadn't wanted to talk about it, because unlike Flori, who could be open, it didn't come naturally to him. 'I don't want to talk about it.'

'But I do. I want to know. Why's it so difficult?'

Eventually he'd answered, 'I met her in Taiji'.

'I know that already. You told me and I heard the first time. And?'

'I admired her, she was feisty and principled.'

He could see the way it was going, she was getting stroppy, picking a fight, so what she said next didn't come as a surprise.

'Not like me then?'

'Look, if it's going to upset you, it's better not to talk. She's different to you. Not better, just different.'

It was true, it had been Amami's active commitment to marine ecological issues which had first attracted him. She

222

never protested when he went away on a project, whereas this was something Flori hadn't been able to do. He'd never told her this, but he could tell by her next remark that she knew already.

'So she's got courage and patience, and I haven't, and she supports you and all your causes, and I didn't.'

'I didn't say that, and I didn't think it.'

He'd lied at this point. He was trying to keep the peace but it hadn't worked because she upped the anti and what she said next came to him like a blow to his solar plexus.

'So why did she get pregnant? You must have fancied her as well. It couldn't have been just her principles that attracted you. You're a man. You fancied her and she got pregnant. It never happened to us. I never got pregnant.'

'No, it never did. It wasn't right for us then.'

He thought for a moment, decided to tell her the truth. 'It was a mistake, she forgot to take contraception.'

'That's not true. That's what she'd say. I've heard that one before. It's the kind of thing women say, that they forgot their contraception, but there's usually an ulterior reason for it.'

She glared at him, waited for him to rise to the bait, but his response was reasonable.

'Whatever. The fact is, it's caused us,' he searched for the right word, 'problems and we've had to confront the consequences. Amami doesn't believe in abortion, not for herself, that is. It's an issue I'd never had to face, but then I had to, I was part of the problem, and I couldn't just abandon her.'

'Very principled. Do you love her?'

It was a question too far, he didn't want to go any further, but he'd said so much already, there was little point in holding back any further. She wasn't about to give up.

He sighed. 'I can't answer that. What's love? I have no idea. I don't know, but whatever it is, I know I love Nami, my daughter, and it wasn't her fault that we were careless. We, I, have had to face up to the consequences.'

'And does Amami love you?' Her questions were forensic.

He said, 'Flori, is this an inquisition? Who knows. Maybe yes, maybe no. Look, I don't know.'

'So it's a marriage, a partnership, of convenience. For the baby.'

'There's a bit more to it than that. Let's stop there. That's enough, I'm not answering anymore.'

'What more is there?'

'Enough, I said. Don't ask me anymore. I've said more than enough.'

They'd continued in silence. He'd felt psychically bruised. He'd seen himself through Flori's eyes, knew now that he wasn't as strong as he'd thought but like everybody else, was subject to the influences of life's vagaries and not, as he'd taken pride in thinking, always guided by personal principle and self-control. The frosty atmosphere continued until they got to the Lakes, where they stopped for the night.

While Flori settled Owain in the Land Rover, he pitched his tent but half an hour later, it seemed she could bear the atmosphere no longer and as he was getting into his tent for the night, she'd called to him. He turned round. She was standing by the Land Rover. She'd apologised and said it was because she was upset knowing he was in another relationship. He hadn't responded. He'd walked away back to the tent, still angry, as much with himself as with her. But he couldn't sustain his anger for long and by the time they arrived in Tayvallich they were talking to each other as if they were still together and there'd been no separation.

It was dark and a light rain was falling when they'd arrived in Tayvallich. The drive from London had taken two days but there'd been no crises along the way. On the motorway they'd seen police patrol cars, but they hadn't been stopped and neither had they broken down.

The final part of their journey to Lagg, the small hamlet on Jura, was to be reached by sea and for this, he'd arranged to borrow a boat from his friend Angus, a fellow marine biologist. It was moored along the shores of Lock Sween and

Flori had asked whether his friend was curious why he was travelling by boat at that time of night. He'd told her he'd have assumed he wanted to catch the night tide but he could tell she was anxious because she'd said, 'I hope you know the way to Jura because there's a whirlpool at the end of the island and it's dangerous.'

He'd wondered then how she knew about the whirlpool but he made no comment, other than, 'Aye, I know about the Corrievrechan Whirlpool. I've passed through it many times, on my own and with Angus. Dinna worry, Flori. I know these waters well.'

They'd bumped along for half a mile, the Land Rover's headlights lighting up the deserted loch side before coming to a halt by a short jetty. The boat was red, powerful-looking, with a large wheelhouse and along the side of the hull was written, 'University of Glasgow Marine Biology Department.'

'Flori. This it. Let's go,' he'd said and jumped out and using the Land Rover's headlights began transferring their luggage into the boat. It didn't take long but Owain had cried when he was woken up to be transferred into the boat and Flori, he remembered, had been concerned the noise and lights would attract attention. But it was deserted. There with no nearby vehicles, houses, or pubs. They were surrounded with the silence of the darkness.

With their belongings packed in the boat, he'd helped Flori down into the boat, then he'd turned off the lights and the engine of the Land Rover, locked the door, jumped back into the boat and turned the ignition key.

Within the hour, they were away. The engine sprang into life immediately, the water making a gurgling noise as it hit the propeller and they'd cruised slowly down the dark loch towards the open sea making their way to Lagg. It was on the western side of the island and where Rose had arranged for Flori to stay.

The lights at the front of the boat lit up the black water, and as they got nearer to the open sea, the wind picked up, causing an increasing wave swell, and the boat to pitch. There was an element of risk crossing the Sound at night because of the combination of poor night time visibility, and the half-submerged skerries dotted through the loch's waters, but he'd been confident he knew the obstacles, submerged or otherwise. By the time they left the weather had improved and the clouds which had drifted across and partially concealed the full moon cleared.

It had been a perfect night for their journey and he'd been in his element. Once he'd turned round to speak to Flori. She was leaning over the side of the boat trailing her hand in the stream of white water, watching the white bubbling wake left by her fingers. He'd asked if she was alright and she'd looked up at him and said, her eyes shining, 'It's beautiful. It's heaven. I want this moment to last forever.'

He'd warned her not to lean out too far then, increasing the boat's speed to its maximum, he'd opened up its throttle until the noise of the engine reached a crescendo, and the bow of the boat lifted out of the water. It didn't take long to cross the Sound and for the Paps, the three central mountains of Jura to come into sight and as they drew closer to the island, he'd slowed the boat down to cruising speed until the noise of the engine quietened. The landing stage could be seen straight ahead and he brought the boat to rest alongside before stepping out and throwing a rope round a bollard. He'd glanced at Flori. She was looking apprehensive.

'Flori, we've made it. Welcome to Jura.'

She hadn't replied. She was staring straight ahead with an expression on her face he couldn't quite make out.

He offered to walk with her to the croft, his torch lighting up the narrow track which led from the jetty to the small hamlet of four or five houses. All was in darkness. The wild vegetation growing outside each door showing that there were no permanent residents. Rose had told Flori to look for a croft with a green door but as there was only one with a green door, she soon found it. She peered through the windows, before she turned her attention to finding the key which had been hidden by the owners of the croft under a pot of lavender. He'd walked back to the boat to begin unpacking.

Before he carried some of the boxes into the croft, he'd stood looking around. The air was fresh and the night still. He could see very little but he sensed the solitude and lonely atmosphere of the hamlet. He wondered then how Flori would cope with this solitude and he'd asked her this. Initially, she'd seemed pleased and said it was what she'd been looking for, this hadn't lasted.

Even in the short time he was there, he'd noticed there were moments when she became withdrawn. He'd looked at her, keenly aware that after he'd left, she'd be alone with Owain with only her thoughts to keep her company. It seemed as if she was in a dream. He'd asked her to check the rooms and to tell him where she wanted him to put her things, but she hadn't answered. She'd carried Owain up the stairs, settled him in his buggy for the rest of the night and then she'd come down to the kitchen and she'd sat at the table. She'd stayed there as he unloaded boxes, not speaking but holding a note in her hand. She'd found it lying on the table and she'd looked puzzled.

When she'd opened the fridge, her mood had changed to one of anger. There was a plate of fresh skinned rabbit and fish and this had disgusted her. He'd laughed and although he'd told her it was intended as a welcome from the croft's owners, she'd responded as if insulted. His further comment that the islanders were probably all carnivores seemed to upset her further.

He'd continued unloading the boat and when he returned with the last box, he found her still sitting in the kitchen staring at a vase of flowers in the middle of the table. He'd asked her what was going on and she'd said their bright colours were like jewels in the centre of a drab room, but they looked a long way away from her. She told him she felt strange. She'd wondered who'd put them there and when he said it must be the owners, she seemed perplexed and not to understand. He stood watching her. She seemed disconnected, as if she wasn't quite there, and was sleepwalking or drugged.

He'd seen her occasionally like this before during their summer together and he'd never understood what triggered it off and, watching her now, he became more concerned about her. It even passed through his mind to question whether it was wise for him to leave her, but he'd had to go. He had planned to return the same night, but he'd stayed because she was so clearly upset and panicky at the thought of his leaving.

It was as he was about to go that she'd become distressed and he'd tried to remind her, 'You know, you do know, I have to go Flori, that's the agreement we had?'

She'd bit her lip and looked down at the floor. She had the appearance of a distressed child and this had made him feel mean and insensitive. Mean for laughing at her disgust with the fish and rabbit, and mean because he was going. He'd gone over to her, put his arms round her, held her close, tried comforting her.

He'd tried reassuring her by reminding her Rose would be visiting soon. 'It's going to be alright. I know it is. And Rose will be here soon.'

'But she won't be with me long. She can't stay. She'll leave me, she'll have to go back to Oxford.'

She sounded so sad, he felt moved. It had reminded him of their early days, when they'd been together, and of how angry she'd become before he left to go away on an environmental campaign. But now, she wasn't angry, she was close to tears. He'd thought grimly her anger was easier to cope with, because now her pain seemed to come from somewhere deep, as if she'd regressed to being an abandoned child and she didn't have the resources to cope. He didn't know how to help her. He didn't have the right words to reach her.

But she knew how to reach him, how to get through to him and whether she was aware of this or not, in the end he'd stayed the night. She'd said, almost as if talking to herself,

'Remember Solva? Our first night. You stayed with me that night, until dawn. I was frightened, of the sea, of the storm. It's the same now. I'm frightened and I want you to stay with me again. Only tonight. Will you, Matt?'

Her words had reminded him of the song, 'I need you tonight', the one she'd sung on the way here. He'd hesitated and in that moment he was lost. The promises he'd made to himself to go immediately after he'd unpacked were forgotten. He wasn't going. Not that night. He couldn't leave; he didn't want to, it was impossible. He'd glanced at her. She must have known by the look on his face he would stay. She'd put her arms round his neck and drew him close. He'd held her.

He'd thought that after London, he wouldn't sleep with her again, but he hadn't kept his resolve. Driving with her to Scotland had been an error, a mistake, one of the first order, the time spent together had brought them closer. Their attraction for each other was too great, and their relationship, their need for each other, even after all this time, bound them together. He'd been in turmoil, aware he was behaving like a bastard. Being disloyal to Amami and cruelly irresolute with Flori. His conversation with Flori on the way here had shown how weak he could be.

Yet again, he'd thought, he had to keep away from her, whatever she asked of him, and whatever was going on for her. It was over. It had to be. His priority must be to Amami and their daughter, but this would be the very last time. He stayed with her that night because that's what she wanted and he'd left soon after dawn hoping, he thought that this would mark, the end of their relationship.

They'd woken early the next day. Owain had slept right through, and he was still asleep as Flori pulled back the bedroom curtains to catch the morning sun. He lay in bed watching her as she stood at the window. She'd turned to him and asked whether he wanted to watch the early morning sea mist rise and clear slowly from the Sound with the rise of the temperature. He could hear the distant sound of a foghorn.

It was beautiful. The sound mysterious. He'd got up, put his arms round her and, holding her close, had said, 'I have to go now, Flori.'

She seemed to accept his going, because she said, 'I know, but have breakfast.'

They'd dressed, sat silently opposite each other drinking coffee in the tiny kitchen. He hadn't been able to take his eyes off her and had asked if she'd come back to bed with him but she refused. She said it would be harder to say goodbye. They'd walked silently side by side to the boat tethered to the jetty. There was no wind and the water was like a mirror. No one was around. No cars, no tractors on the roads, no boats on the water. It was perfect for the crossing but as he was about to go and he'd stepped into the boat, she'd caught hold of his jacket and pulled him back. He'd turned round.

She'd said, 'Is this the end?' She hadn't waited for him to answer and had added, 'When are we going to meet again?'

'It's impossible,' he'd said. 'You know that.' He had meant to be decisive but instead he'd sounded brutal. She'd turned away and ran, heading for the croft. He'd been taken by surprise but knew from before how she'd always felt humiliated by her distress and how much she'd hated him to see her vulnerability.

He'd called out. 'Wait, Flori,' but she hadn't stopped even when he'd shouted loudly. 'Don't run.'

He'd had to chase after her. She hadn't been running to the croft, but away, up the track, and into the hills. When he'd caught up, he'd held her. He held her by her shoulders and looked at her, face on. She'd avoided his intense gaze, pulling away. She was crying. He'd been moved by her distress, but still he had to leave and he'd searched for what he might give her, something solid that she could hold onto, something that would give her strength and would remind her of his love. He'd put his hand in the pocket of his jacket and felt the familiar small white pebble, washed round and smooth by the ceaseless ebbing and flowing of the sea. He carried it everywhere. It was a kind of talisman and a reminder of when they'd first met in Wales.

He'd looked into her eyes and said, 'Flori, this is from Solva. I picked it up the day we met, when we went to the harbour. Do you remember? We played about among the boats? Keep strong and keep it safe. Keep it for me. Understand, I still love you, Flori, and always will and I'm truly sorry for what's happened.'

She'd taken it and, turning it over in her hands, she'd smiled at him.

'I know this isn't the end. We will see each other. Whatever happens.'

He kissed her again, and said, 'Until then. Whenever and wherever it is.'

He'd stepped into the boat, started the engine, pushed the boat away from the jetty and then, turning the boat around, he'd left. He'd opened up the throttle to maximum, and headed for the mainland. He'd looked back only once; she was still there, waiting, watching for him and the boat to disappear into the mist.

He dragged his mind back to the present. Solva would always hold the bittersweet memories of their first meeting but now, despite their separation, here he was still thinking of her. It had been this exact same spot when four months ago he'd picked up his mobile to ring her. Contacting her had been unplanned, spontaneous, all he'd wanted to do was to touch base. That's what he'd thought but how naive he'd been, if not disingenuous. He'd been drawn into her life and trying to help her had only complicated his life further. He should have stood up to her, insisted the baby was handed back, but it was too late now.

She was on the run and the end was imminent. She might even have been picked up already. He sat on the wall for hours, watching the tide flow back and forth over the sands, his mind on Flori, hoping she'd survive the police chase. An image of her came into his mind. It was when he'd first met her. He'd loved her that first summer, but now? He wasn't sure of his feelings. He'd thought he'd fallen out of love but having seen her recently and made love with her, he knew he was still bound to her. It was as if they couldn't live together but neither could they live apart.

Their attraction for each other was powerful, but was it merely sexual and nothing more? There was no definite answer. He experienced an intense pain. Not physical but emotional. He must put the relationship behind him and accept it would never work, concentrate on the present, stay with Amami and his daughter. Whatever was happening now was Flori's problem. He could do nothing.

He slowly walked back to the Land Rover and drove home. Amami had been cooking while she waited for him. She was irritable, told him she'd wanted him to look after the baby while she went to the labs. There were some research results she said she had to check but he hardly listened. She drove off. She'd left him a list of things to do. She was like that, methodical, predictable, you knew where you were with her. After she'd left, a profound feeling of boredom came over him.

He fed Nami her supper and as he held her in his arms, she'd smiled up at him. Her innocence touched him. A wave of sadness passed through him. Somehow he knew then his relationship with Amami wouldn't last. He held her closer, as if wanting to make up to her the inevitable breakdown he knew would come. He held her until she fell asleep and then, settling her carefully in her cot, covered her with her cot blanket. It was one she liked, the one with the yellow rabbits.

He didn't feel like eating. He sat down and aimlessly put on the television. It was the news. He watched. At first impassively. The inevitable had happened. The top story was Flori. She'd been caught on Jura. She'd been brought from Scotland to London. There were shots of the press surging round the car, trying to get a photo of her. The crowd stood by silently until there was a shout. 'Baby snatching bitch.' Then it started, the chant. 'Baby snatching bitch' over and over. As Flori left the car, she tried to keep her head down but there were glimpses of her face. She was terrified. She looked like a hunted animal. A police woman threw a blanket over her face and led her stumbling in to the police station.

He switched the television off. Sick at heart, he went straight to bed. He heard Amami return. She was late and he pretended to be asleep, but he didn't sleep that night or the following nights.

For days he was in a state of shock, avoiding people, watching television or reading the papers. He walked alone, long walks following remote parts of the coast path. For weeks he kept himself to himself.

Amami noticed. She spoke to him, wanting to know what was wrong. He said he was worried about a project and she'd come to him, tried to show him affection but he wasn't interested. He pushed her away. One evening she confronted him. She said, 'I don't believe it's a project, because you'd have mentioned it, if it was. It's something different. You've changed. You've lost interest in me and the baby.'

He hadn't answered, had turned away.

'I'm not a fool. It's a woman, isn't it?'

He'd got up and walked into the kitchen.

She followed him, spoken coldly. 'Don't walk away from me. It's Flori.'

He'd looked directly at her then. 'It's better I say nothing.'

She'd said no more, but her manner became distant. Only their baby kept them together. Neither referred to the change in their relationship. It was easier to pretend everything between them was as before.

15

Rose had been dreading the interview with the psychiatrist. She sat facing him across a large table, watching his every move. He was tall, tanned, slightly scruffy but seemed friendly enough. She could tell by the faint smell of nicotine which hung around him that he was a smoker. He opened his briefcase, took out an A4 pad of paper, placed it in front of him, took out his biro, and pressing it on the table, snapped it open and shut. He looked past her, his eyes fixed on the wall, then stood up, walked to the window and stared out before returning to his seat.

He sat looking thoughtfully at her before he spoke. She noticed immediately his slight Scottish accent and his habit of saying 'you know', but he seemed kindly enough. 'Rose, you know why I'm here and who I am. I explained at our first meeting that I have to present the court with a report, an assessment on you. We need to help the court understand what drove you to become involved with the abduction of the baby.'

Rose didn't reply. She was looking at his eyes, wondering what was going on inside his head and whether he was thinking something different from what he was actually saying.

'It concerns me, you know, how a successful young woman such as yourself, studying anthropology, and from a privileged background could become involved with this crime.' He paused. 'You do understand this is a crime?'

'Of course I do, I'm not stupid.'

'So why?'

Rose shrugged her shoulders. 'That's for you to work out.'

'I can only do that with your help.'

Rose bit her nails and studied him carefully. She wasn't quite sure what to make of him so she said nothing.

He paused. 'You may be wondering if you can trust me. Let me say right now, I'm trying to help you. I'm not against you.' He stood up, wandered over to the window again, stood against the light so he was silhouetted, then turned round so he was facing her and crossed his arms. 'I recognise it's difficult for you to talk, but I have plenty of time, you know, and I'll stay as long as it takes.'

He began pacing round the room, stopped and, looking directly at her, said, 'Tell me about Flori. She's your best friend, isn't she?'

'Is? No, was.'

'Because?'

'Our friendship is over. How can it continue? I've let her down, she'll hate me.'

'Why should she hate you?'

'Because.'

He sat down, leant over the desk towards her. 'Yes?'

'Because I made her tell me about her past. She'd never told anyone and I forced her. I had to know, and once I knew, I had to do something. It was impossible.'

'Impossible for you to remain friends?'

'No, I wasn't thinking that, not at the time. Impossible for her to continue looking after Owain.'

'The baby?'

'Yes, Owain, that's what she called him.'

'Can you tell me more?'

Rose was silent, looking everywhere except at the psychiatrist's face.

He sighed. 'I know it's difficult. Maybe you're frightened of her, what she might do to you.'

'No, she's not like that. It was more what she might have done to the baby.'

'You were frightened she might harm him.'

'Yes, once she'd told me what happened, after, I thought she might be like her mother. She was behaving in a way I'd never seen before, it was frightening.'

He took out his pen, wrote something down, looked at her and said, 'Some instances.'

'What about?'

'Why it was frightening.'

'She took a knife to me, told me to get out, but the thing was, the thing was, I realised, she thought I was going to steal Owain and harm him and she was confusing me with her mother.'

'And she wanted to stop you.'

'Yes.'

'And what did she tell you about her mother?'

Rose was silent, looked down at her hands. 'I can't say.'

'You must. Can't you remember?'

'I can remember alright.'

'Then say, tell me, tell me everything, every nuance, every feeling, every pause. I want to know, Rose. I want to know what she told you. It's important we know the details because then we can understand.' Rose put her arms on the desk, slumped down over them, hiding her face and was silent. 'You know you're in serious trouble. The more you tell me the better...What was going on?'

Rose sat up, looked at him straight, then averted her eyes.

'You want to help her, don't you? Or perhaps you'd like to punish her?'

'For what?'

'For getting you into this mess. You have no record of previous.'

'Don't say that, I don't want to punish her. It was hellish for her.'

236

'So. Help her and yourself.'

Rose looked at him quickly before looking away again. 'Have you ever heard of Flori Rees?'

'I'm sorry. I'm not sure of the relevance. That's Flori's surname, I believe.'

'Yes, and if you look that name up, you'll find out.'

'I need to know about her from your point of view and, Rose, prevarication won't help you. But as I say I'm prepared to take as long as it takes. I do want to help you and I have endless patience.' He stood up. 'You need a break. I'll return in ten minutes.'

'You're not leaving me, are you?'

'No, but I want you to think about what you've become involved in and your friendship with Flori, because that way you can help her as well as yourself. As you know, you're in serious trouble, but I'm repeating myself. Think about it. I'll be back shortly.'

He returned ten minutes later. He sat down and looking directly at her across the table and said, 'Well, what about it, do you want to help?'

Rose stared at him before she spoke. Then she said, 'I don't know where to begin. I really don't. If I had a choice, I'd say nothing.'

He shrugged his shoulders. 'I can understand that. But it's up to you. It's tough, but try. Start wherever you like. It doesn't matter. Whatever comes to your mind. Say whatever you're thinking.'

There was a long pause, then she said, 'Okay. You wanted to know how and why we got together as friends. I'll start with that, with my friendship with Flori. Because I've thought a lot about it, you know, about what having a friend is about and what brings people together. Before I met her, I'd thought, maybe assumed, that friends are good for you, but there can be a dark side to a friendship and, knowing that, frightens me. People may not be who they seem to be. They may have a history...the thing is, when I first met her, she fascinated me, she was so different. I wanted to be her friend straightaway. It wasn't one-sided. It was both of us. Now thinking about it, I sound like a child and it seems ridiculous but it didn't then. Sometimes I look at a photo I have of us together to try and make sense of what's happened. I have one here. Shall I show you?'

She opened her bag, took out her mobile, searched for the picture and passed it over to him. 'This one was taken outside the London Eye. Before it all happened.'

He glanced at the photo, handed it back to her. 'You both look happy.'

'We were. I love this picture. It reminds me of the good times. It's my favourite. It's a close-up of her face and she's looking straight at the camera. I like the way she smiles, don't you?

'I look at it often. I trace my fingers over her face, over her features, to try and get to know her. I want to bring her back, as we were, and as I thought of her then, but I can't do that now. It's too late, too much has changed...when we were on Jura, after she'd told me what had happened, I noticed something about her. It was her eyes. Her eyes had always got to me, they were watchful, green, like a cat's, and when she looked at me, I'd wonder what she was thinking. She'd look innocent, but in a moment that could change. It was as if she knew something the rest of us didn't, which actually, she did. She knew how things can go badly wrong, that people aren't what they seem and she'd lived through something I'd never have imagined or want to imagine. But, even so...she has a sweet, expressive face, don't you think?'

The psychiatrist said, 'I think you're still in a state of shock and whether she has a sweet face or not is neither here nor there. My concern is for you. She has a hold on you. Why, I don't know, but you're infatuated with her.'

Rose glanced at him and didn't speak straightaway, then she turned her chair sideways on so she didn't have to look at him. She said, 'It's true, what you say, but not anymore. Our friendship is over. It has to be. Nothing can ever be the same. We'll probably never meet again. I miss her and I think a lot about the times we spent together.'

There was a long silence before she continued. 'Once we went to Tate Modern and for some reason that day sticks in my mind, maybe because we'd been so happy…we arranged to meet at the entrance to the turbine hall. I'd heard about an installation and it appealed to me and I thought it would Flori, too. The artist came from Scandinavia, but maybe I've got that wrong, maybe it was Germany, but it doesn't matter anyway where he came from…The turbine hall had been taken over by twisting metal funnels. The artist called them sculptures. They looked bizarre, like a futuristic nightmare and they came from the ceiling to the floor, so they were like gigantic slides, only they were covered in, so more like tubes. You could go on them. Slide down from the ceiling to the floor. There were long queues for them and we wanted to slide in them, too. I think we wanted to feel carefree, like children are supposed to be. We only tried it once. That was enough.'

She paused, looking down at her hands as she remembered the occasion. 'I was first down the slide. It was terrifying… as soon as you were in the tube, you started sliding, and you couldn't stop, you were sliding so fast you were out of control. It was like hurtling through space, and the further you fell, the faster you went, there was no escape, you had to go through with it, right until you got to the end, then wham. It stopped. You hit the floor. You'd been thrown out onto a mat…I think of this as a kind of a premonition of what happened. Do you know what I mean?'

She stopped and looked at the psychiatrist.

'As a metaphor for what you've been through?'

'Yes. When it stopped and I hit the floor, I thought I was going to die. There were people standing around watching and it was a bit like, have you ever thought, you know, imagined, what it might be like being born, being inside the birth canal, and there's no one to help you, you don't know what's going to happen, you don't have words, you can't see. Well, that's how it was. The experience passes, a second could be forever, because while it happens, there's no understanding of time. How could there be? Time is relative, isn't it? It's all relative. How terrifying to be born, and not know what's happening. We didn't want to go again. But I think it's strange. The artist was a man. I do remember that. How would he know about all that? You know, giving birth. Maybe he imagined he was a baby. But his name, I've forgotten, but it doesn't matter.'

She started biting her nails, looked at the psychiatrist. 'Shall I go on?'

He nodded, the expression on his face grave. She continued. 'It unsettled me so much, Flori suggested we go to the Tate bookshop and have a look at the books. I bought one about sculpture, modern sculpture. I've still got it somewhere. Then we went to a Turkish restaurant for lunch.'

She stopped, leant her head on one hand. 'I need to collect my thoughts...It's disturbing. We were like sisters, and maybe in another life we could have been, that's what I used to think, but we're not the same. I try to make sense of it. Why? Over and over, I ask why did it happen, why me, why did I get involved with her. But there's no answer, or none that makes sense. Sometimes I wonder if she thinks about me, because what we've done will last the rest of our lives so we're kind of tied together. We'll be remembered for what we did. The two girls who stole a baby.'

'Where did you first meet her?'

'Harrods. We both worked at Harrods but whereas I worked only in the university breaks, Flori was full time. She lived in a hall floor flat near Paddington Station and after we'd become friends, when I came home from Oxford, if I knew she was at home, I'd give her a ring and call in. It was a pretty flat, full of character, the type of flat I would have expected her to live in, lots of unusual bits and pieces from here, there and everywhere, and the walls and the furniture were painted in a subtle colour scheme. She liked pale sea-green and she liked flowers, fresh flowers, especially red carnations. She has style, no doubt about that. She told me carnations reminded her of someone she'd been in love with once. She'd buy them from the station, but she wouldn't get one bunch at a time, but four or five and she'd group them in a large glass vase. They looked stunning and the flat was full of their fragrance. One day I had a strange experience there. I'll tell you what happened. I was back from Oxford and on my way home I called in to see her unexpectedly. She'd run out of milk, and she asked me to wait while she went to get some from the corner shop. She said she'd be about ten minutes. While she was gone, I started looking round, not for anything in particular, but just to kill time. I looked at her books, at the pictures on the wall, I walked into her bedroom. I'd never been in her bedroom before.'

'What do you think you were looking for?'

'Well, nothing in particular but you need to know this. I didn't intend to be intrusive. I was just curious to see more of her flat because that would tell me more about her, so there must have already been something weird about her. There was a cane room divider stretched across one corner of the room. It looked as if it was hiding something, so I walked over to see what was behind, and what I saw didn't make sense. Baby clothes. Piles of them. Neatly stacked. Some new, still with labels on them, others worn. All washed, ironed, folded and there were others for an older child and they were hanging from a rail…

'It was really weird. I wondered if she'd had a baby, because that's what it looked like, but if she had, where was the baby? She'd never told me about anything like that, but I thought maybe she'd said something but I'd forgotten. It was strange. Creepy. I wondered if I was imagining it. You can tell so much from the atmosphere of a place, I've always thought that. So it felt like there was the ghost of a child in that flat and something bad had happened. I sat wondering whether to ask her but in the end I decided I wouldn't. There had to be a reason why she hadn't told me. Whatever it was or whatever had happened, I thought the best thing to do would be to keep my mouth shut. But I couldn't put it out of my mind.

'By the time Flori returned I was reading, or pretending to read, but she knew something was up. Sometimes we could read each other's minds. She asked me, straight out, whether I'd been in her bedroom and seen the baby clothes.'

'I said I had and I asked her what it was all about, because I couldn't lie to her, she'd know if I did. I noticed when she answered she was evasive and avoided my eyes. She said she had a cousin who lived in the States, and that she was on the breadline and pregnant, so she'd decided to collect baby clothes for her. She said she'd got them in the sales at Harrods or from charity shops.

That story was strange, too. She'd told me she didn't have any relatives, that she was an only child, and that even her mother had died, and she didn't know her father. So why hadn't she mentioned any of this before? But I didn't say anymore. When I think about it now, I realise how little I knew about her, like where she was born, where she was brought up, where she went to school. It suited her not to be known. She liked to hide. It was her personality, that's what I used to think, but there was more to it than that. She'd told me once she intended to live life to the full, and not be coerced by the rules of any establishment. She was so different from anyone I'd met before…'

She suddenly stood up, put her arms behind her back and stretched her out. 'Can I take a break? It's hard talking about this.'

'How long do you think you'll need?'

'Ten minutes…and I'd like a coffee, if possible.'

The psychiatrist stood up. 'Sure. You're doing well, Rose. I'll get someone to bring one in.'

He left the room, returning ten minutes later and sat

down opposite Rose. He looked at her, his attention intense. Rose continued, picking up where she'd left off.

'There's always been a strong bond between us, it's something to do with our feelings and understanding for each other and it's still there. I think when she met me, she thought my life had been easy compared to her own, and maybe she envied me for that. Well, it has been materially comfortable, but it hasn't made me any happier.'

'But what about yourself? How do you think of yourself?'

'I'm ordinary compared to Flori. I'm boring. I'm clever but faded. Everything I've done has been predictable and the right thing. Up until now. I went to the right schools, I had good teachers and it was easy to get into Oxford. I've been lucky but I've worked hard and it's drained the real me. I know the right answers, but not the right questions. Now I feel empty. I have nothing to look forward to and I'm not the family type so I'm not looking for marriage. It's too constraining. In that way, I'm like Flori. I like my freedom, I want to do what I like, go where I want to go.'

'So perhaps she provided you with some excitement, and did you ever wonder how she saw you? Did you ever ask her?'

'Yes. Flori said I was like one of those beautiful women the Pre-Raphaelites painted. That might sound like flattery, but she didn't mean it that way. She had a romantic view of the world, and she fitted everyone into her personal story. She said my name Rose suited me, because that's how she saw me. A pale, old-fashioned rose. When she said that, I said to her, the kind no one knows the name of but you see in the hedgerows of country lanes. She laughed and said you're a wild rose, struggling to grow and survive among the clematis, the honeysuckle and meadow sweet. I liked that image but later I thought actually I'm no threat to anybody, pretty, inoffensive and boring.' She paused. 'She seemed to understand me, value me and she made me feel good. But after she told me...look, I've said enough. I want to stop. Do I have to go on?'

The psychiatrist looked at her. 'I appreciate what you've

told me but I need to know more. I want to know about your time together on Jura, what you did and your conversations with Flori. You've mentioned it two or three times.'

'I've had enough. I'm tired but anyway, I'd hardly call it a conversation.'

He raised his eyebrows. 'What would you call it?'

'Confrontation, denouement, altercation, a run in. It was heavy. Look, I'm tired.'

'Perhaps we should leave it for another time.'

'I told you. Check out Flori Rees. It'll all be there.'

'As I've said, I want to hear it from you.' He stood up, put his pen away, replaced his notebook in his briefcase and leant across the table. 'Thank you, Rose. I know it's really difficult for you.'

He'd reached the door when she said, 'Will I see you again? Do you know enough to draw some conclusions, write your assessment?'

He turned and, half-smiling, said, 'I have enough to go on and to make a start. I'll talk to your barrister and take it from there.'

'Are you going to recommend prison?' Rose was looking anxious.

'Certainly not. It would be of no help. Both you and Flori have psychological issues…in her case, serious, and it's unfortunate that you came into contact with each other.'

'So what caused us to behave the way we did?'

'There was a mirroring between you, a symbiotic bond that ultimately turned out to be unhealthy, although it needn't have been that way. I'll explain my diagnosis to you when I've written the report.'

16

Central London, summer and it was hot in the way only cities can get hot. Flori walked towards the tube, beads of sweat on her forehead and arms. There was no wind and the air seemed to pulsate. It bounced off the shiny metal of cars pushing and shoving in lines up along Shaftesbury Avenue and danced in waves off the pavement. It slithered down the steps into the tube, melting the passengers who stuck clammily and reluctantly against one another.

She reached the entrance, took a swig of water from a bottle and paused briefly at the top of the steps to watch the tide of humanity surging towards her. The journey could only get worse. Travelling by tube in the heat of summer was like an assault course, but she had to go. She had an appointment. Across London twice a week, regularly, whatever the weather, she made the same journey. But once she was there she liked it, although she'd never admit it. Only a lone mother bumping her pushchair up the steps interrupted the ceaseless flow of travellers. Flori bent down to help her and noticed the occupant, a tiny newborn baby girl with an abundance of dark hair. Her mother had put a bright pink ribbon round her head; the colour clashed with the baby's red gingham dress. The baby was asleep and looked blissful, her eyes tight shut and her mouth pursed, totally oblivious to the noise and mayhem surrounding her and her mother.

Flori continued down the escalator into the tube. More people seemed to be coming up than going down and for a brief moment she felt as if she was swimming against a tide of human flotsam and jetsam. She wondered whether there was a scientific reason for this; that more people were walking in the opposite direction but decided this wasn't so much to do with an unknown law of physics, but more to do with herself. She'd always gone against life's flow. She smiled to herself as she remembered the occasion when she'd seen a thin, dishevelled man position himself at the top of the escalator. He must have seen the crowds as sheep, and as they'd passed round him he'd made loud baaing noises. No one had smiled, except her. She'd wanted to catch his eye and wink, but then realised he was serious and for him this was no joke. He hadn't looked at her. What he saw were sheep and in his head he was a farmer in a field.

She was heading for Highbury Corner, which meant changing at Euston. She did a quick mental check on the numbers of tourists. She could spot them a mile off. Their numbers made the difference between an acceptably crowded tube or totally mind-bending claustrophobic closeness, but she was determined to catch the first train, crowded or not. She didn't want to be late. She reached the platform, stood in an advantageous spot and waited. She didn't have to wait long. A rush of musty hot air from the filthy tunnels forced its way along the platform announcing the tube's imminent arrival. The tube squealed to a halt. The doors opened. The crowds pressed forward.

She walked to the end of the platform looking for a less-crowded carriage, noticed a tiny space in one of them and squeezed in. Someone had opened the windows in the end door of the tube to give some respite from the sticky heat, so a welcome draft of slightly cooler, but still foetid air, swept in and circled round the carriage. Flori waited for a seat to become vacant, then grabbed it and sat down to read the free paper until she reached Highbury Corner. She got off, crossed over the road to walk past Highbury Fields, then turned off, heading down the back streets towards Leigh Road. It was a familiar journey, one she'd taken twice a week for the past year.

She'd arrived. She looked at her watch. She had to be bang on time. She was a little early but she didn't want that, either. Hannah insisted she came twice a week and always at the right time. This was part of the work, she'd said. She still had another two minutes before she'd ring the bell. She moved away from the house and stood waiting down the street. She didn't like standing right outside the house. It made her nervous. Sometimes she'd noticed Hannah's previous client and she never knew whether to greet her, but it wasn't only that, she didn't want Hannah to know she was impatient to see her.

Today she knew what she would talk about. It was a special day, she'd always remember the date until the day she died. It was an anniversary, a horrible one, she had to admit but still an anniversary. It would be two years tomorrow since she'd taken the baby and so much had happened since then. She planned to talk about Rose, and Owain and her own baby, Nixie. She'd had a picture of Nixie on her mobile for ages but she hadn't trusted Hannah enough to show her.

When she'd first started with her she'd feared if she talked about Nixie that Hannah might contact the social workers and tell them she wasn't looking after her properly. But now she trusted her. Hannah had reassured her. She'd said that what went on in the sessions was confidential. If she felt the baby was at risk, she'd tell her first and they'd talk about what they should do.

She took another glance at her watch. It was time. She made her way back up the street, walked up the steps and rang the bell. Hannah was always there. She'd found her weird when she started. She couldn't make her out. How could anyone always be so reliable, predictable and calm? And she never said much except sit and listen to her, although she knew she was taking in what she said. She remembered the details, even weeks later. Everything about her was quiet – her dress, her voice, her room. Visiting her had become like a confessional, a sanctuary and eventually, after some months, she'd decided she was alright and she liked her.

Hannah opened the door, smiled and led the way to her room. Flori followed behind. That was something else; she liked her to begin talking with whatever was on her mind. Every session started like that, so that was predictable, too. Flori sat down. She looked around, checked whether anything had been added or removed from the room, then took out her mobile and found the picture of Nixie.

'Would you like to see a picture of my baby?'

'Of course,' she said, 'I'd love to.'

Flori handed across the picture of Nixie. Hannah looked carefully at the picture, smiled and then said to Flori, 'You're very alike, same colouring and she looks a happy little girl.'

'You can tell?'

'Yes, I'd say so. Who did you say you leave her with?'

'I leave her with Betty, her childminder, she's the one my social worker fixed up. She's not far from where I live.'

'Nixie, that's an unusual name.'

'It means water sprite and she does love the water. She's not afraid of it. I'm going to take her to Wales soon, to where I used to surf and where I first met Matt, he's the father, but Nixie was conceived later. On Jura, that's what I like to think. I've told you a bit about him.'

Hannah nodded.

'Today though,' Flori paused, 'today I thought I'd talk about Rose. It's two years tomorrow since I took Owain. Did you know that?'

'I didn't.' Hannah was looking closely at Flori.

'I've never said much about her to you. Maybe it's too painful. When we met we were both working in Harrods. It was by chance. We were in a coffee shop across the road and somehow we got talking and became friends. I used to think of her as a sister. I trusted her, so you can imagine how

I felt when I discovered she'd betrayed me.' Flori stopped and looked at Hannah who said nothing. 'You know what I'm talking about, do you?'

'I'm thinking that it was when she went to the police and that, for you, was a betrayal of your friendship.'

'Yes, that's right, but there were signs she'd let me down before she did that. It was when we were first on Jura, I became suspicious. We'd watched *Crime Watch*, and after that she became really angry and paranoid. She told me we'd be found out so we might as well give up. We rowed and I said she was saying that because she wanted the reward and was planning to go to the police. She denied it. But I was right after all, wasn't I, because she did go.'

'Might there be another way of looking at it?'

'Like what?'

'Such as she was concerned about you and wanted to help you and protect the baby.'

Flori was silent for a moment. 'Well, anyway whatever her motives were, it was a real shock and it was all brought up in court. She said I'd been strange and she had to force me to tell her about the, uh, you know, my childhood, the accident.'

She stopped, looked down, her fingers twisting round and round, a sure sign of her distress.

'When you say accident, you mean when your mother...?'

Flori cut across her. 'No. Don't say anymore. I'll talk about it, but not now. Another time. She thought it funny.'

'Who? Rose?'

'Yes, she started laughing, she was going on about how we gate crashed a party and ate the food. There was no one there, you see, so we helped ourselves. She was laughing, but for me that party was horrible and she'd forgotten what happened after that and why I took the baby. She did apologise. She asked if I remembered about the food. I said I didn't but really I did, I was testing her, just to see what she'd say and if she believed me. And she did.'

'I'm confused.'

'She believed me when I said I'd forgotten. That showed me she thought I was mad. But I hadn't forgotten. It was kind of crazy. We found food laid out for someone's birthday. We ate all the best bits, we took the cream off the cakes, we danced round the table, then we went back upstairs and met Phil and Dave and we went off separately with them. That was all before I took Owain.'

'Tell me more. How it all unfolded. You did say you wanted to talk about her.'

'Yes and no. Want and don't want. But I should. It bugs me. All of it. Thinking about her. It seems so long since the police picked me up on the beach in Jura. But I think about it almost every day. It's like it was yesterday and I miss Rose, even after everything she did. When I saw her in court, what she said, and yes, I know, it's true what you have said, that everyone was kind and they seemed to understand, but she let me down...I've been thinking more about that court hearing. The worst time was when I first saw her. We were outside the court and she walked right past me. She was with her lawyers, as if they needed to protect her. She didn't look at me. After everything we'd been through together. It was as if I no longer existed. When she was standing in the witness box, she told them I'd threatened Owain. She said she was frightened of me, that I'd harm him. But I can't remember that. I can't remember that. I didn't threaten him. It's not true. She said that if he'd died, it would weigh forever on her conscience. Never. I'd never have harmed him. But it was her word against mine.'

There was a long pause. Neither spoke as Flori struggled with her feelings.

'I know I'm angry but it was hard. Really hard to listen to her and to know for sure that what I'd suspected was right. She couldn't be trusted and when she spoke out against me, it was as if I'd been stabbed. That's how terrible it felt. That she, of all people, could say that about me. I couldn't bear it, and it was like, like how years ago when they told me what had happened to Tids. It made me rethink everything about our friendship. How we met, things we'd done together. The conversations. The places we'd been together...I searched for signs. Signs that she'd let me down, that she was unreliable, but she'd always been there for me, backed me up. There were no signs, so none of it made sense. She deliberately duped me.

'I started blaming myself as if, as if it was my stupidity and she'd been watching me all the time and she'd secretly been judging me and I hadn't noticed and it frightens me that I don't know who I can trust and that people aren't who they seem to be and they can say one thing but think another, you know.'

Flori came to a stop and looked down at her lap to avoid Hannah's eyes. 'I'm so angry. Sorry, everything's pouring out today but I had to tell you.'

'Flori, I can see how upset you are but you know we have talked about this and you've agreed there are other ways of looking at it. You said at the time you were hearing voices and that sometimes you got mixed up between Tids and Owain.'

'That doesn't mean anything. You're judging me, like the rest of them. People don't understand and it makes me angry. Look, she was my best friend, she had a half-sister she'd never met because her father had had an affair. I was the only one she told. Only I knew, that's how special I was. But it's all over now. Our friendship, I mean. You see. I did know about her but I was young and yes, I could see she wasn't right. It was when I went to school and I began meeting others. By then it was obvious there was something not right in her head. But I couldn't tell anyone. I wanted to be loyal. She only had me. She couldn't help how she was. She wasn't in her right mind.'

'You mean your mother?'

'Yes, not Rose, my mother. When I was on Jura with Tids. I loved him, did you know that? I miss him.'

'Do you mean Owain? You were on the island with Owain, not Tids.'

'Yes, you're right. A slip of the tongue, I did mean Owain.

I still get mixed up sometimes when I'm upset and I go back in time. I was surrounded with water and mountains then, like a womb, really. They couldn't reach me, not easily. But the voices...'

She stopped and looked suspiciously at Hannah. 'What are you thinking?'

'I'm thinking you've been through a lot and you're struggling to make sense of everything. It takes time, Flori.'

'Yes. The voices. Maybe it was just in my head. They weren't real but it felt like they were. One of the voices was my mother.'

There was a long silence. Neither spoke for five minutes.

Then Flori said, 'Did I tell you, I've got rid of that scrapbook, the one in my flat with the cuttings about the fire, and Tids' death? It upset me knowing it was there so I threw it away. Only a week ago, no point in keeping it.'

'That sounds a good thing to do.'

'Yes, the voices, I did hear voices. I admit it. So what? I wasn't well and don't say it again because you've said it already, that they were my voices from my mind and they weren't real...I know that already. I would have been alright. Except she was in my house. Under the same roof. It was so creepy. The atmosphere. Terrible. Terrible. But I'd never have harmed him. Never.'

Flori stood up. 'I need to go the loo. I won't be long.' She returned a few minutes later and said, 'I feel low at the moment, but this will pass. I just need to think that it'll go away because I've been like this before. I need to have faith... Tids, I loved him and you shouldn't have taken him. I'd have looked after you. Both of you.'

'Who are you talking to now, Flori?'

Flori looked momentarily confused. 'Who? Who do you think? My mother. It wasn't my fault. She did it. Not me. I wasn't even there. I was on Jura when it happened. But if I had been there, I'd have stopped it. Tids. That's short for Tiddler, my pet name for my baby brother. You know

252

that already. I told you once. You don't listen. You need to remember. You've forgotten. But my baby brother. I'll never forget him. My Tids.'

'What's going on for you? How are you feeling now?'

'How do I feel now? What do you think? Put yourself in my shoes, and don't ask fucking stupid questions. It doesn't help. I'm sorry. I didn't mean that. Sometimes I feel desperate, especially when you don't understand. It's just that it hurts. Hurts like crazy. Let me get my thinking straight.' There was another long silence. 'It's as if they think we planned it. Then Rose reneged on me. But it didn't happen that way.'

Hannah paused before she next spoke, 'Sometimes, Flori, after we've talked, you can see it another way, and you can see how difficult it might have been for Rose. You know, it does persecute you thinking that Rose betrayed you. It's not helpful at all.'

'I suppose so. Yes, and I suppose it could be seen in another way. I do know your view, you've told me before. You think that Rose was protecting me and the baby. But from what?'

'What do you think?'

'I'll tell you. She did renege, because she didn't tell me what she was going to do, and that's what I'm still struggling with. Maybe that'll change, with time. I need time. We all need time, don't we?

'I still get journalists contacting me and because of the date, I'm apprehensive the phone calls will start again today. Why is it so fascinating? They want to know about me, and her, and our friendship, but I refuse to tell them. I don't trust any of them. How should I know? That's what they don't seem to understand.'

'But you do know, Flori.'

'Yes, you're right. I suppose so. But when, when did it get out of hand?'

'It was a process, wasn't it? One thing led to another and once started, it was difficult to stop. You and Rose were both caught up in a kind of madness.'

'Yes, that makes sense. I'm wondering how Rose feels today. I guess she might still be upset. We're not supposed to see each other, a court Order, but I don't want to anyway. It's better that I never see her. We weren't good for each other. They did a deal. Don't know if I told you, the barristers and the psychiatrists, they said we suffered with 'Folie à Duex'. That means, if you don't know, we shared the same psychosis, as if we were one and that's why she supported me and why I knew she would and why she thought I was great. One person, two bodies. Strange, isn't it? Now we can't see each other, but I don't care anyway.'

'Is that right, you say you don't care, but I think maybe you do, Flori.'

Flori looked away, her eyes full of tears. 'Actually you're right. I feel like crying. They say time heals but how long does it take? It feels as if it's forever. I do think about her. Quite a bit actually. Well, you can't go through all those times, experience so much together and just delete your memory, like on a computer. It must have been tough for her too, and I hope she doesn't blame me for all that's happened. I had asked her for help, so I pulled her into it. It didn't cross my mind, she'd refuse…I suppose. When I think of her now my principal feeling is of regret.'

'Flori, it's difficult, but we must stop now. I'll see you on Thursday and we can pick up from where we finished.'

'So soon. I feel as if I've only just started. Okay.' Flori stood up. 'I meant to ask you earlier, my childminder can't do the next session. Do you mind if I bring Nixie with me? I don't want to miss my session. She's very good, she won't be a problem.'

Hannah paused. 'I don't usually.' She looked doubtful.

'You've never seen her and I'd like you to. If she's noisy, we can leave.'

Hannah smiled, 'Yes, bring her with you, Flori.'

17

Flori pulled the buggy up the steps, wheeled the baby into Hannah's room and placed the buggy so Nixie faced her. She'd dressed her in a blue striped dress with a little white sunhat that tied under her chin. It didn't quite cover her curls. She was sleeping peacefully.

'Do you mind if I leave her just here? She's flat out to the world at the moment, and as it's a strange place it's better she sees me as soon as she wakes.'

'That's fine.' Hannah walked across the room, bent down to look at her. 'Her hair is like yours, it's very dark, almost black. She's a pretty little girl.'

'Yes, funny she's a girl. I always thought I'd have a little boy so I was surprised when she popped out. Well, she didn't actually pop out but you know what I mean. I'm so lucky to have her.'

Hannah stood up and looked at Flori. 'And how much longer will Social Services be involved?'

'I'm hoping not too long. There'll be a Case Conference in two months but everyone is pleased with me.' She sat down and glanced down at Nixie. 'I haven't forgotten about Owain. Owain was the name I gave him. They called him Bertie, but he was Owain to me and he'll always be Owain. It's a Welsh name and I gave him that name because he reminded me of Matt in Wales.'

She paused, looked across the room at Hannah, smiled

255

and said, 'I've got something important to tell you in a minute, but I'll finish what I was saying. When I think back to then, you know, Jura, I really loved Owain. He was lovely, totally innocent, like my Tids had been. When we went for walks, he'd get all excited and laugh and that made me laugh. I'd talk and sing to him, read him poetry, and show him things he'd like, like the sun shining through the leaves, and I'd say, listen, listen to the sound of the wind.'

She leant forward and began to gently rock Nixie's buggy, smiling down at her. 'She's asleep and I don't want to wake her. I'm planning to take her to Wales. I used to surf in a place called Newgale and there's a little coastal village nearby called Solva and that's where I met Matt. I want her to keep in touch with her Celtic side. That's why she's got black hair, although his hair was reddish. He came from Scotland; black or red hair, that's the Celtic influence. When she wakes, you'll see she has vivid blue eyes. Like Matt.'

She continued gently rocking the buggy then she said, 'You know, the last time I was here we were talking about Rose. When I got home I Googled her. She's not on Facebook because I check every now and again but this time something came up. An article in some obscure academic anthropological journal, or it was obscure to me, anyway. It said it was based on her research for a doctorate. When I saw what she'd written…unbelievable. Maternal psychosis among the Inuit. She must have done well in her finals. Do you think what I told her, you know about my mum would have helped her with that?

'I skimmed it. But what she'd written reminded me of her…she must have suffered with it. That was referred to in court. Post natal depression. She had it badly. Now there's a lot more known about it. Perhaps, perhaps sometimes good things come out of the bad. That's what I like to think anyway.'

Flori paused and then looking directly at Hannah, she said, 'But that reminds me, there's something even more important I want to tell you and it only happened yesterday.

It makes me happy, very happy; so happy I could sing and I want you to be the first to know, because I trust you and because you've stuck with me and I know I can be difficult.

'After I've been here and get home, I've taken to going to a favourite café for a coffee. It's an Italian one quite close to where I live. No one speaks to me or knows about my past, or if they do they keep their mouth shut, so it feels safe.'

So, two days ago. I had Nixie with me, I'd collected her from the child minder, and then I'd picked up a letter from my flat. I wanted to open it on my own as I drank my coffee. Sorry, it's something I hadn't told you about, the reason being it might never have happened. The letter was from the London Metropolitan University. It had the name on the front and I knew it was from them because I'd applied to do a course there. So I had this letter with me and I walked to the café, said hello to the proprietor, picked up my cappuccino and sat in my usual place in the corner. It was almost empty, so I had the place to myself. I sat with my back to the door and took out the brown envelope.

'I tore open the envelope and read it quickly. It was from Professor Elliot, the Head of the Department of Psychology and it said how impressed they'd been with my interview, and...he was delighted to offer me a place on the undergraduate forensic psychology course and that I could start the next academic year. He said there might be difficulties in funding, but to get in touch with his secretary who'd help with information regarding bursaries and secondments.

'That was so wonderful. You can imagine. Truly wonderful. I felt like one big smile. I felt like the cat that'd got the cream. I felt like the cow that'd jumped over the moon. I felt like the owl and the pussy cat that went to sea in a beautiful pea green boat.

'I sat there feeling so happy, but you know what, that was when I missed Rose and I wished she'd been there. I know that sounds weird but she'd have been pleased for me. I kept thinking, about me, me, me being a student, and how hard I was going to work, and how I was going to help women, women who'd got in trouble with the law. I want to understand them and I want to help them because I'm one of them and I've been helped.'

Hannah smiled broadly. 'That's wonderful news, Flori. Congratulations. I'm so pleased for you.'

'But wait, there's more. Something, something, that's made me even happier. Nixie was with me and I was still holding the letter in my hand and daydreaming, so I half-notice the noise of the street and the traffic had flooded inside the café, and out of the corner of my eye I see a man walk into the coffee shop. I didn't look up because I wanted to stay inside my own big smiley world for as long as possible.

'He walks over to the counter and places his order. Then he crosses over and walks towards me but I didn't look up because I was re-reading the letter and in my own world. He comes over and sits down at the same table as me but in the chair opposite. I get annoyed then, he's annoying me. There was plenty of room and lots of empty tables in that café where he could sit, without him invading my space. That's when I look up. I was going to say, "Don't crowd me." But then I see who he is. For a split second, I'm frightened. I wonder if I'm losing my mind again, because he looks so like Matt, and I haven't seen him since he left me on Jura over two years ago.

'I stare at him. He's looking at me with a quizzical look. But then he smiles. His smile. Mmm. Yes. Well, it was like when we first met along the St David's Road and I first fell in love with him. He says my name, "Flori" and then he comes round the table to my side, pulls me out of my chair, puts his arms round me and pulls me so close. He's the same. Smells the same, looks the same, his eyes are the same. I can feel his arms round me. He's stroking my hair. It takes me back. I know then. He's real. Sorry Hannah, I'm about to cry.'

'Well, anyway, seeing him that morning brought back the memory of the first day I was left alone with Owain on Jura. It came right back to me, so vivid, so unbelievably vivid, it was as if it was happening all over again. I was standing on the foreshore and watching him disappear into the sea mist.

'I thought he'd gone forever from my life but no, there he was, sitting right by me in that steamy London cafe. He took my hand and held it and smiled again. It felt like it used to be, like when we'd first met in Wales.

'But then I thought, that maybe he hadn't heard about the court hearing and that I should say something about that. "Matt," I said, "You know what happened, because of what I did with Rose, I had to go to court and I can't see her anymore and I have to see a therapist under a Community Treatment Order. I'm bad news."'

'He looked upset. He didn't answer straight away but then he says, "I know, Flori about that, but I've known for a long time. That summer after we met and we were together…your moods, your sudden anger and the little things you inadvertently mentioned, I guessed something terrible had happened. I decided to keep my mouth shut because you'd tell me when you wanted me to know. I loved you but then circumstances intervened. I blame myself. I shouldn't have left you.

'Since leaving you on Jura I've thought so much about you. I think about when we first met, the storm, our first night together, the good times we had. But what's happened, has happened, and it doesn't change my feelings for you. I'm here and I won't leave you, now or ever."

'My heart has been broken too many times. I couldn't stop myself, I had to know. I said, "But what about Amami and Nami?" He looked away, then he said, "After we'd met again in London, Amami put two and two together. I'd told her about you when I'd first met her so she knew how strong my feelings were for you. After we'd met again in London, she and I had a terrible row and we drifted apart. We both knew it wasn't going to work. She's gone back to Japan with Nami. They've been gone for a year now."

'"But what about your baby? Don't you miss her?"

'"I do, I skype her and her mother and we've agreed that

when's she's old enough, she'll come and stay with me."

'I didn't know what to say to that and I was thinking more about it, when he continued, "Then I searched for you. I knew you'd gone into hiding to get away from the press and it would take a while to find you, but here I am."

'I looked at him. "How did you find me?"

He said, "Don't forget, Flori, I have contacts and I know my way round. I've been undercover off and on for years." He smiled.

'It was then Nixie woke up. She was making a noise and trying to get out of her buggy. I looked at her. I said, "Wait a minute, baby," and then I said, "What about Nixie? Have you thought about her?"

'"Nixie, who's she?"

'"My baby, here, surely you noticed I have a baby with me?"

'He looked taken aback. He said, "I did, but I didn't think she'd be yours. I'd assumed she was a neighbour's."

'"No, she's mine,' I said. 'She's my daughter."

'He still didn't get it. "And the father? Is he the Greek Aussie you told me about, the one you slept with at the party before you took Owain?"

'"No, he's not the father."

'"How do you know?"

'"Because I know who the father is and it's not him."

'I looked down at Nixie. She was looking at me with her big eyes waiting for me to pick her up. I picked her out of the buggy, held her close and then, looking into Matt's eyes, I pass Nixie across to him. He looked surprised but he took hold of her. He held her slightly away from him and made funny faces at her. She was puzzled but she didn't laugh or cry, she was gazing at him, wondering who he was, probably and he was looking closely at her.

'Then I say, "Nixie, meet your daddy. Matt meet Nixie, your daughter."

'I don't know what reaction I was expecting but Matt

looked really, really upset. Upset and confused. He says, "What? How come? Are you sure I'm her father? But when?"

"'Of course I'm sure, it was the last night we spent together on Jura and the last time we made love. I'd asked you to stay with me. I was upset, frightened that you were going.'"

"'But why, Flori, why didn't you ever tell me that you were pregnant?'"

"'Because I said I wouldn't. I said I'd never contact you. If they'd found out, they'd ask questions and it would all come out and they'd be after you too. I'd promised I wouldn't. If I'd broken it, we'd both have been in court then. After I was charged, I told them I was pregnant but I didn't know who or where the father was. I said it was someone at the party and I was drunk. I told them I didn't know where he was and that I didn't want him traced.'"

"'So you've kept all this a secret?'"

'He passed Nixie back to me and I sat her on my lap so they could see each other. He was bemused. He didn't know what to say. He was looking out the window. "Well," I said, "What now?"

"'No idea," he said. He looked from me to her and back again. "She's lovely, so lovely, she looks like you. My daughter. Our daughter."

"'Funny", I said, "That's what I thought, that she looks like her daddy. It's when she smiles.'"

"'She hasn't my colouring.'"

"'True. But do you doubt me? That she's not your daughter?'"

"'Nope. I believe you. I just need to get my head around it. It's what we do next.'"

"'What are you thinking?'"

"'I'm thinking of how the song goes and of our first night together in Wales. He took my hand and looking into my eyes sang very quietly, that line, the one that used to tear me apart, 'I'll show you a sunset if you stay with me till dawn.' Then he says, 'I'm thinking of the night we danced together and after, when she was conceived." He says, "It was meant to be."

'I said, "Matt, I never knew you could be so romantic."

"'I've changed. Age and circumstances have mellowed me."

"'What do you want to do?"

"'Right now? Make love to you."

"'You're silly." I smiled. "But..."

"'It doesn't appeal?"

"'It does, but later."

"'You're playing hard to get. Your address? No, don't bother. I know it. You've moved, haven't you?"

'He was looking intently at me, and said, "We've so much to catch up on." He stood up. "I want you to come away with me. You and Nixie."

"'Go away with you? When?"

"'Why not now? 'Till the sun finally sets in the sky' but I'm embarrassing myself, so *w*hile you think about it, I'm going for an apple strudel."

'I said, "Every time I hear that song, I get upset all over again."

"'Well, don't get upset. I'm here now. I'm going nowhere without you."

'He stood up and walked over to the counter to ask for a apple strudel. I remembered that had always been his favourite and when he returned, he took my hand again and we just looked at each other until the waiter called out to say the apple strudel was ready. Matt brought it back to the table. It had cream and cinnamon on the top. He placed it between us. "We can share it."

"'What about Nixie?" I stood up. "I'll get something for her."

"'I said we, and I'll give Nixie as much as she wants of mine."

'He took a piece of the apple strudel, covered it with cream, put it on a spoon and gave some to me and then Nixie. She took it from him. He looked at me and smiled as I stirred the froth off the top of my coffee.

'I said, "You're the cream in my coffee."

'He laughed but then he looked serious. "I want to ask you something. Whether you still have it. Something I gave you the morning I left Jura. Remember?"

'I knew what he meant. I put my hand in my pocket and drew it out. I put the beautiful, white, smooth stone on the table. I told him it was more precious to me than a diamond ring. It was our stone. It had taken centuries to make and it was irreplaceable. He smiled that half-smile, the one that had melted my heart. We looked at each other for a long, long time.'

Hannah hadn't said a word.

Flori stood up. 'I know it's time to go.' She pushed Nixie to the door, turned, and, looking directly at Hannah, said, 'I'd like to see Rose again. I want her to know about me and Matt. And I want her to meet Nixie. I'm going to find her and no one will stop me.' Without looking back she bumped Nixie down the steps to the pavement.

Lightning Source UK Ltd.
Milton Keynes UK
UKOW02f1041040914

238026UK00001B/32/P